Between Fire and Flame

Stephanie Wells Mason

ISBN-13:
978-0692389423

ISBN-10:
0692389423

Manufactured in the United States of America

To my daughter, America.

This one's for you!

Prologue

May 2004

It was a perfect evening for May. Spring had turned everything green, giving life to the dormant trees and flowers that had slept through the long winter. The first butterflies of the year winged silently above the newly planted annuals in reds, purples and golden yellows. Squirrels chased each other across the expansive lawns and an occasional song bird could be heard from the swaying branches of hundred year old pines. The grounds of the historic Conrad Mansion were immaculate, the perfect setting for a wedding.

Brad Stevenson stood and turned with the small crowd to watch London Elliot walk up the aisle. She looked beautiful in a simple white gown with classic tailoring. Tendrils of her dark hair framed her face below a gauzy veil and sparkling tiara. In her hands she held a bouquet of red and white roses accented with baby's breath. Brad knew it was the first time she'd had the chance to walk down the aisle dressed as a bride. Her first wedding—if it could be called that—took place at the court house in front of the local Justice of the Peace. Now, beside her walked Corkie, her seven year old son dressed in a tuxedo, the red cummerbund at his waste perfectly matched to the boutonniere pinned on his lapel.

Brad saw the smile on London's face, the absolute serenity in her countenance. Her brilliant blue eyes locked with the man she would marry. He winced at the heavy pain in his chest as she passed by, stepping forward to take the hand of Ammon Moffatt.

Chapter 1

July 2004

Traffic in the park was not unusually heavy. It was always crowded in July as tourists flocked to northwest Montana to take in the incredible beauty of Glacier National Park, but that didn't stop Brad from feeling annoyed. He was hot, tired, as hungry as one of the bears he'd passed on the trail that day, and anxious for a shower. The hike he'd chosen for the day was one he hadn't done since he was a boy. He remembered it was difficult and his dad had pushed him to the summit with words of encouragement and praise. Time hadn't changed the layout, and he found it was just as difficult today, only there was no one urging him onward, just his own desire to push himself harder, faster, and longer until his physical exhaustion overtook all other feelings. He'd beat out most of the crowds by getting an early start, but the Going-to-the-Sun Road was now littered with cars and people slowly inching their way along the narrow winding road that would lead them back to their campsites.

He noted as he passed that no one was alone. There were the famous red touring cars full of passengers stopped along the turn-outs so that those inside could capture the breathtaking views with their cameras. There were couples posing for pictures, the numerous waterfalls their background, parents with children, groups of motorcyclists, families, friends, old, young; and not one of them alone. Not like him.

A part of him—the part he tried to listen to most often—liked being alone. There was nothing quite like hiking through wildflowers and waterfalls with no one to disturb the sights and sounds. Alone was peaceful. Alone was a time for reflection. Then there was that other part of him that he couldn't seem to push aside completely. The part that reminded him all too often that being alone was lonely.

Only last year he had driven this road with London and her kids. He hadn't minded listening to the incessant banter between Corkie and Marty. He'd enjoyed joking and laughing with them. Seeing the wildlife had been all that much more exciting when there had been someone there with whom to share it. They'd never been able to hike as far as he could alone, but he never regretted it. He'd seen more through Corkie's six year old eyes in one afternoon than he'd seen in years of hiking on his own; every rock was unique, every cloud was a cartoon character, every waterfall made a rainbow.

Stop! He told himself. Those were exactly the kinds of thoughts he was trying to clear his mind of when he'd pushed himself to the summit earlier. She was another man's wife for cryin' out loud. He had no right to keep thinking about the past. It was time to move on.

He was happy for her. Really he was. She practically glowed since the wedding. And it's not like he could fault Ammon. It wasn't his fault things hadn't worked out between them. Brad could admit Ammon was a pretty decent guy. He treated London well, loved the kids, and provided well for them.

It still irked him that religion seemed to have pushed a big wedge into the friendship he'd once shared with London. It was fine if she wanted to go join some strange church and drag her kids into it, but he'd be hanged if she was going to push him into it. It wasn't that he wasn't Christian, but ever since she'd returned from New York last fall she couldn't stop talking about God and Jesus Christ like they'd personally come down from heaven and changed her life. Yeah, like that could really happen. And wasn't it convenient that Ammon belonged to her new church.

London had asked him to come to her and Marty's baptism, but he hadn't gone. He'd used work as an excuse. In truth, he was somewhat curious about it, but not enough to give up his hurt feelings over the whole situation. When she had first told him about her trip, about reading that book, and about meeting Ammon, he was angry. More than that, he was downright red with rage. He felt betrayed and the hurt was deep. After all, he had helped her out by doing her paper route while she was away, he'd kept up her yard and took care of things, all with the hope that the time away would help her see that they should be together. Instead, she found someone else, became someone else.

It took some time, but he realized she hadn't really changed, at least not in a bad way. She was happier. She was more confident. She was more independent. And all of that translated into her needing him less. Ouch! It wasn't easy to admit that his ego had been bruised. Once he did admit it, however, he realized he had changed. He'd quit being her friend. He hadn't helped her nearly as much as he should have when she was trying to move to her new house. Ammon had still been in New York, coming to visit once a month and here she was, trying to go to school, work part time, take care of two busy kids, and keep a long distance relationship going. It took a few months for the pain to dull, but finally he'd swallowed his pride and tried to be the friend he had once been.

It wouldn't be so bad even now, he thought, if it weren't for the fact that every time he watched her with her new husband and their seemingly perfect life, it was a stark reminder that he was still alone.

Brad exited the park gates and headed towards the small town of West Glacier. The cell phone he kept tucked in his pocket started vibrating followed by the muffled singing of Bruce Springsteen. Pulling into a parking lot, he flipped it open, "Hello?"

"Hi, Brad," Corkie said enthusiastically.

"Hey there Buddy. What's up?"

"You're still coming aren't you?" the seven-year old asked. "Mom wanted me to call and remind you in case you forgot."

"Um..." Brad hesitated. He had forgotten. On purpose? Maybe.

"I've been calling all day," Corkie continued, "And I've left you lots of messages. How come you never called back?"

"Sorry, I've been up hiking all day and there's no cell phone service on the mountain. I'm just heading back to town now," Brad informed him.

"Good, then you can still come. Dad's making homemade ice cream."

It stabbed at his heart to hear Corkie calling Ammon "Dad," a title he wished belonged to him. "Corkie, I'm kind of tired—"

"You have to come!" Corkie insisted, "You promised!"

How many times had those words come back to haunt him lately? He was going to have to be more careful about making promises. Keeping them was turning his hair gray.

"Why don't you put your mom on, let me talk to her a minute." It would be easier to offer his excuses to London than to this little boy to whom he couldn't seem to refuse anything.

"Okay, but you're coming!" Corkie insisted before Brad could say another word. He heard Corkie shouting for London and laughed at the commotion in his ear just as London came on the line.

She started right in where Corkie left off, "Brad, you have to come. You haven't been over all summer. I feel like I've hardly seen you since the wedding, and besides, it's the Fourth of July. If I didn't know better I'd think you were avoiding me?" She raised her voice just enough to make it a question.

"I'm not—it's just that I've been hiking all day, and—"

"No excuses this time!" she said emphatically. He sighed on the other end, so she tried another tactic, "Please, Brad. We really want you to come. It would mean a lot to me."

He could already see it in his mind, just how the evening would be. He'd wrestle with Corkie for a while, spend a few minutes teasing Marty. Ammon would probably be manning the grill and he'd have to talk business or horses with him, pretend he didn't envy everything the guy had. He'd watch London preparing the table, getting after the kids, sending glances towards her new husband. They'd all sit down to pray and eat, all the while him feeling like a fifth wheel. Added to the fact that he was tired, both physically and mentally, he just didn't think he could do it.

"London," he started to offer his excuses.

"Please?"

How was a guy to hold out when the woman he loved was begging him?

"What time?" There was obvious defeat in his voice.

"Seven," she said triumphantly. The phone disconnected before he could change his mind.

"So, you managed to convince him?"

"Yes," London replied smugly. "He's coming." She walked over to her new husband, put her arms around his neck, and kissed him. "And, for your information, it didn't take too much convincing. I simply asked him to come."

Ammon felt sympathy for Brad, man to man sympathy. He knew how hard it was to resist the woman he now held in his arms. He had yet to be able to do it himself. He also knew that Brad's feelings for his wife ran deep and so did their friendship. Brad had already been an important part of her life before she met Ammon. The ugly green envy monster had surfaced a time or two in the past year when he'd still been in New York and she'd been two thousand miles away in Montana with Brad. Those months of maintaining a long distance relationship had been brutal, but through it all he had trusted her, never doubting that she loved him. And it was some relief knowing she wasn't there all alone. She had at least one good friend to rely on if something major happened and he couldn't be there.

It had been a bit awkward, that first introduction to Brad, each knowing how the other felt about London. Ammon expected Brad to be a cocky Montana cowboy, much like the guys he'd gone to high school with, who drove a big truck, kept a wad of tobacco tucked in his cheek, and talked of nothing but hunting season.

Instead, he found Brad to be a genuinely nice guy who enjoyed the outdoors, took his job seriously at the fire station, and could carry on a decent conversation about global finance. It was a little disheartening, though, to see that he was also at least three inches taller than him and had a build that would leave most women swooning.

The cold shoulder he'd anticipated hadn't been there. Brad had been downright friendly, and he wasn't sure if that was his way of trying to show London he was the better man, or if he'd simply lost any romantic interest in London. Perhaps if Ammon hadn't been so in love himself, he might have missed that look in Brad's eye, but he recognized it for what it was—defeat? Resignation?

Either way, it touched something in him, and he felt sympathetic towards Brad. After all, she was wearing his ring, kissing him good night, telling him she loved him, and Brad stood by and watched it all without complaint. Perhaps he *was* the better man, Ammon mused.

So, sympathy turned to respect. He knew Brad loved London. What guy wouldn't? She was beautiful, intelligent, capable, fun to be with—she was everything. And she was his.

He knew if he was in Brad's shoes, it would nearly kill him to see her with another man. It stood to reason that ever since the wedding, they'd hardly seen him. It probably was killing him and he was simply trying to avoid a slow and painful death.

London didn't seem to see it that way. He'd tried to explain, but she insisted Brad no longer felt that way about her. He knew she was wrong. He could still see that love in Brad's eye every time he looked at her. He must be going through hell, he thought. He'd spent enough time with Brad in the last year to consider him a friend, but he didn't fault him for not wanting to hang out together when it meant torture to the guy's psyche. Ammon wished Brad could find another woman to fall in love with, but he also knew it would take time and wasn't something that could be forced on him, no matter how hard London tried.

"He's not going to like this," he chastised his wife. "You're just going to make him stay away longer next time."

"He doesn't know I've invited a few other guests and it's not like I'm going to be obvious about it. It was our night to feed the missionaries and by inviting Crystal over too it just looks like she's accompanying them."

Ammon smiled at her knowing there was no changing her mind.

"He's still not going to like it."

"You just mind your own business and go start the grill."

"Yes ma'am," he chuckled on his way out the door.

Poor guy, Ammon thought again as he checked the propane tank and scrubbed the grill. Not only would Brad be cornered by two eager young missionaries, he'd have to face another not-so-subtle-attempt by his match-making wife to set him up—again—both of which he guessed would be seen as highly unwelcome situations. Ammon knew all too well what it was like, having people push religion on you when you weren't ready and trying to set you up on dates with women you weren't interested in. He knew London meant well, and it was because she was so happy, both in her relationship with God and him, that she wanted that for Brad. He couldn't fault her for wanting those things for her friend. He wanted them for Brad too, but Ammon knew from experience that neither type of relationship was one that could be forced.

Ammon, a returned missionary, had fallen away from the church for ten years. In that time, he'd been in and out of worldly relationships looking to fill the void that he felt in his life. He had money, a successful career, a great apartment in Manhattan, and more. None of those things mattered though if he didn't have someone to share them with. So, he dated women, even lived with a woman, looking for the right one. It wasn't until he put his relationship with his Heavenly

Father in order that things in his life really came together. He just wished it hadn't taken the death of his mother to push him in that direction.

No amount of pleading or lecturing from his parents had been able to persuade him that he was on a path of self-destruction. He'd been raised in a loving home, taught the gospel from birth, and served an honorable mission. He figured he was home free. In his arrogance, he let his guard down and Satan stepped in, using subtle weaknesses to bind him until Ammon had turned away from his family and his Savior.

Looking back on those days made Ammon's heart ache. Even now he was paying the price for those choices. He had faced a disciplinary council and was still waiting for the time when he could once again partake of the ordinances that brought salvation and eternal happiness. He was working each day to regain what was lost, to prove himself worthy again so that he could take his new bride to the temple. Remembering the days when he had once shared the gospel with the people of Australia, he wished he could share it with Brad, and that Brad could also have the same joy that came from an eternal family.

Chapter 2

Just before seven Brad pulled his Jeep behind the white Chevy Malibu in front of the Moffatt's home. It was still weird to think of London with a new name. It was at this same house that he'd first met her. He was on duty at the fire station when a call came through about a possible heart attack victim. He and a fellow fire fighter had driven behind the first response vehicle carrying two other paramedics from the station. Following the dispatcher's directions, they'd rushed upon the scene to find a young woman administering CPR to an elderly woman. When Brad found her, there was blood on the victim's clothes and the floor surrounding her, but once they had her stabilized and on the gurney, it was ascertained that the blood wasn't from the victim, but from London. It turned out that while delivering her nightly paper route, London had heard a call for help and found the unconscious lady. In her panic she had been totally unaware that she was kneeling in broken glass from a shattered vase while she struggled to give life sustaining support to the elderly woman.

It was while pulling shards of glass and bandaging her bloodied hands and knees that Brad had had his first glimpse into the frightened, but beautiful eyes of London Elliot and knew he was a goner. Something about her struck him right to the heart. It was all he could do to remember his basic first aid skills. He counted himself lucky that they ran into each other later at the hospital when they'd both arrived to visit the woman that had been so fortunately saved that morning, Mrs. Elsie Moffatt.

Their relationship had blossomed from there. He'd taken her on her first date since her first husband was killed three years before. All summer they'd gone on picnics and hikes, went boating at the lake, and played games in the park. He'd quickly fallen in love with her and her children. He'd watched her come alive, free from the grief she'd surrounded herself with after the many tragic events in her life. He liked knowing he had a hand in that, even if it was just a small hand. It devastated him when she refused his proposal. Though she claimed to love him, it was only as a friend. Not long afterward, she'd met Ammon.

"And to think, it all started right here..." Brad said aloud to no one in particular. He hopped out of the Jeep and pressed the electronic keypad on his ring to lock it. He was just rounding the other car, wondering who it belonged to when Corkie came bounding out of the fence to the back yard.

"You're here!" he shouted as he ran towards Brad and grabbed his hand, pulling him in the direction from which he'd just come. "It's about time! Mom said we couldn't eat until you got here and I'm starrvviiinnggg!" Corkie drew the word out as though he hadn't eaten in a week.

"Good to see you too." Brad laughed as he allowed himself to be dragged to the backyard.

Corkie pushed the gate open, revealing an inviting patio lined with colorful planter boxes in full bloom. In the middle sat a large outdoor dining table already set for dinner with red, white, and blue paper plates. The smell of grilling meat filled the air and the sizzle of melting fat as it dripped onto hot metal could be heard coming from the large stainless steel grill on the far side of the patio. A dark haired man with apron strings dangling down his back stood in front of it with a spatula in his hand. For a second, the scene reminded Brad of an old Frankenstein movie he had loved as a kid with the mad scientist busily working away at his creation. He chuckled at the recollection.

Startled, Ammon turned, spatula in mid-air, "Oh, hey Brad," he said, slamming the grill's lid closed, "Glad you could make it."

"You look like you're cooking up something sinister there," Brad teased.

Ammon put down the spatula on the side board and began wiping his hands on the apron around his waist. "Well, only if you consider barbeque pork ribs to be evil," he said. He looked at Corkie and began rubbing his hands together and trying to cackle like a wicked witch. "Go tell your mom these are just about done…oohhh hah hah." He gave him a loving swat on his backside just as Corkie reached the sliding door. Foregoing his Dr. Jekyll impersonation, he walked over and extended his hand to Brad, "Good to see you, my friend."

"Good to see you too," Brad said as he gripped Ammon's hand in a friendly shake. "I'm glad you're only offering me your hand," he said lightheartedly, nodding at the apron tied around Ammon that boldly displayed a large cartoon frog with large puckered lips above the words 'Kiss the Cook.'

"I like you Brad," Ammon asserted, "But not that much!"

London stepped out to the patio balancing a large bowl in one hand and a full glass pitcher in the other. Seeing her handle the heavy items, Brad rushed over to relieve her burden and rescue what he presumed to be the rest of dinner. In her wake were three other women, only one of which he recognized. Acknowledging his help, she gratefully handed him the pitcher and exclaimed, "Brad, I didn't know you'd arrived yet." She quickly set the bowl on the table and gave him a welcoming hug and kiss on the cheek. "I'm so glad you came. I've missed you." And then, as if to confirm her words she hugged him again before turning to introduce him to the ladies left standing behind her.

"Brad, this is Sister Ericson and Sister Rojas. And you remember Crystal?"

Brad shook their hands as each was introduced, half-heartedly offering a "pleased to meet you," to each of the sisters and a nod at Crystal letting her know that indeed, he did remember her as London's former neighbor. Catching sight of the name tags adorning each "sister's" lapel, he inwardly cringed. He instantly felt a little annoyed with London for practically begging him to come when he could see right away her intentions—even if they were well meant. Briefly he glanced at Ammon and was offered a knowing look of pity that seemed to say, "I'm sorry, I couldn't stop her."

Until now he had successfully dodged any attempt by London to be in the presence of the missionaries. She'd talked non-stop about them all winter. He knew she met with them often and had them over for dinner frequently. Her invitations to him for dinner had been no less frequent, but he always made excuses not to attend when he knew she had the missionaries coming as well. He had no desire to learn more about her new-found religion—he got enough of it from her.

He also didn't appreciate being forced to partner Crystal like a blind date. She was attractive enough, with her pixie-short, blond hair and green eyes, but with him being a good foot taller than her, and her having a sometimes over-exuberant personality, he couldn't seem to get past thinking of her as his little sister. Crystal was a frequent visitor at London's house, just as he had been, so he knew she was two years out from a messy divorce. She wasn't shy in the least when it came to talking about the emotional stress that her ex-husband continued to cause. Brad wasn't about to get involved with someone that carried that kind of baggage. Still, he was polite and kindly pulled out her chair when London announced it was time to eat.

After offering a blessing on the food, Ammon tried to clear some of the tension around the table by making small talk with the sisters. "So, where are you from Sister Rojas?"

"I'm from Arizona, but I was born in Mexico. My dad served a mission in Mexico City. He later went back and that's when he met and married my mother," she answered.

"What about you Sister Ericson?"

"I'm from a small town in Southern Utah called Loa. Most people have never heard of it." Turning to London, Sister Ericson complimented the food. "This potato salad is delicious, Sister Moffatt. I hope you didn't spend all day in the kitchen."

"Well thank you Sister Ericson, but I really didn't do much," London said modestly. "If it weren't for Brother Moffatt's talent with the grill, well…" She smiled at Ammon almost demurely, making Brad want to roll his eyes. He knew she was an amazing cook in her own right, but never gave herself enough credit. To prevent himself from getting too sick from the familial flirting going on between the newlyweds, he quickly changed the subject.

"Aren't we missing someone? Where's Marty?" he asked.

"She went waterskiing with a friend, but she should be back anytime now," said London.

Never one to miss an opportunity to embarrass his big sister, Corkie added, "She doesn't really know how to water ski, but she thinks Lauren Pryor's older brother is really cute and likes to watch him ski."

"Corkie!" London admonished. Without missing a beat, Ammon asked, "How do you know that?"

"Cuz I heard her say so when I listened on the phone to her talking to Katie Holmquist about going today."

"Corkie!" said London even more appalled. "You shouldn't do that!"

"I know," he said sheepishly and put his head down. As the adults continued to talk he risked a peek at Brad who slyly winked and offered a knowing smile. Corkie and Brad had often shared man-to-man discussions about the intricacies of having a sister. There was definitely a shared bond of understanding between them.

"So Brad," Ammon began, "Corkie mentioned you were hiking today. Where'd you go?"

"I took the Garden Wall trail that joins the Loop Trail in the Park."

"Did you see any bears?" asked Corkie.

"A few cubs and a mama bear," said Brad. "Things are looking really dry up there. Some years there is so much snow you can't hike that trail until late July. I think the bears must be coming down to eat and look for more food, especially near the campsites. I heard one ranger telling some people they'd had so many sightings down in Apgar Village they might have to close the campground."

"That's going to be pretty disappointing for all those tourists coming in." Ammon confirmed.

"Yeah, but better safe than sorry. With the high temperatures and rain shortage, there's just not very much water left up there. Not even the Weeping Wall was weeping very much today. Almost bone dry."

"Does that mean we're in danger of fires?" London asked. She turned to the sister missionaries and explained, "I remember a couple of years ago when there was a drought. Seems like there was a fire in every corner of the valley and you could smell smoke in the air all day."

"Hopefully it won't be too bad if people are careful," said Brad. "If only we could control the weather. It seems ironic that we need the rain so desperately, but with the rain inevitably comes the lightning. Most of the forest fires I've ever worked on have been started from a lightning strike."

"I didn't know you fought forest fires," said Crystal.

"I don't usually, but I've had experience so when they get desperate for man power I volunteer. The Fire Chief is pretty good about letting me go, even though it means extra shifts for the other guys at the station."

London picked up where he left off, "Last year he went and helped with that big fire they had over in Seeley Lake. A couple of men were killed in that, weren't they Brad?"

"Yeah, it was terrible. A few got trapped behind the fire lines when the wind shifted. There wasn't much that could be done."

"Well I hope that doesn't happen this year," said London. "I was worried about you for two weeks solid."

"I guess we'll just have to wait and see." said Brad. "Weatherman says we're in for some thunderstorms day after tomorrow."

One of the sister missionaries asked a question and the conversation switched to another topic.

Talking about the forest fire from the previous summer forced Brad to remember, and instead of listening to the lively banter going on around him, he was lost in memories of another time, a time when the fresh blue eyes of the woman sitting across from him weren't trained on another man.

It was so hard being around her now, seeing her so happy, so lively and confident, and yet, he could hardly begrudge her those things. A part of him wanted to hate Ammon, but he couldn't. He was nothing like he had imagined; a snob in a fancy suit who looked down his nose at small town people and their small town ways. But as it turned out, Ammon Moffatt was a humble, sincere, and funny guy. Life could be so cruel.

In the small amount of time they'd spent together, Brad continued to look for a reason to dislike Ammon. There just wasn't any. He couldn't even use their differences in religion as an excuse. Not once had Ammon ever brought up the subject that seemed to be such a cementing element between him and London. She was constantly talking about her new church as though if she talked enough he'd get curious and want to know more. He didn't. Not now. Not ever. He believed in God, tried to keep the Ten Commandments, and be nice to people. Wasn't that enough?

So while London pushed, Ammon backed off. And while Brad knew Ammon participated in all that stuff, he assumed he just wasn't as fanatical about it as London seemed to be. That's why he knew that his eating dinner at the same table with two Mormon missionaries had to be London's doing and not Ammon's.

And the whole Crystal thing? Well that was something he'd have to make clear too. He wasn't interested. Period. He was too in love with London to ever love another woman.

London was just bringing out dessert when Brad's pager buzzed. He looked down and checked the message. Immediately he stood, apologizing, "Sorry about that, looks like I gotta go." Nodding at Ammon he said "Thanks for the ribs, they were delicious."

"You're going to miss the best part," Corkie added. "Homemade ice cream."

"Sorry kiddo," Brad rubbed Corkie's head affectionately. "Duty calls." He gave London a quick kiss on the cheek, "Thanks again."

He was already out the gate running for his Jeep and barely heard London call, "Be careful!"

Chapter 3

Screeching sirens pierced the air as two fire engines barreled down Main Street. Brad heard the heavy horn honking as was protocol when nearing an intersection. Cars that had pulled to the side of the road for the emergency vehicle were making their way back into traffic, slowing his progress. In order to avoid the traffic light, Brad turned left onto a side street and headed towards the heavy smoke that was already visible above the trees. A right turn and another left put him directly behind the fire engines. A crowd had gathered in the street and the people parted like the Red Sea when the horn sounded again.

An old turn-of-the century house was quickly being consumed by flames. Littering the street and yard was the remnants of firework containers, spent rocket launchers, firecracker debris and empty Roman candle sticks. The shrubbery surrounding the house was on fire and it had spread to the wooden siding. Two men were beating at the flames with blankets and towels while a third man sprayed a garden hose at the house, all to no avail. The yard and house were too tinder dry to escape ruin.

Slamming the brakes, Brad threw the Jeep into park and ran towards the danger. Police cars had arrived on the scene to act as crowd control, keeping the people at a safe distance from the fire. He waved at one officer he knew would recognize him and pushed past the crowd.

Two men jumped from the first fire truck and four more from the second. They worked in practiced sync, each knowing their job perfectly. Those responsible for pulling hoses off the truck ran with the end to the nearest fire hydrant and had it secured in under a minute. Those whose job it was to spray, held the heavy hose and braced themselves against the force of 350 pounds of pressure as water came gushing out.

"Glad you could join us!" one firefighter called to Brad and tossed him a helmet. Brad caught it easily then turned and started pulling more gear from the truck. In no time he was suited up in fire proof pants and a coat. He quickly shoved his feet into a pair of boots then paused long enough to look around and see where his help was needed most.

While his co-workers attacked the blaze with water, Brad pulled aside one of the men who had been beating at the flames. He was young, maybe twenty or twenty one. His t-shirt and shorts were black with soot as well as his hands. Brad yelled above the roar of crackling wood and fire, "Are you hurt? Is there anyone inside?"

"I don't think so, man. We were just lighting some fireworks and--"

Brad cut him off, "Are you positive there's no one inside?"

"Man, I don't live there," he yelled back belligerently. "It's the neighbor's house. I don't think anyone's home."

Brad let the man go and instructed him to stay back. "Idiot," he muttered under his breath. Fireworks were illegal within city limits, not to mention, warnings had been plastered all over the valley about the extreme danger of fire during the current drought. It never ceased to amaze him that people continued to act so selfishly and ignore public notices. This was the third fire this week due to an errant spark from fireworks.

A woman came forward having pushed past the crowd and police officers. She was screaming, and Brad managed to grab her before she could get past him to the front door that was already in flames. "My babies!" she cried. "My girls are in there!"

Heat from the fire was intense. One of the first floor windows exploded as Brad restrained the hysterical woman. "What?" He yelled above the noise. "How many?"

"Two. My twelve year old daughter was babysitting my two year old."

Without further explanation, Brad ran to find a partner. He grabbed Casey Dye who was helping at the truck. The two men pulled oxygen tanks from the truck and secured them to their back. Casey just had time to reach for his helmet and pull it on as Brad indicated they should go around back.

The two burley men each used a foot to kick in tandem, breaking open the back door to the house. The fire had not yet reached the back, but thick smoke hovered in the air making it difficult to see inside. "Hello?" Casey called and Brad repeated. They searched the main floor, flinging open doors in hopes of finding the girls. When that proved fruitless, they went up the stairs, continuing to call out at intervals.

In the bedroom closest to the front of the house, they found the two girls on a bed. Whether they were asleep or had passed out from smoke inhalation, there was no way to know, and no time to assess. A television screen glowed eerily in the haze and it appeared as though they had been watching and fallen asleep. Neither girl was responsive when the two fire fighters shook them. The room was quickly growing hot. Without wasting any time, Casey grabbed the two year old and headed back to the hall followed by Brad with the twelve year old in his arms.

Another siren pierced the air, this time an ambulance. The police had radioed for medical back up when they learned that there were possible victims inside.

Brad and Casey didn't wait for the ambulance to pull up. They rushed through the crowd, meeting the truck halfway down the street. The mother, seeing them carrying her lifeless children rushed after them.

The door in the back of the ambulance was flung open before the vehicle had come to a complete stop. Emergency medical personnel jumped out with a bag of equipment and instructed the men to place the girls on the grass of a neighboring house. Immediately they set to work securing oxygen masks around their small faces and searching for a pulse at each tender neck.

The mother, still crying hysterically knelt at their sides. The firefighters didn't wait to hear the outcome. Instead, they hurried back to the fire truck to assist with the blaze, but they heard the ambulance siren ring out as it raced the short distance to the hospital.

Two hours later the fire was out. The Victorian-era home was nothing more than a blackened frame. The yard was soggy with mud and so were the neighboring yards. Debris and broken glass lay everywhere. Members of the fire crew coiled hoses and secured the property with yellow caution tape. Brad worked beside Casey, arranging the air tanks and other miscellaneous equipment back on the truck.

"That was a close one. I wonder how those girls are doing," said Casey as he handed another tank to Brad.

"Yeah, no kidding. I hope they're okay." He paused, still holding the tank and turned to survey the destruction. "I love my country, but I sure hate the Fourth of July."

"I think every fireman hates the Fourth. It's part of the job description. You put a bunch of explosives in the hands of the masses, including those that can't even read how to use them properly and you have a recipe for disaster." Casey nodded at the mess before them. "There's proof positive, my friend."

"You're right. With so little rain this spring there's bound to be more like this." Brad said as the explosion of celebratory fireworks echoed through the valley. He wiped at the sweat dripping from his forehead. "I could sure use a drink."

Casey checked his watch. "I'm off shift in five. Tell you what, I'll buy if you drive."

Brad thought for a minute. It had been a while since he'd spent any time hanging out with the guys, but the truth was, he just wasn't up for socializing. The one person he wanted to share his day with, rehash everything he'd seen, heard, and felt, was unavailable to him. He imagined she was home enjoying the festivities with her family. The very thought made his heart ache and his mood lousy. He knew he wasn't fit company for anyone. "Nah, you go ahead. I think I'll just head home and crash for the night. It's been a long day."

Chapter 4

The theater crowd lingered outside enjoying the summer evening during intermission. Some held glasses of wine, others held bottles of beer or water. People meandered around munching on cookies and candy purchased at the concession stand from the lobby. Sky Ryder pushed past them all, seeking some fresh air and a little solitude.

She moved down the sidewalk until she felt she could finally breathe. Looking down at the diamond on her hand she noted how it glimmered in the sunlight. It was beautiful; it looked like it was at least one full karat, princess cut, surrounded by an intricate band of platinum that was embedded with even more stones. It was a show piece that glowed like a spotlight against the brown skin on her small hand. She stared at the exquisite ring with mixed emotions. The proposal had taken her completely by surprise.

A man walked up behind her and slipped his arm around her waist. "Well, what do you think?" he asked observing her inspection of his ring.

"I…It's beautiful, Tom. It's absolutely beautiful."

"How's the fit? Too big?"

"No. No, it's perfect."

He kissed her affectionately on the lips. "And so are you. We'd better get in, I think they're about to start the second act." Sky allowed him to lead her back into the crowded theater, leaning on him just enough to compensate for the fact her legs were still shaking.

Inside they found their seats again, squeezing past the elderly couples that frequented the theater on summer nights. The lights dimmed and soon the audience was laughing at the arrogant antics of Henry Higgins as *My Fair Lady* resumed. Tom reached for Sky's hand, holding it securely in his. The sensation was somehow different this time. Instead of the warmth of his fingers encircling hers, all she could feel was the press of her fingers against the thick band of her engagement ring.

Engagement ring? Was it for real? She could hardly believe this was happening to her. A thousand thoughts ran through her mind. The actors on stage were now only a blur of sound and movement.

She was engaged.

She was getting married.

To Tom.

Sky looked over at her new fiancé. He was engrossed in the play. She studied his profile; the angular jaw with just a hint of dark beard beginning to show. His nose was straight and narrow, his brow deep. His hair was perfectly sculpted with no signs of a receding hair line. As she watched him she could feel him unconsciously twisting the ring on her finger, playing with it like a new toy, constantly reminding her that she was his. She had said yes. In the not-too-distant-future she would belong to this man, just as he would belong to her.

As though sensing her eyes on him, Tom turned and looked at Sky. In the dim light she met his eyes, hoping to convey all her hopes and happiness in that one look. He brought her hand to his lips and kissed it before turning back to the scene on stage.

By the time the show ended she had composed a mental list of everything she needed to start doing; check the calendar for dates, find a dress, reserve the church, check the cost of catering. There would be even more to do over the summer now. Her heart pounded in sync with the applause as the actors and actresses made their final bows.

As she walked out of the theater with Tom's arm around her shoulder, she felt a little like Eliza Doolittle; transformed from an old spinster to a new bride.

Sky Ryder was getting married!

"So are we still on for next Tuesday?" Tom asked.

They were standing at his car where he'd turned her to face him. Slipping his arms around her waist, he kissed her gently first on the forehead, then her nose, then one cheek, then the other until finally having worked his way to her lips, he hovered there until she leaned in and kissed him soundly in return. "Of course. But not until after my meeting."

"I'll pick you up at the church." He kissed her again.

"I'll be waiting," she returned with a kiss.

"Happy?" he mumbled against her warm mouth.

"Mmmmm."

"I love you."

Sky pulled back enough to look him in the eyes. He looked content, and a little bit like the Cheshire Cat. It wasn't completely unlike him. He did tend to be confident and self-assured.

When she didn't say anything his brow puckered and his expression faltered. "Well…don't you have anything to say?" he urged.

"Hmmm, let me think…" she teased. He started to pull away, but she held on. How about, I love you, too."

"Works for me!" he said and kissed her again.

Chapter 5

"Okay girls," Sky called for attention, "Make sure you take home your supply list. I'd hate to have you forget something. It looks like we might be in for a few storms this weekend but things are supposed to clear up again by midweek. Everyone pray for sunshine."

"Sister Ryder?" asked an older girl in the group, "What about those of us going on the over-night hike? What are we supposed to bring for that?"

"Good question, Emma. For those of you going on the over-nighter, I've made an additional list of items you'll need to bring. Make sure you pick that up from me on your way out. Any other questions?" Sky waited a few seconds before continuing, "Who will offer our closing prayer?"

Everyone folded their arms and bowed their heads as one of the Laurel-aged girls said a quick prayer. There was a chorus of "amens" and then an outbreak of conversation and giggling as girls began talking excitedly and gathering their things before exiting the cultural hall.

This had been the final night of preparation before girls' camp. Sky had walked them through the basic steps of first aid as outlined in their Young Women Camp Manual. It wasn't the intensive training she offered to her nursing students at the college where she occasionally taught, but she was nearly as exhausted as having spent a whole day teaching rather than just an hour. It had been all she could do to keep the girls focused on her as she demonstrated such skills as CPR and how to handle severe cuts. Only a few of the quieter, younger girls had paid much attention during her overview of poisonous plants and what to do for burns and dehydration. The others seemed to think that discussing the newest teen heart-throb or texting was more important than survival skills. She only hoped they were right and none of them would ever have to employ the things she'd taught them over the past few weeks.

It had come as a complete surprise when Bishop White had called her into his office in early May and asked her to be the Young Women Camp Director. Sky willingly accepted the calling, but not without some reservations. At twenty nine, Sky Ryder was still single, and she had never considered herself to be good with kids. She had a handful of nieces and nephews who she adored, and she'd done her share of babysitting, but being in charge of twenty-something young girls for a week was more than a little daunting.

Born and raised in Montana, she was an avid outdoor enthusiast. She loved to hike, camp, fish, rock climb and ski. She had spent a fair amount of time traveling too, always looking for the next adventure whether that was a 100 mile run in Alaska or an Olympic triathlon in Hawaii. But being asked to serve the young women seemed like the biggest adventure yet.

"Are you sure that's what the Lord wants me to do, Bishop?" she'd asked him. "I don't know anything about girls."

"You're a girl aren't you?" he asked sarcastically. "Besides, I'm sure, Sister Ryder. But more importantly, you can be sure. All you have to do is ask Him. If you'd like to take some time and think about this, pray about it before accepting the calling, you can."

"No, Bishop. My mother taught me never to turn down a calling."

"I appreciate that, Sister Ryder. And so does the Lord."

"I just feel really inadequate. I don't know anything about the young women."

"Of course you do, you're a young woman yourself. And your talents will be of infinite value to these impressionable girls. I know you enjoy camping and hiking."

"Yes…but, I'm not even married yet. I don't know if I can be the kind of example the Lord wants for them." Sky remembered her own Young Women leaders. They were amazing women who had taught her so much. Because of their enthusiasm and devotion to the gospel they had instilled in her, she had gone on to serve a full time mission for the church. She had felt privileged to share the restoration of the gospel with the Navajo people. They shared an ancient Lamanite ancestry that she loved telling them about.

When Sky returned from her mission she had hoped to get married, raise a family, and teach them the gospel, as well as the many wonderful traditions of her Native American heritage. She watched as one by one her siblings got married and started their own families, some moving far away, others remaining close to the ranch where they'd grown up. But things had not worked out like she'd hoped they would. Finding her own "Mr. Right" was not so easy.

She started taking college courses at the community college in order to meet more people. She attended all of the young single adult activities hoping to find the right guy. The college courses had given her a successful career as a nurse and as an instructor at the same college, and the single adult activities had kept her busy serving in the church. But finding the right man to share eternity with was taking longer.

"Aren't you dating that nice young man? What's his name?"

"Tom?"

"Yes, that's the one."

Sky thought about Tom and the few dates they'd been on. He was fun to be around. He was certainly good looking. She wasn't sure where it would lead, but she hoped... Would he start dating someone else if she was gone for a week at Girls' Camp?

Pulling her mind away from Tom, she tried to focus on the bishop's words.

"The Lord obviously thinks you have something to share with these girls, or He wouldn't be calling you." Bishop White said. "I want to remind you of an oft-used statement in the church," he continued, leaning forward to look intently at Sky's nervous eyes, " 'Whom the Lord calls, He qualifies.' You may not feel like you have what this calling requires, but He will give it to you."

"Thank you, Bishop," said Sky. She stood and reached to shake his hand. "I'll do my best."

"That's all any of us can do, Sky."

Sky waved good-bye to the last girl and began gathering her materials.

"Are you ready yet?" Sky's fiancé asked anxiously as he walked into the gym past the young women going out. "The movie starts in fifteen minutes."

He was wearing designer jeans and cowboy boots with his dark hair smoothed back with hair gel. Tom Allred looked like he could have walked right off a billboard advertisement for men's cologne. He was stunningly handsome with a polished Montana look that showed he'd been born into money.

"I'm just gathering my things."

"Okay, but hurry, I don't want to miss the beginning." He stole a quick kiss.

"I know. It's just been a little crazy tonight," Sky pointed out. With her papers in hand she turned out the gym lights and checked that the door was locked after it closed. "This was our last meeting before camp next week."

Tom put his arm around her shoulders, urging her to walk fast and match his pace. "I know. I'm trying not to think about it. I'm going to miss you so much, Babe."

Outside the church, he quickly unlocked the car with his key fob and jumped in. She climbed in the passenger seat, and with her arms full of books and papers, managed to pull the door shut just in time. Seconds later Tom had the red Camaro in drive and was speeding out of the parking lot.

Sky sat silently as he drove too fast through town. "Tom…" she began, but stopped mid-sentence as he swerved to avoid a bicyclist and nearly hit an on-coming car before sliding back into the north-bound lane of the highway.

"Sorry 'bout that, Babe."

"Could you slow down?" she pleaded, just managing to keep back the fear she felt at his reckless driving.

"Ah, don't be mad, Babe. I saw it coming." He reached over and squeezed her knee reassuringly, but didn't slow down.

"I'm not mad," she insisted. She hated when he drove like this. It scared her. His impatience tonight reminded her of the young girls she'd just been with. Wasn't he supposed to be more mature? Her good mood was quickly turning sour. She was probably just tired and a little stressed. Deep breaths, she reminded herself, nice deep breaths. Trying to sound upbeat she asked, "Can't we just do something else?"

"I thought you wanted to see this too."

"I did—I do. It's just that there are things we need to talk about." Sky shifted so she could face him better. The papers still on her lap were in the way so she reached between the seats and managed to put them on the back seat without scattering them too badly.

Tom braked hard at the stop light, the momentum sending everything to the floor behind the passenger seat. Oblivious, he looked over at her, "So talk. What's up?"

"We're getting married in less than two months."

"Yeah. And?" The light changed to green and he gunned the Camaro through the intersection.

"We haven't even finalized the invitation design and we need to pick a time when you can come to the bakery with me so we can decide on the cake. There's just a lot to do still and I'm going to be gone all next week at camp."

"You know that's not really my thing." They had reached the movie theater parking lot. Tom pulled the car into the closest available spot and shut off the engine. "Whatever you decide'll be great," he told her. He leaned over and kissed her quick on the lips. "Come on Babe, this is gonna be great. I know how you love movie popcorn."

"Gee, I can hardly wait," she said sarcastically as she trailed after him to the entrance.

Chapter 6

Brad's shift was nearly over. He'd been at the fire station for three days straight and was looking forward to sleeping in his own bed again. It had been a busy weekend and they'd been called out several times. Luckily only one of the calls had been serious. The thunderstorms which crossed the valley all weekend had knocked out power in several neighborhoods. An elderly man had started his curtains on fire when he attempted to light some candles. The fire had quickly spread up the wall, engulfing the ceiling. By the time the fire trucks arrived, the whole house was ablaze. It didn't help that the wind from the storm kept threatening to carry the flames to the house next door. The man was able to get out, fortunately, but he had lost almost everything. It always made Brad sad to see people lose their possessions like that, even though he knew fire was a formidable foe that never showed any mercy.

It seemed like ever since he had stopped dating London, he'd pulled himself into a sort of shell. Before he met her, he had been good friends with most of the guys at the station. Only a few of them were married and had a family waiting for them to return home. The rest of them would go out for a beer after work or go shooting up in the hills sometimes. Occasionally they would double date if one of them were lucky enough to have a date. Before London, Brad had seemed to be lucky more often than most with his rugged good looks and easy-going personality. Women were drawn to his sandy brown hair and dark blue eyes. The attention Brad got from women was flattering for a while, but when he started thinking about getting serious with someone, he found the pickings to be shallow. It was no wonder London had touched his heart; she was strong and deep.

This was the first weekend in a long time that he'd felt that old camaraderie between the guys at the station. Instead of keeping to himself by reading a book or just watching TV, he'd joined their poker game between calls, losing nearly twenty dollars in small change. They'd talked and laughed around the table for hours. The guys welcomed Brad back into their circle, but not without relentlessly teasing him about having been love sick for so long. He took their jabs with the good humor in which they were intended and found it easier to laugh at himself and the whole situation.

"So let me get this straight," said Josh, leaning back on his chair so that he was balancing on the back legs, "She dumps you, marries some suit from New York, and you still hang out together?"

"She didn't dump me," Brad insisted.

"Okay, but she didn't marry you," said Bill. "Who's dealing?"

"Brett's turn," said Brad.

"Isn't not marrying you the same as dumping you?" asked Josh.

"It is in my book," said Casey. "Any girl says no to this, is history," he said, standing up to display his biceps under his uniform t-shirt.

"You get any more stuck on yourself, man, and you'll have to marry yourself," Brad said jovially.

"Hey, I'm just sayin'…"

"Quit saying and start playing. Are you in?"

"Yeah, I'm in," said Casey throwing his ante into the growing pile of coins.

"You know what you need?" said Brett as he dealt cards to the five men at the table. "You need to meet my sister-in-law, Carrie. I think you'd really like her."

"Man, he doesn't need another woman," said Bill. "Why is it that every guy that's married thinks all the rest of us should be too? No, what he needs is to go out hunting with the guys. Get himself a twelve point buck and forget about women. They're all the same; trouble. That's what. They're all trouble.

"Well, it's easy to see why you aren't married, Bill," said Josh. "Seriously Brad, if you want, I could set you up with Candy's roommate. She's pretty hot."

"I don't need anyone setting me up. I get enough of that from London." Brad proceeded to tell them about London's match making attempts with Crystal. "I'm sure I'll meet the right one someday. In the meantime, I'm forced to hang with you sorry lot of hopefuls while you cheat at cards."

Despite Brad's disinterest in his co-workers' attempts to set him up with another woman, he appreciated their concern. The outer jibes made it easier to forget the inner turmoil.

When they weren't on call, putting the truck back together, or playing cards, they watched the news for updates on a new fire that had begun in the Bob Marshall Wilderness Area. The same storms that had knocked out the valley's power had started a series of fires. The lightning had been fierce with over three hundred strikes in only a few hours and though the clouds had been ominously black, little rain had fallen to douse the flames.

Fire Chief Jerry Fitch called to Brad just as he finished gathering his few personal items to leave. "Can I have a word with you, Brad?"

"Sure, Chief. Be right with you."

Brad stuffed his dirty socks and sweatshirt into a duffel bag, slung it over his shoulder and walked to the Chief's office. Fitch was near retirement, having served more than thirty years in the Kalispell Fire Department. He wasn't tall, but he was burly and the men knew he could carry more than any of them. He demanded respect from the men and they gave it, wholeheartedly. He also demanded perfection which was why the department boasted an outstanding safety record since Fitch had been made fire chief. He was old enough to be a father to most of the firefighters and that's how he tended to treat them, like sons; praising and encouraging most of the time, reprimanding some of the time, and loving all of the time, even if it was hidden under a gruff demeanor.

"Come on in, Brad," said Chief Fitch walking over to close the door behind him. "Have a seat."

"Everything okay, Chief?" Brad asked. He felt like he had just been summoned to the principal's office by the tone of Fitch's voice. He'd spent his fair share of time in the hot seat as a kid to know that this invitation was more than just a social update. There was obviously something serious on the Chief's mind.

"You tell me, Sergeant."

"Is there a problem?" Brad racked his brain trying to think of anything he'd missed lately. "I finished up those reports you asked me to do except for the one from Lake County. We're still waiting for their information."

"Fine, fine." The chief sat back in his chair, distractedly clicking the top of a ball point pen. "No, your performance at work is top notch as usual. But I'm a little concerned about you, Brad. How are you doing?"

"I'm fine," was Brad's even reply.

"You've been closed up, quiet, withdrawn. This weekend's the first time I've seen you smile in months. What gives?"

"Nothing, Sir. I'm fine. Just a small personal problem. Nothing that won't pass in time."

"Anything I can help with?"

"No. No, it's all good."

"Well, good. I'm glad to hear you say that, it makes asking you to leave easier."

"Leave, Sir?" Brad asked tentatively, wondering just what the Chief meant.

"I hate to send any of my best men, but they're asking for help and God knows they need it. Those lightning strikes this weekend have stirred up a mess over in the Bob not too far outside of Swan Lake."

"Yeah, I've caught a couple of the local updates on the news," Brad confirmed. "The last report said it had burned twenty thousand acres already."

"That's just for starters," said Fitch. "They've got three main fires burning now. One is up high, making it hard to access. The other two are lower but they're threatening some of the campgrounds and could spread to private lands and cabins. The forest service has already called up men from Missoula and Stevensville, and of course men from Polson and Ronan are already there. I just got a call and they're asking for all the men that can be spared within a two hundred mile radius. The winds are fierce, the ground tinder dry, the rivers all low. It's gonna burn a lot more than twenty thousand acres before it's over. Predictions put it near one hundred."

Brad didn't need anyone telling him how bad the situation was. He had seen that for himself just the other day when he'd been hiking. The mountains were a tinder box waiting for someone to ignite them. This time it wasn't a careless camper with a forgotten fire, or a smoker with an errant cigarette butt, but rather Mother Nature's fury. She had let loose with a vengeance.

"I hate to even ask," Fitch went on, "being as how you helped them out last year. I know this isn't part of your job, but they need experienced men on this one. I figure after what happened last year, you've pretty much seen it all. I'm asking you to go with Casey and Dye."

He had seen it all, at least as much as he hoped to ever see when it came to burned and bloodied bodies. He could still picture the three men who had lost their lives near Seeley Lake when they got trapped by the flames from another forest fire. He knew Chief Fitch was thinking of them too. They'd both been there the day the bodies were recovered. No one who had been there would forget. Knowing the risks involved, the extreme conditions, the physical demands, and emotionally draining hours of work didn't stop Brad from accepting the request. He'd begun his career as a volunteer, fighting forest fires, so although he knew all those things were real, he also knew it was exciting; a huge adventure. He could use a little adventure in his life about now, just the thing for a broken heart.

"No problem, Chief. When do we leave?"

Chapter 7

The lush greenery of the Swan Mountains created a magnificent backdrop, rising up hundreds of feet above the deep blue water of Holland Lake. Sky glanced up at the cloudless expanse of blue above the trees. She was grateful for the sunny skies above and the stiff breeze that helped to alleviate some of the heat as she helped the girls set up their tents.

She had always loved this area as a child. Her family had spent many campouts along the serene shore. She'd swum in the cold water with her brothers on hot summer days and hiked to picturesque waterfalls. On the edge of the Bob Marshall Wilderness, the area was rich with wildlife, forest and flowers. From the valley floor to the top of Holland Peak, the pinnacle point of the Swan Range, was a never ending expanse of untamed beauty.

Wiping the sweat from her brow Sky offered a silent prayer of thanks that it wasn't raining. She was nervous enough as it was, being in charge of twenty eight girls for the next five days. Of course, she wasn't alone. Sister Chapman, her assistant camp director, was there, and there would be other sisters from the Young Women presidency coming up throughout the week. The High Priest Group Leader was also there representing the priesthood, but for the most part, she was the one in charge. That thought scared her to death.

"Sister Ryder?" Emma asked, "Brother Hunt wanted me to ask you where you want the coolers stored. He's trying to finish unloading the trailer."

"Oh, um…ask him to put them next to the metal folding table, for now," Sky told her, pointing as she spoke. "We'll use that as our preparation table so we'll have room to sit and eat at the picnic tables. We'll have to put them back in a car at night so the bears don't get into them."

Emma rushed off just as two other girls carrying a tent bag between them stopped in front of Sky, seeking her directions. "Where should we put this up?"

Sky turned in circles looking for another level area close to the one currently being erected by another group of girls. When she spotted one that looked promising she said, "Let's try it over there girls. See if you can get Mandy and Anna to help you set it up. I'll come over as soon as we finish with this one."

The questions continued throughout the morning as camp slowly came together and there was some sense of organization. She was just glad she had told all the girls to bring a sack lunch for that day so they didn't have to prepare a meal until dinner. By the time the girls were gathered and eating, Sky was exhausted and it was only noon. She'd never known camping to be so tiring, but then again, she'd never been in charge of a group this large. Normally it was just her and a friend, or her and one of her sibling's families. On those occasions, she had nothing more to worry about than her own pack and sleeping bag. God give me strength, she prayed.

"Girls, girls!" she called loudly and waited until she was certain she had at least some of their attention. "I want to officially welcome you to Girl's Camp. You can all give yourselves a big round of applause for a job well done; camp looks great." Sky waved her arms around the clearing, indicating the tents, the tables and general organization of the remote mountain site. "Thank you for your help." She clapped with them in appreciation.

"While you're eating, I want to go over a few things that you'll need to know in order to make this a fun and safe experience for everyone. You'll notice I've posted the schedule and the rules by the food preparation table. I want to review those with you," Sky said. She looked down at her clipboard and read them off as she had written them the week before. "The number one rule I want you all to follow is never—and I mean never—go off by yourself. We're on the edge of the Bob Marshall Wilderness which is inhabited by both black and grizzly bears as well as mountain lions. They'll most likely stay away when there's a big crowd making noise, but you could be lunch if you're alone. So always take a partner, preferably a group even if it's just to visit the outhouse. Second, keep all the food in the coolers or car.

Again, we don't want any unexpected visitors to our camp and they'd just love to get a free lunch. If you've brought snacks with you, don't keep them in the tent." Sky continued outlining the rules, trying to keep the tone light but emphasizing the seriousness of obeying each of them. She reviewed the dress code as outlined in *For The Strength of Youth* and reminded them of the standards they had been taught in dress and behavior. She knew that for most of the young women these things were not an issue, but there were a few who needed reminders.

"As for the schedule, we'll be breaking up into groups for games this afternoon. You'll need to check the board to see which group you're in. Also, be sure to see what meal you're scheduled to help prepare. The menu is posted next to the schedule, but I'll be available to help if you have questions or can't find something. After dinner tonight we have a special speaker and then a devotional followed by s'mores around the campfire. You'll have free time each day, during which I hope you'll take advantage of the certification stations we'll have set up. This will be a great opportunity for you to practice some of the skills we've already learned as well as learn some new camping and survival skills.

"For those girls going on the overnight hike, you'll need to get your certification done tomorrow since we'll be leaving early Thursday and won't return until Friday evening just before dinner and our testimony meeting.

"Now, I know some of you might be planning some pranks," she looked at two of the Mia Maid girls who had specifically asked her about ideas at one of the camp preparedness meetings that summer. She winked. "But let's remember to keep things nice, and be respectful of others and their property." Sky shared a brief story about a time when she had gone to Girls' Camp as a Beehive and an 'innocent' prank had ruined one of the tents. "Also, I'm not your mother so I won't be picking up after you. Keep your tents clean and the camp tidy. You're all old enough that I don't think I need to tell you when to go to bed either, but I will remind you that our flag ceremony is at 7:30 and you're all expected to be there," she said authoritatively. The girls were getting antsy and Sky was tired of lecturing so she finished by saying, "Now, go have fun and we'll see you back here at two o'clock."

There was an instantaneous break in the silence by twenty eight giggling girls as they resumed their talking and scattered to the surrounding camp area. Sky sat down in the fold-out camp chair behind her and inhaled deeply, relieving some of the tension she felt over being in charge and trying to capture the joy she usually felt while camping in God's great wilderness. With the sound of girls in the background, it wasn't possible to hear the chirping of birds or the creaking of branches as they swayed in the wind. Still, the beauty of the pines and their heavenly scent reminded Sky just how much she loved the outdoors. Her fears were not completely allayed but she had faith enough to know with God's help she'd get through this week, and maybe—just maybe—she'd come away having enjoyed it as well.

"You're doing a great job," Sister Chapman said taking up another fold-out chair next to Sky. Rochelle Chapman, who was serving as the assistant camp director, was also the wife of the Second Counselor in the Stake Presidency. At fifty five, she was still young at heart and enjoyed being with the young women. She had served for years in the Young

Women organization, often as president, but found it even more enjoyable to step back and assist the new generation of leaders like Sky. "The camp looks great, the girls seem happy…"

Sky looked around her, noting the firewood stacked neatly next to the fire pit, the tents all standing erect, the coolers lined up under the trees all neatly labeled with their contents. "It does look good," she said with a touch of humility in her voice, "although I don't think it was because of anything I did. The girls were great at pulling it all together. They've worked hard this morning. I just hope it all continues to work together."

"It will," Rochelle said confidently. "I think it was one of the general authorities who said 'the success of any event begins with organization'."

"Which one of them said that?"

"I don't know for sure, but it sounds like something they would say. You've got everything for this girls camp more organized than I've seen in all the years I've served. Based on that alone, it's going to be a great week."

"Thanks, but I couldn't have done it without your help. I'm so glad you're here with me. I still feel completely inadequate when it comes to dealing with the girls. Camping I can do. Girls…that's a different story."

"I know it's not easy trying to connect with some of them. I've served in Young Women's for over thirty years and I still feel like I'm just learning what to do. Times have changed, the girls have changed, and it's hard to keep up with it all. I've cried with them and laughed with them. I've watched them grow up and make mistakes. I've seen them fall away from the gospel and find their way back. I've stood with them in the temple as they take that next step into womanhood. Sometimes there's heartache and sometimes there's joy. But always there is love. The secret is to just love them through it all."

"I'm trying," Sky confessed.

"I know you are," said Rochelle warmly, "And that's why you're doing such a great job."

"I'm just glad that I get to give them all back at the end of the week. I don't think I'm cut out to be a mother."

"Of course you are. Aren't you getting married soon?"

"Yes"—Sky hesitated for a moment, thinking back to the conversation with Tom the night before. He had sounded so angry. He was upset that she was leaving for the week, but it wasn't like she could back out now. The girls were depending on her. She'd accepted the calling and was seeing it through. Tom was a strong member of the church so why, she wondered, was he giving her such a hard time about fulfilling a calling. Her feelings were hurt by his attitude, but she tried not to let it show. He hated it when she got emotional. It was probably all just pre-wedding jitters. "October third we'll be going to the Cardston Temple."

"Congratulations, that's wonderful."

"Thank you. I'm a little nervous," Sky admitted.

"That's normal. But when you're in the right place with the right person, all that nervousness will go away, you'll see."

"Still, I can't imagine being a mother any time soon."

"You've still got plenty of time to start a family."

"I don't know, I think if Heavenly Father wanted me to be a mother He'd have sent me prince charming sooner,"

Sky said with a touch of regret. "At the rate I'm going, I'll probably be too old when we finally decide to have kids."

"I don't believe that for a minute!" emphasized the older woman. "You're still plenty young. Look at Abraham and Sarah or Zacharias and Elisabeth. Now they were old. I bet you're not even thirty yet."

"Thirty on my next birthday," she stated matter-of-factly.

"How does your fiancé feel about starting a family?"

Sky thought for a moment, remembering conversations they'd had.

They'd only dated for two months before he'd proposed. Tom had shown up at one of the young single adult activities early that spring. Apparently, he'd grown up in California but his family had moved to Montana while he was on his mission. After serving in Maine, he'd returned to California to work, and as Sky had found out later, to surf. He was visiting his family for the summer when they met. He was so charismatic and full of life, it was hard to resist his charm. All of the young sisters had been drawn to him, Sky included. She felt flattered when he singled her out and asked for a date.

He was younger than Sky by four years. Sky had long since come to terms with the fact that she was past the age when most eligible men would look her way. She knew she wasn't sporting wrinkles yet, and her long dark hair hadn't begun to gray, but hers was no longer the face of a giddy twenty year old. She was a mature woman with a career who had traveled, experienced different cultures, and lived on her own for quite some time now. Experience and wisdom taught her that these were not the things men were looking for in a wife. Besides, it wasn't as if there had been that many eligible men around, at least not worthy men. Too many of the guys she met at the single adult dances and actually dated turned out to be struggling with their testimony; often times they didn't even have a temple recommend. Sky had determined long ago that when she did finally marry, it would be in the temple to a worthy priesthood holder.

Tom hadn't seemed concerned at all about their age difference though, in fact, he told her he appreciated it. Besides, they had so many common interests, what difference did a few years make. Together, they'd gone rafting, horseback riding, even skydiving. When she hadn't been working or planning for camp, he'd consumed her free time with every exciting thrill the valley had to offer. He was like a small kid at an amusement park, wanting to experience it all and it had been incredibly exhilarating for Sky to share it with him.

But kids? Family? Had they ever discussed it? She just assumed...

"I'm sure he wants a family at some point," she answered vaguely.

"Well then, maybe it'll happen sooner than you think." The older woman stood and stretched, looking about her and smiling. Holding her hand out to pull Sky from her chair she said, "There's a rock over there by the lake with our name on it. What d'ya say we cool our toes for five minutes."

Taking Rochelle's hand, Sky stood. "I say it sounds heavenly!" And the two ladies walked arm in arm towards the water, giggling and laughing with no less energy than their young charges.

Chapter 8

Brad stopped at the grocery store on his way home. He had a few items to pick up before leaving for base camp the next morning. He'd learned from experience that having a ready supply of Power Bars when he was fighting forest fires was essential. He needed something to keep him going during a twelve hour shift. The protein bars weren't the tastiest things in the world, but they would sustain him.

He walked through the aisles searching for other quick and easy meals that he could prepare over a fire or on a propane stove. He added a couple cans of chili to his cart, three cans of chunky soup, and several cans of mandarin orange slices.

In the snack food aisle he added some packages of beef jerky and a few canisters of nuts. He was just picking up a container of Pringles potato chips when he heard Ammon Moffat's voice behind him.

"Hey Brad," Ammon greeted him cheerfully. "How are you?"

Brad turned around and returned the greeting. "Hey Ammon. I'm good. You?"

"Couldn't be better."

Of course he couldn't, thought Brad, he had the perfect life. Brad picked up another two cans of potato chips and dumped them into his cart.

"Ahh, the bachelor's life, canned soup and junk food," Ammon commented, indicating the other contents in Brad's shopping cart. "Never having to eat vegetables if you don't want to," he continued teasingly, holding up a basket of tomatoes, bean sprouts, and cucumbers.

"True," Brad admitted. "But you may live longer eating the healthy cooking of your wife."

"How are things at the fire station?" asked Ammon, changing the subject.

"Good. Actually I'm just picking up some stuff to take with me. I've been called out to help with a forest fire that started in the Bob a couple of days ago.

"You mean the one that started this weekend? I thought they used volunteers and forest service guys for those."

"They do, but it's out of control so they're calling for more help. Chief Fitch has offered as many of us as he can spare."

"Oh, well…How long do you think it'll take to get it under control? London's been wanting us to get together again."

"I don't know. Hopefully, not more than a few days if we're lucky. It's hard to say though." Whew! He didn't even have to make up an excuse this time. Now he wouldn't have to suffer through another awkward evening at the Moffatt house.

"Okay, well I'll just have to tell her to put her plans on hold."

"Thanks, Ammon. I appreciate it," Brad told him. Then, as though just thinking of it he continued, "And do me a favor, would you? Just don't mention my leaving to London or the kids." It would be nice to think that London was home worrying about him, but it wouldn't be right. "I don't want them to worry."

'You want me to worry all by myself?" It was a rhetorical question that Ammon didn't expect him to answer. "I won't say anything so long as you promise to be careful and not die," he said, only half joking.

"You afraid of a little competition?" came Brad's mocking reply.

"From you…?" Ammon left that thought hanging while he laughed halfheartedly. Brad chuckled and knew the jibe was taken as it was meant. "Seriously, pal," Ammon cautioned, trying to keep the tone light while stressing that he understood the gravity of the situation, "Be careful."

"Yeah, I'll do that." He paused for a minute then continued as an afterthought, "And if something—"

Ammon heard the hesitation in Brad's voice and wouldn't let him finish the thought. "It won't! Just be careful!" he emphasized again before slapping Brad on the shoulder. "I'll be praying for you."

"Oh... Thanks." Awkward! Brad thought pushing his cart toward the check-out counter. He appreciated the thought, but had little hope it would do him any good.

Brad pulled his Jeep into the clearing that had been designated for parking and looked across at the sea of tents, emergency vehicles, port-o-potties and men. It reminded him of a large Boy Scout jamboree, with the difference being no one appeared to be having fun. The men were all dirty from the soot on their faces to the scarred and blackened clothes they all wore. A few were in uniform and some were suited up in full fire gear, ready to take their shift on the front line. The one thing they all had in common; they all looked tired. Brad was glad to be one of their reinforcements knowing that someone could now get a few hours of much needed sleep.

"Come on," he said to the two other men who'd driven up with him. "Let's find out who's in charge and get suited up." He slammed the door of the Jeep shut and clicked the locks in place with his key chain remote. Already the sun was hot and the air tangy with smoke. Brad pulled his sunglasses over his eyes as he searched the sky for clouds. "It's gonna be a scorcher today," he mumbled to no one in particular.

The three men wandered the site seeking someone who could tell them who was in charge. All hands seemed to point in different directions, but after picking their way among the scattered tents and cook fires, they spotted a large, burly man with a clipboard standing in front of a large green pump engine.

"You the man in charge?" Brad asked.

"Chief Charlie Carruthers," he answered without looking up from the clipboard. The radio in the truck behind him beeped to life with static and muffled voices. He grabbed the hand receiver from the dashboard and held it to his mouth, "Repeat. I said repeat."

Static continued to muffle the voices but Brad could clearly hear the incoming message, "Wind shifting southwest. Retreating to 113 degrees 7 minutes west, 47 degrees 113 minutes north."

"Roger. Copy that," called Chief Carruthers and replaced the radio on its hook. "Damn wind," he cursed. Turning back to Brad and his co-workers he asked, "What can I do for you?"

"Brad Stevenson, Kalispell Fire Department. This is Casey Dye and Brett Fisher." Each of them shook hands as they were introduced. "Chief Fitch sent us up to help, sir."

"Good, we could use it," he said sternly. It was obvious Chief Carruthers was a no nonsense kind of man, his voice gruff and his sentences clipped. "Equipment?"

"Yes, we brought two suits apiece, tanks, masks, gloves," Casey listed.

"Good. Suit up. We've got tired men up there. You'll take a shift with Sargent Powell's team at 0800. Shovels are on the trucks."

It was, as Brad had predicted, a scorcher. Dressed in full turnout gear with a thirty pound gas tank strapped to his back, he spent six hours digging ditches under the blazing August sun. There didn't seem to be enough water in the whole state of Montana that could quench his thirst. When Chief Carruthers called up and assigned the team Brad was working with to move to another location, it was a relief to take a break on the truck, if only for the twenty minutes it took to drive there. For the next six hours he traded his shovel for a chain saw as he and the nine other men on the team cleared dead growth from the forest floor trying to expand the no burn zone.

It was exhausting work and not the kind of thing one imagines a fireman doing, but Brad knew from his years as a volunteer for the forest department that stopping a forest fire required cutting off its fuel supply. While helicopters and planes worked to douse the flames from above, ground crews worked to clear areas of old growth and dead trees that would burn hot and fast. Ditches were dug and dirt thrown up to create a barricade, much like a moat surrounding a castle. Only this castle had no prince or princess, thought Brad, just one mean, fire-breathing dragon.

By nine o'clock that night when the truck pulled back into the clearing, his whole body ached, and it was only the first day. He'd forgotten the physical demand required for this job, and longed for a cool shower to ease his aching muscles, not to mention the need for rinsing the crusting layer of salt that had formed over his skin from all the sweat.

"I can't decide what I want most," Casey groaned, "Food, a shower, or sleep."

"Whichever requires the least amount of energy," Brett supplied. "I don't think I can even get my hand to my mouth. I might just have to lick any food I find off the ground."

"I hear ya, man," agreed Brad. "If I didn't think these clothes would permanently stick to my skin, I might just sit here 'til we're called up again." He tossed aside his helmet and tank and laid back in the long meadow grass. The sun was just setting and the temperature was finally dropping to a more comfortable level.

"Do you think Dominoes delivers up here?" Casey asked, dropping his gear beside Brad's and plopping down next to him. "I could eat a dozen or so." Casey Dye was a big man at nearly two hundred eighty-five pounds, most of which was muscle if you discounted the large beer belly that hung from his six foot three inch frame.

"That's just an appetizer," said Brett. "What'll we have for dinner?" He had a much smaller build, but Brad had once watched him eat fifteen hotdogs in fifteen minutes; and lost twenty bucks to Chief Fitch for it too.

Brad slowly got to his feet and the three men began taking off the heavy outer jumpsuit that protected their bodies, piling it neatly next to the Jeep where it would be ready for their next shift. Too exhausted to speak anymore, they silently unloaded the Jeep and pitched their tents. Brad settled for a gallon of water and a Power Bar before sleep overcame him. For the first time in several months he was too tired to even dream about London.

Chapter 9

"Are you sure you'll be alright?" Sister Chapman asked Sky. "Maybe you should wait and have a couple of the brethren go with you when they get here."

"No. The girls and I will be fine. Quit worrying so much. You'd think we were crossing over the mountains, not just going up the trail six miles," Sky replied good-naturedly. The six of them would be hiking to Upper Holland Lake along the Sapphire Lake trail. It was a strenuous hike and would push the girls, but she was confident they were up to the challenge. The trail was actually a loop and they would be able to return back to camp the next day by an easier route. Sky had chosen to take the more difficult assent because it was used less by pack animals and it had more waterfalls to enjoy along the way.

"I know. But you could run into a bear or something."

"You're right. And he could wander in here to camp just as easily." Sky continued shoving items into her pack as she spoke. Looking up at Sister Chapman's worried expression she joked, "Are you sure it's us you're worried about and not all of you here without our extra noise for protection?"

For the past two days of camp there had been plenty of noise to keep all wild animals at bay, including squirrels and chipmunks. The girls had giggled and screamed to their hearts content with no one but the birds to answer back.

Sky was pleasantly surprised at just how well everything had gone so far. The girls had all behaved wonderfully. There were no squabbles among them, and they seemed to be getting along with each other. It had warmed her heart to see some of the older girls helping the younger girls master the certification skills. All of the typical barriers that would keep the girls in groups seemed to have broken down and now they were all just one happy, noisy, and very dirty family.

They had stuck closely to the schedule Sky had devised before camp began. Each morning began with a flag ceremony and devotional. The girls, sleepy-eyed and grumbling, were not happy about the early morning routine, but it was Sky's favorite part of the day, when the air was clean and crisp and before the sun was blistering hot.

That first breakfast had been an adventure in and of itself. Sky worked with the girls to get a fire going in the pit, while Sister Chapman showed them how to use a propane cook stove. The first morning they'd eaten burned eggs and pancakes, but by the second morning things had improved and the girls used their newly learned skills to avoid another blackened breakfast.

Outdoor cooking, in Sky's opinion, was one of the best parts of camping. Food always tasted better cooked over the fire, even hot dogs. Her mouth would water over the thought of Dutch oven barbecue chicken. There was no comparing a pineapple upside-down cake cooked in the heavy cast-iron pot to one cooked in a traditional oven. Camping meant s'mores and banana boats stuffed with melting chocolate, gooey marshmallows, and any other sugary treat the imagination could think of to stuff into a banana before it was wrapped in foil and tossed onto the red coals of a campfire. Perhaps it was the added preparation needed to make the meal, or maybe just enjoying it in the beautiful mountains that made it better, she wasn't sure. But she knew for certain it all tasted delicious and made the whole experience that much better.

Their afternoons had been filled with activities and crafts. The girls had strung homemade bead necklaces and tied friendship bracelets with embroidery floss. Several of the girls walked around camp wearing the silk flower headbands they'd made. The wooden plaques with temple pictures modge-podged to the front had turned out particularly nice and the lesson on temples had encouraged the girls to keep them displayed as a reminder of their future goal of temple marriage.

They'd played games that had them all laughing so hard, Sky thought she would pull a stomach muscle, especially when the smallest Beehive, Sadie West, had blown the largest bubble gum bubble, winning the contest just before the pink goo exploded, covering her face completely.

The trust-building exercises had been powerful lessons to the girls and Sky felt like they'd learned something valuable from the experience. She'd watched anxiously as each blindfolded girl had listened carefully to 'the still small voice' that would guide them through the maze of obstacles, back to the safety of their leaders. It had brought back memories of her own girls' camp days when she, too, had been blindfolded and had to listen for the quiet voice of her camp leader to give her directions. It was a lesson she relied on often as an adult when she was seeking for answers to prayer; listening carefully for the whisperings of the Spirit to show her the way.

Two days of camp had brought laughter and fun, but there were quiet times that were also enjoyable. Each day the girls would take their journals and scriptures and seek out a place within the camp to read and reflect. When camp was quiet, the stillness broken only by the sound of rustling branches and occasional bird calls, the Spirit would speak to Sky and she would revel in gratitude for the beauty that God had created all around them. It was at these times that she also shared her gratitude for this experience and the Lord's trust in calling her to this assignment. Surely, she was benefiting more than the girls.

She felt like Girls' camp had been a huge success so far and the fears and insecurities she'd felt that first day were all but forgotten.

"Sky, I know you are completely capable of taking the five of those girls on an overnight hike," Sister Chapman continued. "I'm just a little uneasy about it, that's all. It seems to be getting hazier. I hope that doesn't mean it's going to rain on you guys."

Sky finished shoving the last of her gear into the pack that already had her sleeping bag and bed roll fastened to the bottom with the pack's stretch cords. As she stood, she hefted it just off the ground to test its weight. Satisfied that it was balanced, she swung it around to her shoulders with a groan and snapped the harness around her waist. She smiled triumphantly. "Don't worry, 'mother,' we'll be fine," she repeated again. She looked up at the sky. It did appear to be getting hazier, the blue less distinct, but it was probably just high cirrus clouds. Nothing to worry about. "If it does decide to sprinkle, a little rain never hurt anybody. And if we see any bears we'll be sure to avoid them. Now, stop fussing and help me gather up these girls. We've got to get on the trail before it gets any hotter. I'm already sweating!"

"Are we almost there?" Laela called from behind Sky. The dark haired, black-eyed sixteen year old, Laela Stone, trudged slowly, bringing up the tail of the small group of six hikers. "My shoulders are killing me," she complained.

"Mine are too!" Heather joined in from just in front of her. At sixteen, Heather Cordin was only two months younger than Laela, but with her willow slim build that had not begun to mature and her doe-like brown eyes she appeared to be much younger. Her twin sister, Amanda, followed closely behind Sky as she led them up the trail. The two girls were identical in looks only; their personalities completely different. While Heather tended to be loud and always in the thick of things, Amanda was quiet and timid. Amanda wouldn't dare complain, even though her shoulders ached from the heavy pack and she was limping slightly, probably from a blister rubbing uncomfortably against her shoe.

Emma Knudson and Annie Marquardt were the oldest girls of the group. Sky knew Emma well since she'd been her babysitter when Emma was only five. She'd spent a lot of time as a young woman watching the Knudson's children. It hardly seemed possible that at seventeen, Emma was as old now as she had been when they'd first met. She had grown into a beautiful young woman who was also intelligent, responsible, and caring. Sky knew she was planning to attend BYU in a year and she wouldn't be surprised if Emma went on to serve a mission. With the depth of her testimony, she would be an asset to the Lord's army.

Annie Marquardt was new to the ward and the area. Sky didn't know much about her besides her name and age. She was pleasant enough and Sky had watched her participate in the camp activities, but she didn't interact with the adult leaders very much. She thought the overnight hike might give her a chance to get to know Annie better and have more time to talk one-on-one.

"We've got another mile to go," Sky called to the trail of girls behind her. "We'll take a break in that shade up there and have some water."

There were cheers from behind that brought a smile to her face. She had to hand it to them, they were all doing a great job, despite the occasional complaints. It was a grueling hike made all the worse by the heat. Her own back was soaked through to the skin and she longed to find a stream and jump in. The distance from the camp was only six miles, but the elevation gain was near twenty three hundred feet which meant they'd been hiking uphill for almost the entire morning. With the sun nearing its zenith, it felt more like the depths of hell than the stairway to heaven.

They had stopped occasionally along the trail to admire the scenery and catch their breath. One section of the trail followed the contour of a river as it snaked through the forest. The river was low from the drought, but there was enough water in it to create some stunning waterfalls. They had all luxuriated in the cooling spray of fine mist that emanated up from the base of the falls. And when at last they felt rejuvenated enough to go on, they would continue climbing past the boulders covered in a carpet of moss until finally they reached the switchbacks that would take them the last stretch of their journey.

"Okay girls, you can take off your packs and have a seat." Cheers arose all around her as Sky gratefully undid the belt bracing her pack around her waist and slid the heavy canvas bag to the ground. Guzzling water from her canteen, she watched as five exhausted girls did the same, plunking down packs and falling to the dirt, regardless of getting dirty. Grateful for the shade and a chance to rest, they rummaged in their packs for their lunch that would restore their energy.

"I'll trade you," Heather said, holding a granola bar out to Amanda. "My chocolate chip for your peanut butter?"

"Yeah, sure," Amanda agreed before eagerly ripping her own granola bar open.

There wasn't much conversation as the girls greedily ate the sack lunches they had packed that morning. The peanut butter sandwiches that had seemed so unappetizing only a few hours before were now quickly being devoured by hungry females.

"Are you going to finish those potato chips?" Laela asked Heather.

"Yeah, of course," she answered, "I'm starving."

"Me too. And since I'm bigger, I probably need more food than you do to keep me alive so you should share yours with me," Laela suggested with a smile.

"No way! Just because I'm small…well all that means is that I have a high metabolism. I probably need more than you because I don't have much in the way of reserved energy."

"Was that a fat joke?"

"No." Heather laughed with Laela. "Now get away from my chips." The girls played tug of war with the bag until Heather succeeded in getting it away from Laela. The two then started a version of keep away, drawing the other girls into the melee and tossing the bag to Emma.

Sky leaned back against her pack, watching the girls play and tease. Either the food had renewed their strength or the hike hadn't been too hard on them. She knew there'd be some blisters, tired feet, and aching shoulders tonight, but she hoped their sense of accomplishment would outweigh all of those.

The site she had picked out earlier that summer was only another mile up the trail. It was flat enough to camp without sliding down hill while they slept, and best of all, there was a small freshwater spring not far from them where they could refill their water supply. Water was heavy and not easy to carry so she was happy to not have to haul their needed overnight supply with them. Without that spring they'd have to be more careful about how much they drank, and in this heat, that was hard to do. It was too dangerous to drink from streams and rivers, even though they were in a protected wilderness area. The chance of getting giardia was too much of a risk. She didn't want to send any of the girls home with a horrible bacterial infection that would land them in the hospital. Better to be safe and drink only from springs coming straight from the rocks.

Annie sat leaning against the opposite side of the tree Sky had chosen for shade, her eyes closed. She hadn't joined with the others as they ate and played, only sat back watching and smiling as she ate her own lunch. Sky hated to disturb her reverie, but they needed to get back on the trail. It was likely to take them another two hours just to go the last mile.

"Are you okay?" Sky stood and stretched, pulling her sweat-dampened t-shirt away from her back. It was tempting to stay right where they were. The thought of putting the heavy pack back on her shoulders was as unappealing to her as she knew it would be to the girls.

"Yeah, I'm fine, just resting." Annie answered.

"Have you been drinking water? I don't want you getting dehydrated."

"I've gone through one of my water bottles, but I still have one left."

"That's good. You'll probably need it. This last mile is going to be… challenging," Sky said, trying to sound optimistic. Taking the opportunity to learn more about her, she asked, "Have you done any backpacking before?"

"No." Her answer was short, but not rude.

"Have you done much camping before?"

"No."

"You don't like to talk about yourself much, do you?" Sky asked, deciding the only way to get to know this young woman was to be blunt. "I feel like I've gotten to know most of the other girls, but you don't seem to say much. I hope it's nothing I've done." She turned then allowing Annie some time and making it clear that she didn't expect a response if she wasn't comfortable giving one.

Sky called to the other girls who had wandered off a ways to get their packs on and get ready. She hefted hers onto her shoulders and secured the belt around her waist once again. She knew it wasn't possible, but the pack seemed to have gained ten pounds since they'd stopped for lunch.

Turning back to Annie, she offered her hand and pulled her to her feet. Sky silently held up Annie's pack so she could slip it on.

"You got it?" She asked, as she heard Annie's belt click.

Annie turned around. "Yeah, I got it," she said.

All around them, girls were groaning as they too hoisted their packs and secured them to their backs.

"Sister Ryder…" Annie said quietly as they all headed back towards the trail. Sky heard the tentative voice and urged the others ahead of her.

"What is it Annie?"

"It's…Well, it's…I just wanted you to know it's not you. I mean, I think you're great and all…like, you're actually pretty cool."

"Well, thanks. I think you're pretty cool too," Sky returned the compliment. She kept walking, bringing up the tail end of the small group of hikers with Annie just ahead of her and Emma leading them up the trail. It was an awkward place to hold a conversation with the trail too narrow to walk two abreast. Sky wasn't even sure if they were having a conversation or if that was all Annie wanted to say, but she didn't want to pressure her into saying more either.

They took several more steps before Annie stopped and turned to face Sky. "I'm just not used to having anyone care, is all."

Taken aback by her sudden admission, Sky wasn't sure how to respond. Curiosity raced through her mind; Who is this girl? What's her story? What about her home life? Doesn't she have any friends? Such a beautiful young woman, how could she think that?

Before she could respond, Annie turned back and moved quickly up the trail, closing the gap between her and the other girls. Sky could hear Laela starting a round of 'I'm going on a trip and I'm going to bring…' just as Annie caught up with them.

"Curiouser and curiouser…" Sky whispered to no one in particular before she too joined the group.

"Your turn Sister Ryder," Heather called back. "We're going on a trip and we're going to bring an MP3 player, sunscreen, water bottle, curling iron, bear spray, cell phone, Volkswagen Beetle and what else?"

"A gallon of ice cream!" she called out, laughing. "A gallon of chocolate chip cookie dough ice cream!"

Late in the afternoon they reached the clearing where they would camp for the night. They had passed the two Sapphire Lakes, the highest point on the trail consisting of a steep set of switchbacks along the cliff's side. Eventually they'd begun a short descent into the valley where Upper Holland Lake sat nestled, surrounded by highland meadows and subalpine forest. Towering mountains surrounded three sides of the meadow, and to the west they could see a panoramic view of the snow encrusted Mission Mountains. Wildflowers in every color mixed with the high mountain grass, red Indian Paintbrush, purple Lupine, golden Yarrow, blue Forget-Me-Not, and large white puff balls of Bear Grass. It was beautiful, but the girls hardly took notice of the flowers and view in their relief to unload their packs and stop for the night.

"This is it girls," Sky said, turning circles and gazing at the mountain tops surrounding them. "Isn't it gorgeous!"

Emma dropped her pack next to Sky's and rolled her aching shoulders before collapsing to the ground as though she'd just run a marathon. "I so deserve a medal for this!" She squinted against the glare of sun and looked up at Sky. "But you're right, it does look like totally amazing from down here."

Heather, hands braced against her knees, panting, said, "It's a good thing it's beautiful, or I might have to kill someone for putting me through this torture. I am so never doing this again!"

"No kidding! The next time I go backpacking, it's like gonna be through the hall at school," said Laela.

"What about you, Amanda," Sky asked, "what do you think? Are you ready to kill me for dragging you up here?"

"No. I have to admit there were a few times back there when I had serious ideas about revenge, like sticking a snake in your sleeping bag or something, but now I'm thinking it's totally worth it!"

"This is the closest I am ever getting to nature," Laela continued. "I don't think people were meant to live without running water."

"Not to mention flush toilets," Annie added.

Sky was happy to see Annie was warming up to the group and joining in the banter.

"Speaking of which, there aren't any, as you may have guessed. Let's be sure to all take someone with us when we have to visit the woods; we don't want any unexpected grizzlies sneaking up behind while we do our business. And remember to grab the shovel before you go and dig a pit like I taught you," Sky reminded the girls. "We do have running water, of sorts, though. Come on, I'll show you."

Sky lead them to the base of a large boulder not far from where they had set their packs. The ground surrounding the rock was damp, almost marsh-like and on the other side of it was a small stream hidden in the tall grass just deep enough to submerge a water bottle without stirring up the mud below.

"This is a freshwater spring," she explained. "You can fill your bottles here. It's safe to drink."

"But you told us we should never drink water from a stream," Amanda reminded Sky.

"You're right, I did. But this isn't a stream. It's a spring. It comes from deep in the earth where it has been purified."

"You mean all those water companies have to hike way up in the mountains to get spring water for the grocery stores?" Laela asked.

"No, the spring water in the grocery stores means they collected it in the spring so it's fresher than summer water," Heather answered.

"Really?" Laela looked at her with amazement. "I never knew that."

"Not really, Laela," Emma corrected.

"You're so blond sometimes!" Heather laughed and dodged Laela's retaliating swing before it could connect with her arm.

"There are springs all over the place, you just have to know where to find them. And I wouldn't be too certain that spring fresh water at the grocery store is bottled from a spring like this. It's probably more like positive advertising to get people to buy it," said Sky.

"Kind of like you telling us this hike would be 'kind of difficult'?" Heather asked, making quotation marks with her fingers in the air. "I think you should have advertised it as 'extremely brutal and potentially life threatening!'"

"There was no false advertising," Sky protested. "It was definitely kind of difficult."

"Sister Ryder, I think your definition of difficult and mine are totally different!" said Emma. "But I will be the first to drink this mountain spring water and hope I don't die!"

The girls each took turns refilling their water bottles and quenching their thirst. The heat of the afternoon sun was less intense now that it was past its zenith, but the air was still warm and dry. The wind had picked up as well and blew steadily across the meadow.

As day drifted into evening, Sky gathered the girls in a circle and they sat on the ground reviewing some of the skills they should have learned from the Girls Camp Manual. They practiced identifying plants, flowers and clouds while they munched on trail mix and licorice.

Heather lay next to Laela with Amanda on the other side of her, each gazing into the blue expanse above them. "I think that one looks like an ice cream cone," Amanda said, pointing to a group of clouds in the east.

"No, I think it's more like a really fat dude with his hands on his hips, kind of like when Principal Donovan is staring down some kid in the hall and you know he's totally in trouble," said Laela.

"Ice cream cone," agreed Heather, "definitely ice cream cone."

"Aren't we supposed to be identifying these?" asked Annie.

"That's what we're doing," answered Laela.

"No, like with real names and stuff."

"Yeah, but that's not as much fun as 'fat dude,'" Heather laughed.

"Looks like smoke to me," was Emma's contribution.

"Those are probably cirrus clouds straight up," said Sky pointing above her. "And those large cotton-looking ones are cumulus clouds. They can develop into storms if there's enough moisture, but I don't think we're in danger of that tonight. The weather report said no rain."

"I'm dying for it to rain!" exclaimed Heather. "I planted a garden for one of my value projects and I've had to keep it watered all summer because we haven't had any rain. It's such a pain. I hope my mom hasn't let it die while I've been gone this week."

"Have you seen how low the rivers are?" Laela asked. "My dad and I went rafting last weekend and we had to like practically carry the raft over a couple of spots because there was like almost no water. It totally bummed me out. It was like you could feel the rocks under the raft. I ended up with a huge bruise."

"I heard if we don't get rain soon they might start rationing water in the valley," said Annie.

"I've heard that too," Emma confirmed. "My dad always jokes that there are really only two seasons in Montana; winter and fire."

"Well, we've certainly had our share of fires in the past couple of years," Sky said. "Luckily we have lots of uninhabited land so when there is a fire it doesn't usually threaten people's homes like in California or Colorado."

"Yeah, but we did have that fire not too long ago that made them close down the lodge in Glacier National Park," Amanda reminded her.

"True. That was mostly a precaution though. They were able to get it contained before it got dangerously close to the lodge."

"All this talk about fires is making me hungry," complained Heather. "When are we eating dinner? And what's it going to be?"

Dinner that evening consisted of re-constituted freeze dried meals cooked in boiling water in a makeshift aluminum can over a propane flame. As they sat devouring macaroni and cheese, chicken with potatoes, and pasta with marinara sauce, they each agreed that food had never tasted quite as good.

When they had finished eating, Sky showed them how to string up their packs and hang them from the trees just in case a hungry bear came sniffing around. Once everything was secure for the night, they settled down and played card games on top of their bed rolls while they waited for the sun to set.

Darkness was slow in coming and only Heather, Annie, and Emma were awake to watch the stars come out with Sky. Laela and Amanda had given in to sleep, their bodies exhausted. Even through the haze the Milky Way crossed the heavens like a white ribbon and there were enough stars to make the rest look like grains of sand in the night sky.

"I love this," Sky said dreamily. "Whenever I get the chance to see the sky like this, I am reminded of just how great God really is and that we are nothing but a speck of dust in the big scheme of things."

"Yeah, but we're still His children, so we can't be totally worthless," said Heather.

"Of course we're not worthless," Sky confirmed, trying to share with the girls what she was saying, "just small. Looking at the stars reminds me of God's power and when you think about all the things He has made and all that He can do, the fact that we *are* his children and that he knows each one of us individually is overwhelming to me."

"What is it the scriptures say?" Emma spoke up, "This is my work and my glory, to bring to pass the eternal life of man."

"That's just it," Sky continued. "We *are* His work and glory. In all of this," she said, motioning to the dark expanse above them. "We are the crown jewel of His creations. Kind of makes you think doesn't it?" Sky reached over and squeezed Annie's hand, hoping the gesture would convey the thoughts she dared not speak aloud with the other girls listening. "We're never alone in all of this. He is always there for us. He loves us above all things." It was a simple testimony, but it felt good to share it with these incredible young women she was learning to love more and more with every minute they spent together.

"We'd better get some sleep or we'll be too tired tomorrow," said Sky.

"Yeah, the good news is, tomorrow will be all downhill," said a sleepy Emma.

"The bad news though," said Annie, squirming in her sleeping bag as she struggled to find a comfortable position on the hard ground, "we have to put those dumb packs back on."

"Please! Don't remind me," groaned Heather.

"Good night girls," Sky whispered. "Sleep tight and don't let the mosquitoes bite!"

Chapter 10

Brad awoke with a start at the sound of his cell phone beeping next to his ear. He had set the alarm on it to wake him before his next shift. It had only been six hours since he'd fallen asleep, but sleeping like the dead had left him refreshed and ready for another exhausting day.

He nudged the sleeping bag next to him with his foot. "Hey Casey, you awake man?" Casey Dye shared the four-man tent that Brad had brought. Brett Fisher, the other man they'd brought up with them, had opted to sleep in the open.

"Uuugghhh," Casey groaned and rolled onto his back. "It can't be time already. I was just about to answer the million dollar question. I had all the answers too."

"It's time." Brad sat up, pushing his sleeping bag off and reaching for his boots. He slipped them on and stood up outside.

Brett was already up, his sleeping bag rolled and set next to the tent. Steam, barely visible in the dim light of pre-dawn, rose from the Styrofoam cup in his hand. "Thought you guys were going to sleep all day," he said, taking a sip of the warm brew. "Time's a' wastin', fire's blazin'."

"Any more of that?" Casey asked coming out of the tent next to Brad, and indicating the cup with a nod of his head.

"That way." Brett gestured, looking to his left. "But I warn you, tastes like it was made with yesterday's ashes."

"Perfect," said Brad. "Bring me a cup, would ya?" he called as Casey headed in the general direction he'd been pointed to.

"What's the word this morning?" He asked Brett.

Not good. Still no containment. Winds were too strong through the night and the sucker jumped right over some of the traps we dug yesterday. It's split and now we've got two main hot spots to worry about. Some concern about it heading closer to camping areas."

"You doin' alright?" asked Brad.

"Yeah, I'll make it. Slept good at least. You?"

"Like I was dead."

Casey walked briskly back towards their tent, dodging men, camp chairs, coolers and fire gear, one cup held in each hand. Holding one of the disposable cups out for Brad, he said, "Suit up boys, we've got our orders."

"What's the plan?" asked Brett.

"I ran into Chief What's-His-name--"

"Carruthers," Brad supplied.

"Said if we were ready, he needed us with an evac team. Looks like the dragon's getting awful close to some camp sites and he wants them out of there ASAP. While we're there we'll clear a section, set up a blockade and try to save what we can." Casey gulped the rest of his morning coffee and started gathering his gear from in front of the tent where he'd dropped it the night before.

Energized from the caffeine, Brad joined him and soon the three men were dressed in fire retardant suits, carrying helmets and oxygen tanks towards their transportation.

The evacuation team consisted of six men, Brad, Casey, Brett and three others they'd not met until five minutes before moving out. They rode in silence along the highway, each man keeping his thoughts quiet. Though the sun had not peeked over the mountains, dawn was fully bright, not a cloud in the early morning sky, just a whole lot of smoke.

Brad watched out the window, his eyes searching the grass along the road for deer. It was the time of day when they'd likely be out feeding. The last thing they needed was to hit one and cause a delay.

Time was of the essence as the fire moved closer to the more populated camping areas. Chief Carruthers had showed them on the map the area they needed to evacuate. He had already contacted the forest service and asked that they help by sending rangers out to clear as many sites as possible. Still, there was a lot of area to cover and not many to do it. Camp grounds were bound to be full with it being August.

He pulled his cell phone from his pocket, curious if he had any coverage. He didn't. He wondered if Ammon had told London and the kids where he'd gone. He thought about the last summer and the hiking trips they'd taken together. Gosh, he'd loved that. Loved her. It had been in a similar situation then--fighting a forest fire--that made him realize just how much he loved London and wanted to marry her.

Thinking back over all that had happened since, it was probably for the best that she'd said no to him. This way she didn't have to worry when he was off fighting a fire. It would make doing his job that much harder, he reasoned. She was happier this way, with her husband and kids, her God and church. He didn't need any of it. In fact, he'd totally given up even praying. He figured it hadn't done any good when he really wanted something before, what was the point now when he couldn't seem to have what—or who—he wanted. Life was so much simpler when it was just him.

"We're coming up on Holland Lake," said the man driving the van. He'd been introduced that morning simply as Dan, and seemed to be in charge of the group. "Forest service says there are sixty camp sites but no way to know how many are occupied. We'll have to spread out and tell everyone to clear out." He turned the van off the highway and drove slowly over the speed bumps at the entrance to the campground. "I'm going to talk to the camp host, see if they know how many are here, make sure we get them all. It's early still, you may have to wake some people up, but don't be shy. Remember, stress urgency. Time is precious."

Dan pulled to a stop in front of the camp host spot where a large motor home was parked. A bamboo mat, lawn furniture, and citronella candle torches gave it a homey look. The six men, all in fire suits, jumped out. The smell of smoke hung heavy in the air. Brad wondered if it was from camp fires or from the blaze that was headed their way. Like a well-orchestrated military group, they each moved off in different directions without having to say a single word. Brad and Casey ran in the direction of the B-loop, Brett and a man named Jarvis headed towards C-loop and the other two would take A-loop, where they were currently parked. They had a job to do, and they each knew how to do it.

The first two camp sites were easy enough. One was already packed and ready to pull the chocks from his RV tires when Brad ran up, quickly explained the situation, and directed the campers to stay clear of the area. Casey did the same, in the next site where a man sat enjoying his morning coffee while bacon fried over the open fire pit.

They continued moving leap frog, one ahead of the other, trying to inform campers of the impending danger without scaring them into a panic.

At one site, Brad pounded on the door of a large fifth-wheel trailer. There was no response. Again he pounded the door, calling loudly. Finally he tried the handle. Fortunately, it was open and he pushed his way in. In the back of the trailer, a man and woman lay sleeping, oblivious to the noise. Brad clomped loudly, hoping one of them would wake up before he reached them, but the amount of empty beer cans was a good indication that they were knocked out cold. He had to shake the man vigorously before he came out of his drunken stupor enough to realize there was a stranger in his trailer.

"Wake up!" Brad shouted.

"Huh...? Keep it down--my head!" he groaned and rolled over

"Get up! You've got to leave NOW!"

"Wha--" he sputtered. "Who are you?"

"Fireman! Fire! Now get up and get out of here before you're toast!" Brad had lost all patience with the man.

The woman began to stir and finally rolled over and sat up, her hair standing out and her eyes squinting against the light.

"Look ma'am, you've got to get out of here. There's a forest fire coming this way and we're evacuating the area."

The couple registered his words in unison and began scrambling for clothes. Brad left them, certain they would hurry, despite whatever hangover they were nursing.

Brad and Casey reached the far end of the loop together. There had only been two vacant camp sites. The languorous atmosphere of an early morning in the woods had been replaced with anxiety and chaos. People scrambled everywhere, shoving camping equipment into cars. Tents were dismantled, RVs unhooked. It was like the circus pulling out of town.

The group camping site at the end of B-loop was already alive with young girls gathered around a make-shift flag pole where the Stars and Stripes flew in the morning breeze. Some of the girls were wrapped in blankets, huddled together for warmth against the early chill, and seemed less than awake as they stood listening to a woman talk.

Brad headed straight to the center of the circle, addressing the woman. "Are you in charge here?"

Obviously taken aback by the intruder dressed in a fire suit, the woman stammered, "Uh…yes. Yes I am. Rochelle Chapman. Is there a problem?"

"I'm afraid it's time to go," Brad answered curtly without explaining.

Fully awake now, the girls gawked at the handsome stranger, waiting for more.

"You can't just—"

"There's a forest fire headed this way. You've got to leave. Now! The whole place is being evacuated."

"But we can't," the woman cried, panic beginning to creep into her face.

"Can I help you, sir?" An elderly man asked, coming forward, a note of authority in his voice. Holding out his hand to introduce himself, he said, "I'm Earl Hunt."

Brad shook his hand in a goodwill gesture, repeating what he had just told the others. Then he turned to address them all and began giving instructions. "You can start by dropping tents." He looked around at the staring eyes of twenty young girls, none of whom could be more than fifteen. Behind him, Casey had already begun to dismantle the flag pole, folding the flag with less than the respect it deserved. "Look, I don't mean to be rude, but there's a major fire coming this way. We've got to get you out of here and to a safe location."

"But we don't have enough vehicles to leave," Rochelle pointed out. "We've only got two cars between us. We have more members of our group who'll be joining us tonight and they were bringing the trailer to haul our stuff and bring the girls back tomorrow."

Brad thought for a minute, looking around at the number of people and the amount of gear.

"Okay, here's what we'll have to do. Pack up as much as you can and put personal stuff in your trunks. Each car has room for five?" He didn't wait for an answer but continued talking quickly, figuring in his head. "We've got a 15 passenger van. We'll put the rest in there and stuff as much of the remaining gear in as we can get. You may have to leave some behind."

"I've got room for eight in my Suburban," said Earl Hunt.

"Good, good. Now let's get moving. We don't have much time."

The camp became a riot of noise and activity as girls rushed to their tents to remove their camping equipment. In their panic to leave a few started pulling down tents before they'd been emptied. Girls shouted as their nylon homes came crashing down around them. A few stood helpless, too frightened to move, too scared to know what to do. One even began crying uncontrollably. The woman in charge did her best to comfort her, but there just wasn't time to console her completely.

"Mandy! Carmen!" she called to two of the young women who had just finished pulling the stakes from their tent. "Don't bother trying to get it to fit back in the bag. Just fold it the best you can and roll it up. We'll have to sort it all out and get everything in order when we get home."

"Casey," Brad called. "Run for the van, I'll help finish up here. Maybe bring Brett back with you and he can help."

"I'm on it!" He called, running back towards the host site and waving over his head.

Brother Hunt pulled his suburban around and opened the hatch. Girls holding sleeping bags, pillows and duffle bags swarmed him trying to get their stuff all stowed away.

Rochelle assigned one of the young women to get her things out of the leader's tent while she worked to stuff all of the cooking utensils, bowls, and pans back into the plastic tote bins they'd brought them in.

"Can I ride with you, Sister Chapman?" asked Brianna.

"Sure," she answered, not really paying attention to who had even asked. She was too intent on doing her job to notice. "Here, take my keys." she said, pulling them from her pocket and handing them to the young girl. "Open my trunk and put your stuff in. Do the same for whoever else is going to ride with me."

"Sister Chapman!" Sarah called from the leader's tent. "What should I do with Sister Ryder's things?

Rochelle froze. There was still a group missing. In all the commotion she had not remembered Sky and the five other girls who would be returning to camp in another four, maybe five hours. Did they have that long? How long could they wait and still be safe? And if they left now, there wouldn't be anyone here waiting for them; no cars to drive them to safety. "Oh Father," she whispered, running towards Brad, "Please help them get to safety."

"Hey, we've got a problem," she said to Brad who was bent over, rolling up a large tent.

He looked up, but didn't stop rolling. "What is it?"

Brad watched as panic bubbled to the surface like a geyser. Her calm demeanor she'd maintained at the news of having to evacuate crumbled and tears welled in her eyes. "There's another group of us."

"We'll just have to squish them into the van, bring less gear," he said, finishing with the tent and standing up. He was a good ten inches taller than her and had to look down at the older woman. He noted the tears in her eyes and was worried that she might give him a hard time about leaving behind some of their stuff. It was a lot easier to replace camping gear than people he wanted to remind her.

"No, they're not here," she explained. "They went on an overnight hike. They're due back around noon. We need to wait for them."

The pungent smell of smoke was getting stronger. The dust that had been churned up in the dismantling process floated in the air, visible through the slanted rays of light now peeking through the pines. For one second the world seemed to move in slow motion.

Then it registered.

"We can't wait."

Brad ran to the van that was pulling to a stop in front of the camp site. Rochelle followed at his heels, protesting. "We have to wait. We can't just leave them!"

Brett and Casey jumped out of the van and immediately pulled open the sliding passenger doors and the back cargo door where girls were already lining up to throw in their stuff. Brad reached Casey as he tossed a sleeping bag that a freckle-faced, red head had just handed him.

"Casey, you're going to have to get these guys out of here. Seems I'll be going for a hike." Relief showed on Rochelle's face to hear him say so. He turned and asked, "Where'd they go?"

"They went up the trail to Upper Holland Lake," she said, pointing to the trail head map at the corner of the road. "The leader, her name's Sky, she said it was about six miles, but I haven't been there. Can't we just wait for them to get down?" she asked hopefully.

"Do you smell that?" Brad sniffed the air. He knew that smell too well. He could taste it, see it. There would be no waiting. This fire would be here soon and it was hungry. He turned to Rochelle and saw the worry in her eyes. Reaching deep to find an ounce of compassion that would override his own sense of impending danger, he reassured her, "Don't worry, I'll find 'em."

Chapter 11

Sky rolled in her sleeping bag, stretching her stiff muscles to relieve some of the tension that had built up from yesterday's hike and the rocky ground she'd slept on. Above her, the sky was blue, hidden behind a mask of haze. The sun had yet to appear from behind the cliffs surrounding the meadow.

When she couldn't get comfortable, she decided she may as well get up and get things going. She could get some water boiled for hot chocolate before the girls woke up. Quietly, she inched the zipper of her sleeping bag down and grabbed her boots she'd left close, in case she'd had to get up in the night. Not one of the girls stirred, cocooned in their own sleeping bags on top of the meadow grass. Sky stretched again, releasing more than one kink in her body. She found her small tea pot to fill with water and started towards the spring.

Despite the early hour, the meadow was already alive and humming. Insects hopped from her path, bees buzzing over wildflowers as they ate the sweet nectar for breakfast. Near the edge of the clearing, just before it was engulfed by forest, a doe and her fawn froze at the sound of Sky's footsteps. The dappled light wasn't quite enough to camouflage them from view, but as Sky moved slowly away, they dipped their heads and continued munching the green carpet at their feet, ignoring her.

It was beautiful and Sky was grateful to be a part of it, despite the poor night's sleep. She'd felt restless throughout the night, never getting quite comfortable. It wasn't unusual to feel every rock when sleeping out in the open, but it was more than that. After star gazing, she'd been unable to settle her mind. Even the prayer they'd said before bed had not helped. Being in the mountains was usually enough to bring peace to her soul, but she felt on edge and couldn't see any reason for it. That's why at the first crack of dawn, she was up and anxious to get back to camp. Perhaps something was wrong there, she reasoned.

At the spring, she carefully pulled aside the grass and exposed the little pool of crystal clear water. She dipped her pot, filling it as high as she could without disturbing the dirt. It was only a little more than half full, but it would have to do.

Walking back to the girls, she saw Emma was at least sitting up, if not actually out of her bag yet. Sky breathed deep, smelling a hint of smoke. That was strange. Where had that come from? They were the only campers in the meadow. It was possible that others were camping in the woods and had started a fire already. For some reason, the smell added to her sense of urgency.

"Good morning," she whispered, coming up behind Emma and placing the pot on top of the small Coleman stove they'd brought for cooking.

"Morning," Emma croaked. She was still bleary eyed, unsure of her surroundings. She looked left, then right, as though to remind herself where she was. Heather, who had slept next to her, was now cuddled close and, Emma gave a gentle shove to give herself more room.

One hand emerged from Laela's bag, pushing it down to expose her face. "It's cold out here!" she complained.

"The sun'll be up over the peaks soon to warm things up," said Sky.

"Looks all cloudy," observed Emma.

"No, just really hazy." Sky looked up, and noted the haze was getting worse, not better as the sun got higher. "We'll have some hot chocolate soon to eat with our breakfast."

"What time is it?" Annie moaned, shielding her eyes from the light as she peeked out of her bag for the first time.

"Somewhere around 8:30, but I don't know for sure. I forgot my watch." said Sky. She knew there was no logical reason for not taking things slowly and enjoying the beautiful morning, but she couldn't shake the feeling that they should hurry. She was glad the girls were waking up.

"If you'd all stop talking," Heather mumbled from deep within her downy covering, "I could get some more sleep." She rolled even closer to Emma, seeking warmth.

Amanda sat up and rubbed her eyes. She yawned and stretched then began coughing. "I think I just swallowed a bug," she gasped and continued coughing and spitting.

"Protein for breakfast," teased Emma.

"Ugghhh! That's so gross!"

"What's burning?" asked Annie. She sniffed the air and looked around searching for a fire that would offer some heat.

"Probably some other campers nearby," answered Sky. She pulled a package of instant oatmeal from her pack and poured it into a cup filled with hot water. She sat stirring her breakfast as the girls slowly pulled themselves from their bags and joined her around the little stove.

Within the hour they were all awake and nearly finished eating. The girls were more inclined to laugh and tease each other than to eat. Sky tried not to be frustrated that they were taking so long to finish breakfast. It wasn't as if it was a gourmet meal, just oatmeal and granola bars. While they ate at a snail's pace, she rearranged the remaining items in her backpack. There wasn't much left to carry back and it would be considerably lighter than the day before. Most of the food she'd carried was gone, although she did still have some granola bars, several bags of trail mix, three MREs, some carrots, a roll of Ritz crackers, and four more single serving pouches of Crystal Lite drink mix to add to her water bottle if she wanted something sweet.

"Those campers must really have a big fire going," Amanda noted, "It totally stinks."

Sky too was noticing the pungent aroma of wood smoke that seemed to be getting worse all the time. "Are you girls about finished?" She asked. "We should probably be on our way." She kept her tone light, but there was an underlying sense of urgency in her words.

"I need to get my sleeping bag rolled tighter today," Heather said. "It felt like it was slipping out constantly yesterday."

"Maybe you need to pull the bungee cords tighter around it," said Laela.

"My peanut butter sandwich is all squished," said Annie, pulling a plastic bag from her pack. "Guess I should have eaten it sooner."

The girls were in the process of repacking their own packs when a man's voice called across the meadow "Hey!"

Turning, Sky saw a man she didn't recognize bending over, hands on his knees, practically panting. She didn't have time to answer before he again started running towards them, calling her name.

She knew she'd never seen him before, at least not that she could recall. He was dressed oddly. Definitely not typical hiking attire. His face was flushed and dripping sweat even though the morning was still cool. As he ran towards her she could see his hair was mostly blond with some brown at the roots and he moved with agility, despite the heavy suit he was wearing and the extra- large pack bouncing on his wide shoulders. Alarmed at his sudden approach, she walked to meet him in an attempt to protect the girls in her care.

"Who are you?" she asked.

"Brad Stevenson, fireman," his introduction was short and came in breathless pauses. He'd been running as fast as he could tolerate up the steep trail. When he was too tired to run he'd kept to a steady walk. His job required him to be physically fit and he regularly lifted weights and worked out at the station. He was in good shape and was an avid hiker, but the high altitude and sloped incline had required all his strength. He felt like a Marine, running through the forest in full gear, carrying a loaded pack, only he hadn't had the benefit of cadence being shouted to help him keep pace.

He was tired and winded, but there was no time to stop and take a breather. It had already taken over an hour to reach them. They had to get off this mountain and fast.

"Are you Sky?"

"Yes, I'm Sky. How do you know my name?"

"I was sent up here to bring you back. We've got to get out of here right now!" He paused, gulping air before explaining further. "There's a fire headed this way. We're evacuating everyone."

Chills spread across Sky's spine like exploding fireworks. The haze. The smell of smoke. She instantly recognized the reason for her uneasiness. The Holy Ghost had been warning her all along. Now he was shouting at her, confirming the truth of Brad's words.

She didn't waste time asking more questions of Brad. Instead, she turned and ran back to the girls. "Laela! Heather! Throw your stuff in, we gotta go!" she called, seeing their gear spread haphazardly at their feet while the others were busy tying their sleeping bags onto their packs.

Brad followed behind Sky and without a word bent down and started throwing things into the closest pack without bothering to ask who it belonged to. He was grateful to find them nearly ready to leave instead of still asleep.

Surprised, Heather grabbed her pack and pulled it back before he could stop her. "Hey, what do you think you're doing?"

"Heather, it's okay, he's helping you! We have to go!" said Sky sharply. It was the first time she had spoken to one of the girls in anything less than her nicest voice and it startled them all. It was enough to put them all on alert. Heather, confused and hurt, moved her pack back and allowed Brad to help her shove in her personal items.

"What's going on?" Emma, always level headed and confident, sensed something was terribly wrong. "Who's this guy?"

"He's a fireman. Girls, we have to leave. There's a fire coming our way and we need to get back to camp where they're evacuating everyone," Sky explained, trying to keep calm and not scare the girls.

"They've already left," said Brad. "At least I hope they have. But don't worry," he said, looking around at the anxious faces of five teenage girls, "we'll meet up with them." He looked at Sky. This time there was no smile on his face, just grim determination.

Sky looked back at him. It was strange, but it was as if they were sharing an entire conversation. Their eyes expressed what they dared not say in front of the girls. Sky told him she was worried; about the girls, about the danger, about getting back to the others. Brad acknowledged her fears and reassured her that he understood, all without words.

"Does everyone have water with them?" He asked.

"Girls, each of you go and fill your water bottles at the spring," Sky urged. "And hurry!"

As they ran for the spring, Sky turned to Brad and asked, "How bad is it? How much time do we have?"

"I'm not sure," he told her honestly. "When we left base camp this morning evacuating the campers was only a precaution. But the smoke has been getting thicker. By the smell of things, I'd say it's pretty close. The wind must have sped it up."

"What direction is it coming from?"

"It was headed northwest, at least part of it. The main fire actually split last night and is moving in two different directions as far as we can tell. But this is a big one and we're talking wilderness here. It's hard to get in and fight it when there aren't any roads. If we take the trail down we should be moving away from it."

Sky glanced behind her and saw the girls hurrying back from the spring. They were still smiling and happy, unaware that the situation was in any way dangerous. And that was just the way Sky wanted to keep it.

Before they could hear her, she turned to Brad and said, "I get it. We're in trouble here. But these girls are young and impressionable. I don't want you scaring them. The last thing we need is one of them freaking out that we're going to burn to death. So stick a smile on that face of yours and quit looking like the grim reaper!"

"Get your packs, girls," Sky said, smiling at them. "We've got ourselves an official escort down the mountain."

Brad stood ready to assist them with their packs, but before he could, each girl had hefted her own and slipped it over her shoulders. He nodded approval before he started at a break neck pace out of the meadow and towards safety.

Chapter 12

Brad moved fast following the trail back, down the mountain. Going downhill was easier on his lungs, but his thighs felt the burn. Behind him, the girls were scrambling to keep up. Sky brought up the rear, making sure no one fell behind.

The trail was dry and dusty, full of loose gravel. It was also narrow, traversing the steep embankment of the mountain. Sky watched from behind as the girls practically ran to keep up with their escort. Occasionally one of their feet would slip, but each time they managed to grab a branch to keep from falling. Looking ahead at the distance quickly developing between the small group of girls and Brad, Sky tripped over Annie who fell down just in front of her. Sky managed to avoid kicking her in the head, but like a sudden stop on a bicycle, she tumbled over the top of Annie like she was a set of handlebars, propelled by the pack on her back.

Dazed, Sky lay still for several seconds. Annie was already getting to her feet. "Are you okay?" She asked. "I am so sorry!"

Sky felt the stinging sensation on her palms from having braced her fall against the gravel. She landed on her back, the bulk of her pack taking most of the punishment, but her head had scraped a rock as her body catapulted into a somersault. As Sky sat up, blood from the gash dripped into her eye.

"Oh my gosh!" cried Annie, running forward and stooping to her level. "Stop!" she called so the man in front would give up his mad dash. "Sky's hurt!" Sounds of loose gravel echoed back.

Sky attempted to wipe the blood from her eye, using the back of her hand to keep her dirty fingers from making it worse. Annie continued to apologize and used her own sleeve to wipe more of the gushing blood.

The other girls had stopped and were working their way back to Sky when Brad pushed past them all. He had been so far in front that by the time he reached her, Sky was already on her feet.

"I'm fine," she assured Annie. "Really. It's not your fault."

"What happened?" Brad's gruff voice demanded.

"She fell—" Annie began to explain.

"You're running down this hill like a maniac and we can't keep up," Sky interrupted, angry as much as annoyed.

She attempted to brush off her clothes and adjust her pack into place.

Brad stepped forward and took Sky's face in his large hands. He tilted her face upwards to get a better look and assess the damage like the professional he was, but one look into her dark eyes made him stop cold. He studied her face.

Her eyes were chocolate, not milk chocolate, but deep, rich, dark chocolate. The kind that left all cravings completely satisfied. Her skin was smooth and brown from the sun without a single freckle or blemish. Her straight nose pointed to a set of full lips, perfectly positioned above an obstinate chin with a small cleft in the center. It seemed like forever, staring down at her, a queer tightening in his gut, when in reality only seconds had passed. He mentally shook his head and asked, "Does it hurt?" as he wiped the dripping blood away.

"I'll be fine." She stepped back, shaky from his gaze and not the fall.

Brad dropped his hands. "It looks deep. We'll need to put some pressure on it to stop the bleeding."

"Here," Amanda stepped forward, holding out a bandana. "It's clean," she offered. None of the girls seemed aware of the awkward tension that had suddenly arisen between their two leaders.

Taking the bandana, Brad folded it into a head band, then reaching around Sky, he threaded it under her long black pony tail and tied it tightly around her head, being careful not to pull her hair. "Good?" he asked.

Sky only nodded, still dazed and a bit shaken. She reached up and felt her head, the remaining blood was turning into a sticky patch of brown. "Can we—"

Brad saw her hands, that they were scraped and raw. He pulled them down, turned them over exposing her palms. She allowed him to brush at the dirt with his thumbs as he held her hands in his. She looked up at him again, this time letting her anger and frustration mask any vulnerability before pulling her hands away.

"Can we slow down, please? I thought the whole point was to get safely out of here. If we keep running like this, someone's going to get hurt."

"You mean someone else?" He asked pointedly, rubbing her blood from his hands onto the legs of his suit.

"Exactly!" She scoffed. She reached up and rubbed at her cheek smearing blood with dirt.

Brad's eyes stayed on her. He held his hand out to the side, palm up while continuing to stare. She returned his look, challenging him with her eyes. Stubbornly, she waited for him to say something. Instead he moved his palm in front of her, it was now covered in specks of ash.

Alarmed, Sky reached out and touched his hand, scraping the gray dust off. She rubbed it between her fingers and thumb, testing the feel of it. The reality of it.

"Slowing down is not an option," Brad said quietly, but firmly, his tone ominous. His eyes bore into her the seriousness of the situation. Finally, he turned. Moving quickly to the head of the line he called, "Let's move it!"

Behind him five girls and one woman fell into line. Each raced after him. There was no more talking, no more complaining. The girls moved quicker now, all eyes focused on the trail and whatever obstacles might trip them in their haste to keep up with Brad. Occasionally a foot would slip and the sound of rocks rolling and falling broke the tense silence. Hands reached out, grabbing at branches, using them to secure balance. Without words the girls assisted each other to regain their footing and continue forward on the slippery path.

Around them ash fell steadily, coating them in a layer of fine dust. Smoke continued to choke the air, its acrid smell filling their lungs. The bright morning sun was slowly fading to gray and it looked more like the darkening hours of evening. Each of them were coughing, covering their mouth and nose with whatever article of clothing they could reach without stopping to rummage in their packs.

They were only halfway down the mountain trail when the first falling embers landed on Laela's sleeve. "Ouch!" she yelled, hurriedly brushing them from her arm as they burned her skin. "What was that?"

Ahead of her, Heather brushed frantically at her hair while Amanda patted out the glowing sparks that threatened to send her sister's hair up in flames.

Hearing the commotion behind him, Brad halted and turned. With eyes no longer focused downward on the trail, he could see red dots raining down around them. They were falling gently like snowflakes, but it wouldn't be much longer before they were plummeting like hail stones. The fire was close. Too close. He listened carefully, hearing the rumble that always sounded through the forest as it burned. He listened for the familiar cracking and popping as dry branches ignited and sap, the life blood of trees, exploded from the heat.

"We have to change course," he called to Sky who was still bringing up the tail.

What?" she panted.

"We'll have to change course," he repeated. The fire is getting closer. We're going to meet it head on if we continue in this direction."

"But where will we go?" Emma asked, panicked. "This is the only trail back to the camp."

"We'll have to go off trail." Brad turned in a circle, searching the layout of the land.

Once they'd left the meadow earlier that morning the trail had clung to the side of a steep hillside. Craggy rocks and towering cliff faces rose to one side with a sheer drop down the mountain on the other. That particular section was open to the surrounding mountains with few trees to hide the majestic view. It was narrow and winding and had made their need for speed difficult. As they got further down the mountain, the trail had begun to wind through more and more trees. It was still steep, but the tall douglas firs and western red cedars obstructed more of the view and made it impossible to see exactly what lay ahead.

The forest floor was a jungle of fallen trees and limbs. Weathered trunks of all sizes crisscrossed in random piles, some with giant root systems still clinging to earth and mud, some simply broken and jagged like a snapped pencil. Small shrubs grew up around the dying timber, carpeting the forest with emerald green leaves and hiding the uneven terrain. Boulders as large as cars protruded out of the chaos. It was an old growth forest in which none but the animals traveled, and even they had difficulty picking a pathway through it.

Looking north into the mass of pines, Brad said, "We'll have to head this way."

"We can't go through there," Sky said emphatically, stepping around the girls and coming to a stop in front of

Brad. "There's no trail and we won't know where we're going."

"We'll be going north. More importantly we'll be going away from the flames." He brushed at an ember that landed on the back of his hand as he pointed in the opposite direction, towards the oncoming fire.

"It's going to take an awful long time to cut a trail through there." Sky challenged. "We'd be better off just to stick to the trail and meet up with the others so they can drive us back to town."

"Sister Chapman will be worried about us," Heather offered.

"The others are probably still waiting for us," added Annie.

"I'm scared!" Amanda began crying. Laela, looking none too sure herself, reached out and silently grasped her hand in comfort.

"We're going to be fine, Amanda," Sky reassured her. "We're going to make it back just fine." She looked at Brad as though he was some kind of bully responsible for making the girls cry.

"Look lady," he began and then paused. He took a calming breath and started over in a more reasonable but no less insistent tone, "We're wasting valuable time. We have to get farther away from this fire before it fries us to a crisp. With embers flying like this it could start up around us any minute. We don't know how wide it is which means we can only run from it. I assure you no one is waiting for us at the campground, they'd have all evacuated by now and moved to a safer area. Now, you can stand here arguing with me while it gets closer or you can trust me to get us out of here."

Brad didn't wait for a rebuttal. He grabbed the nearest limb and hoisted himself over a boulder. From the other side he reached down and held his hand out towards the closest girl to pull her up with him. Emma gripped his large hand and joined him.

One by one, the girls reached out and took Brad's hand. He deftly pulled them up and instructed them to move forward into the forest. When it was Sky's turn he reached his hand out, but she stubbornly refused to take it, still unconvinced they were doing the right thing.

She glared up at him before finding her own hand hold and pulling herself up without his help. "What makes you think you can just come marching in here and take over like some kind of drill sergeant? I'm responsible for these girls. Their families are depending on me to get them back safely."

"What do you think *I'm* trying to do?"

"You've been Mr. Doom and Gloom since the moment you came traipsing into our camp. Can't you see these girls are scared?"

"Of course I can. What do you take me for, a Neanderthal? They should be scared! We're being hunted by a forest fire. Have you ever been near a forest fire?"

"Well, no. But I—"

"Then trust me when I say, it's no day at the beach."

"Yeah, I get that." She walked past him angrily. The girls were out of earshot, searching the woods for some hint of a trail that would lead them north to safety. "Girls," Sky called motioning them over.

Brad was beyond irritated. He was doing his job. Drill sergeant! Who did she think she was? Ungrateful little chit! Part of him wanted to throttle her. If she had any idea the kind of danger they were in, she would be thanking her lucky stars he was there to rescue them. But another part of him—a part that was larger than he was comfortable with—wanted to grab her and keep that pert little mouth from arguing with him by planting a kiss on her red lips.

He thrashed his way forward, anger and adrenalin heating his blood, while effort and exertion heated his body.

Meanwhile, Sky had gathered the five young women and the six of them were kneeling amidst the ferns and grass, heads bent, eyes closed. And one hard-headed, dark haired Pocahontas was offering a prayer.

"Great!" Brad muttered. Just great! It's not God that's going to get you out of this mess he thought. Having picked a line of trees to follow, he moved past their circle into the forest. Behind him he heard the unison chant of "amen" and then the tromping, scurrying feet of six women as they hurried to catch up.

Once again Sky fell into line behind the girls as they slowly picked their way through the dense forest. It seemed they'd been walking for hours. Trees above created a dark canopy, making it impossible to tell what time it was. Her mind strayed from the trail, envisioning the other members of the camp. Had they made it to safety? Were they worried? If what the fireman had told her was true, they'd evacuated and were most likely on their way back home. She wished she was with them.

At least the girls ahead of her appeared to have forgotten the danger and were talking and laughing much as they had done the day before when they'd first ventured away from camp. When they had been forced to leave the trail she saw panic written on their faces, heard it in their voices. The quick prayer they'd offered had done much to alleviate their fears and bring comfort. They had asked for safety and guidance, and though there hadn't been time to listen for any answers from heaven, she was sure Heavenly Father had heard and would respond. She just hoped the man leading them knew what he was doing.

Sky watched him at the head of the line. He was a big man, over six feet tall. His shoulders were broad and in his fire suit she thought he resembled the hockey players her brothers loved to watch. He'd secured his helmet to his pack, his very large pack that he seemed to wear like as extension of his body. It had to be heavy didn't it? His sandy blond hair was cut short, his face tanned, or was that just soot? Hard to tell, but the angular jaw and strong profile couldn't be obscured by dirt. And those eyes, she had stared into those eyes for only seconds, but the memory would be there for years. Bottomless blue pools had touched something in her soul and she found herself wanting to swim in them again.
You're just being silly, she told herself. Exhaustion and adrenaline could do strange things to your system, like make you dreamy over a blue-eyed hunk while you ran for your life. Maybe that was being a little melodramatic. After all, the ash had stopped falling and the roar that she hadn't even been

aware of until it was gone, was silent. They had to be far from the danger now.

In front of her, the girls stopped abruptly, shaking Sky from her thoughts. She looked up to see Brad had stopped as well and was kneeling down, rummaging through his pack.

"What's wrong? Why have we stopped?" She asked, picking her way around the girls as they tried to clear a path for her to where Brad knelt.

"Nothing's wrong," he assured her. "If you discount the fact we're running from a forest fire and are far from any known trail. Things couldn't be better."

"Then what are you doing?" She watched as he continued to pull out miscellaneous items from his pack.

Finding what he was looking for, he pulled it free and held it up for Sky's inspection, "It's called lunch." In his hand he held a Power Bar. "I suggest you try it." He proceeded to tear open the package and take a huge bite. As he stood chewing, he began removing the heavy, yellow fire suit. The T-shirt he wore underneath was embossed with the Kalispell Fire Department logo. It was soaked with sweat and clung to his body. He breathed deeply and Sky watched the muscles in his chest and abdomen expand. His arms were browned from the summer sun and the short sleeves only emphasized his impressively sculpted biceps. Unaware that she was watching in awe, he took another bite of his Power Bar. Then holding it between his teeth in order to keep his hands free, he pulled down the suspenders attached to the matching yellow set of pants. Underneath he wore faded jeans, the kind that had been worn long enough to fit like a second skin. Sky couldn't help but admire the view as he bent over and untied his boots so he could pull the pants off. "That's better," he said.

Temporarily at a loss for words, Sky shook her head, bringing her thoughts away from his physique and back to the situation at hand. "Oh, I thought..."

"Yes?" he mumbled through another bite of chocolate, granola and peanut butter.

"It's just that..." she hesitated and watched him swallow. "Well, you were so intent on pushing forward, I just figured you wouldn't want...that we couldn't...or—

"You figured I am such a maniacal ogre that I wouldn't let us stop to eat?" Brad took another large bite followed by a swig of water from his canteen.

"Something like that," Sky said. She turned to tell the girls they were stopping to eat, but it was obvious the girls had figured that out since they had already set down their packs and were digging for food as well.

Taking off her own pack, she set it down with a sigh and rolled her shoulders a few times to relieve the strain. Pulling off the lid of her own canteen, she took a long drink, the cold water a welcome relief to her parched throat. "Are we close?" she asked Brad.

"Close to what?" He countered.

"Close to getting back to some kind of civilization," she said, sitting down next to him and pulling a pre-packaged bag of mini-carrots from her pack. "My other campers are probably wondering what's taking us so long."

"No, we're not close. And chances are they aren't the only ones wondering. My unit is probably wondering the same thing."

"Where exactly are we? I mean, I know we've been traveling north, but we shouldn't be too far from another trail. I've got a map." Sky felt around in her pack pushing aside worn socks, granola bar wrappers, and her mess kit. When her hand failed to find the map, she did all but poke her head in the pack trying to find it. "I swear it's in here somewhere. I remember putting it in my scriptures so I'd be able to find it quickly and then…" she stopped, remembering she had taken her scriptures out at the last minute because she was afraid they would get bent in her pack. She sat up, defeated. "I guess I don't have a map."

"It's okay," Brad said. "I do." He pulled a worn, scarred map from his pocket and unfolded it. Sliding closer to Sky he spread the paper out between them, using their knees as a table. Sky watched his hands, big, strong hands that brushed gently across her leg sending chills up her spine.

"I've been following my compass," he told her, "trying to find a path through these woods isn't easy and I've been trying to avoid the downhill slope too much, just to make it easier for the girls, so we've really been heading more northeast. The trail was here," Brad pointed, finding it on the map and tracing it with his finger. "By my calculations, walking at roughly two to three miles an hour in a steady northeast direction, we'd be about right here," he indicated.

"But that puts us further from the road than we were before," Sky protested.

"Yeah, but it also puts us further from the fire."

"Where exactly is this fire?"

"I'm not sure--exactly."

"But you said—"

"I said it was coming at us," Brad cut in. "When I left base camp this morning, the fire was here and here, moving west," he indicated on the map. "But forest fires often switch directions. Wind changes, drier undergrowth, lay of the land…lots of things can cause it to switch. Obviously, it had to have shifted or we wouldn't have been getting so much of the fallout earlier."

"So what are you saying?"

"I'm saying I don't know for sure where the fire is. It could be moving in several directions. Our best bet is to keep moving north. At least we know it isn't there. We'll try to head more westerly and pick up a river that we can follow so that we aren't heading for the Continental Divide. Eventually we'll find our way back to a road.

"That's your plan?" She asked incredulously. "*Eventually* find a road? And how long do you think that's going to take?" Her voice was gradually getting louder and louder until she was nearly shouting at him. When she stopped talking, a hush fell over the woods. Conversation among the girls had stopped and they all turned to look at their fearless leader. Sky smiled at them then turned back to Brad. Lowering her voice to a near whisper she continued. "I don't think that's such a great plan. I mean, we were only planning on being gone one night. I brought a little extra food just in case, but it's not enough to hold us for another day."

"We don't have any other choice right now. We can't go back to the trail or we'll be burned alive. I prefer a little hunger over being roasted."

Sky took a deep breath and slowly let it out. She was beginning to feel shaky and cold. She had to get a grip on her emotions if she was going to deal rationally with this situation. She dealt with emergencies every day in her job at the hospital. This was no different. She just needed to take careful stock of the situation, form a reasonable plan and move forward. It should be simple. But it wasn't quite the same. This time she wasn't dealing with someone else's emergency, taking charge from the outside of the situation without emotion. She was smack dab in the middle of her own emergency and it felt paralyzing. The responsibility of getting the girls home safely was overwhelming. She couldn't let anything happen to them. She had been entrusted with their care and safety. She'd accepted the calling as camp director with reservations about her abilities and now it seemed they were being tested beyond what she'd ever imagined.

"Okay, okay," she mumbled more to herself than Brad. "We can do this. We'll just keep walking and everything will be fine." She hurriedly began shoving items back into her pack with more force than necessary, continuing to mumble her own little pep talk.

Brad touched her arm, "Hey…" When that failed to get her attention, he held more firmly until she paused and looked up at him. "It's okay to be afraid." Sky closed her eyes, not wanting him to see the tears that were just beginning to pool. It was too late, though. One traitorous drop rolled down her cheek. Brad wiped it away, smearing her face with more dirt and ash. "Being afraid is what keeps you alive. It keeps you cautious."

Sky nodded her head, still too close to tears to speak.

"I've got some emergency supplies in my pack," Brad informed her. He continued to hold her arm, offering comfort. "We'll make it, but you've got to be strong. I can't carry the six of you out of here. And if you lose it, the girls are sure to follow your lead. We're the adults. We've got to act like it regardless of our own fears."

"You're right. I'm sorry. I just freaked out for a second, but I'm okay," Sky asserted. Sniffling away the last of her tears, she secured the clasps on her pack and stood, ready to go again. She turned to the girls and called, "Are you guys going to sit here all day? We better get moving while the sun's still shining."

Chapter 13

"I think this is a good spot to set up camp for the night," Brad said, surveying the leveled and somewhat grassy bank of the river. "We're close to water and the ground seems pretty even here."

Sky turned circles, making her own observations, before approving Brad's. They'd been walking for hours, hoping to find a trail. But with no such luck, their search turned instead to finding a camping spot for the night.

"Okay girls, you can put your packs down. Looks like we get to sleep under the stars again." She hoped her words didn't sound as disappointed and weary as she felt. She undid the mid-strap of her own pack and slowly let it slide off her shoulders, not caring how it hit the ground. It was such a welcome relief to have it off her shoulders. Throughout the day it had gotten considerably heavier as they trudged through the forest, up and over logs, rocks and hillsides. It had been an exhausting day.

For the most part, the girls had not complained, not any more than they had the day before. Brad's presence seemed to have curbed their tongues and though they had walked for nearly seven hours, they appeared to be in good spirits.

"I'm dying of thirst!" Laela said, letting her pack down and reaching for her water bottle.

"Don't drink all of that," Emma warned her, "you'll need some for tomorrow."

"Mine's already empty," said Heather, shaking her water bottle upside down to show them it contained nothing but a few drops of water.

"I'm out of water too," said Brad. "We'll have to boil some more and let it cool tonight so we've got some to drink tomorrow."

"I don't think I've got enough propane left in my stove to boil that much water," Sky informed them. "I didn't think we'd need it for more than some hot chocolate this morning." Brad said, "Then we'll build a fire." He set his pack on the ground and pulled out a mess kit. "We better get started. It's going to take a while with this small pan."

"I've got a similar set," said Sky, rummaging in her pack to find her mess kit. Suddenly the weariness was gone, and she was back to being camp director, restoring some resemblance of order, "Girls, if you've got anything that we can boil water in, pull it out. Three of you go gather some sticks we can burn. We'll need lots in order to keep the fire going long enough to boil the water. The other two, you can help clear the ground for sleeping bags. We'll use the rocks you find to make a fire ring."

Like troops given an assignment from their commanding officer, the girls moved as quickly as their tired bodies would allow, following Sky's instructions.

As the girls moved away she turned to Brad, "Seems kind of ironic, doesn't it."

"What's that?" he asked.

"Building a fire when that's the very thing we've been trying to escape."

"I guess it is. But that's the nature of fire. Friend or foe, depending on who's in control."

"Let's just make sure this one stays in our control."

"Agreed!"

Despite the long hours of walking, the girls worked tirelessly dragging branches from the woods to the small clearing along the river. While some gathered material to burn, the others cleared a spot to make the fire, carefully clearing away all of the tinder dry grass and digging down into the cool dirt. They made a ring of stones to keep the embers away from anything else that might burn. By the time the late summer sun was setting, they had a fire going and three small tins of water on the coals ready to boil.

Now that the work was done, there was time to sit. Dirty beyond all hope of cleanliness, the girls along with Sky and Brad sat on the ground around the fire. Dinner was meager fare consisting of a few shared granola bars, the remaining MRE packs, and Ritz crackers.

"I'm starving!" Heather complained. "Are you sure we can't have just a little bit more?"

"We've only got three more granola bars, two small bags of trail mix, and a pack of gum," Sky pointed out. "We're going to need something for tomorrow."

"I think I'll try rigging up a fishing line in the morning," said Brad. "Hopefully they'll be biting and we can fry up some trout."

"Oooh, gross!" said Laela. "I think I'd rather starve."

"Suit yourself." He shrugged his shoulders then stood up and stirred the coals, pulling more of the glowing chunks towards the base of the pots.

"Here," said Amanda, handing her sister a chunk of her granola bar. "You can have some of mine. I'm not that hungry," she lied.

"I plan to dream about a nice big hamburger and cheese fries tonight," said Emma.

"Oh, that sounds so good," Annie piped up. "Add a chocolate shake and I am all over that."

Heather said, talking while chewing the last of her meal, "I'd rather have a pizza, extra pepperoni--"

"With a huge glass of root beer to drink," Laela interrupted.

"Yeah," agreed Amanda. "And that's just to start. After the pizza comes chocolate cheesecake."

Her mouth watering and laughing at the girls' descriptions, Sky said, "Girls! Girls, stop! You're making my stomach hurt. I think it can hear you and is starting its own revolt."

"I don't know," said Brad. "I think I just gained ten pounds and my arteries are now clogged."

Despite the attempt at humor, he glanced at Sky and there was mutual recognition about the seriousness of their predicament. They needed food to keep their energy up if they were going to walk out of the wilderness. Hopefully, it would only be until tomorrow that they had to endure a few uncomfortable hunger pains, she thought.

As the sun sank behind the trees, the sky changed to every shade of pink and purple, made more intense by all the smoke in the air, before finally fading to gray and becoming black altogether. Sky and Brad kept the fire going, slowly replenishing the water in each of the nine water bottles they had piled together. Too hot to consider drinking now, it would be cold by morning, chilled with dew.

Without the sun, the temperature steadily declined. "You should probably get to bed, girls," cautioned Sky. "We've got another long day ahead tomorrow." They groaned in unison at the reminder. "But at least we'll be home. Let's have a prayer and then you can get settled in your sleeping bags. Would you like to join us?" Sky asked, turning to Brad.

"Uh, no thanks." Brad replied stiffly. "You go ahead. I need to fill these pots again." He stood and wandered to the river, leaving the six women alone in the glow of the fire.

Emma offered the prayer, giving sincere thanks for the safety they'd been blessed with before asking for Heavenly Father's protection to see them safely home. Following the prayer the girls moved off to their sleeping bags where they continued to talk, laugh and gossip, seeming to forget that they were still lost in the wilderness.

Brad stood at the edge of the river listening to the soothing sound of water rushing over rocks while he tried to ignore the words of prayer being offered only yards behind him. He didn't know why it bothered him so much, but it did. He could hear their praise and gratitude, their plea for protection, and felt only annoyance. I believe in God, he thought, but I don't need to go begging for help. Listening to the words, it reminded him of London and the way he had heard her and Ammon pray before a meal.

He realized he hadn't really thought about London today. He had been too tired at the end of yesterday's long shift to do anything but crash into a fitful sleep. There had been too much happening today to think about anything but getting to safety. There had been too much of—Sky.

He turned just enough to look over his shoulder and watch her. Sky, illuminated by the glowing flames, sat huddled before the fire. She hugged her knees with one arm while poking at the coals with her other. She had removed the elastic that had held her onyx-colored hair in a ponytail and now it fell forward, surrounding her face, nearly reaching the ground. Light and shadow danced across her features and Brad was entranced with the performance. She looked like an Indian princess; peaceful, strong, and beautiful.

A sudden burst of giggling from the girls broke his trance. He carried the pails of water back to the fire and placed them on the glowing coals then he sat down, prepared for a long vigil.

Several minutes passed in awkward silence. Forced to travel together all day, they had spoken very little about anything except for matters pertaining to their precarious situation. They were strangers really.

Finally, Sky spoke. "Thank you."

"For what?"

"For being here…for helping us."

"It's my job."

"Job?" She questioned him. "But your job is a firefighter, right? Not rescuing damsels in distress."

"You'd be surprised how many damsels I get to rescue on a regular basis." He shifted his body, finding a more comfortable spot on the rocky ground.

"Yeah, well, this damsel appreciates your help," she repeated her gratitude.

Silence ensued, each of them watching the flames as though mesmerized. Then, one of the embers popped loudly, startling them both. Brad quickly moved, reaching over and patting at an ember that had escaped the makeshift fire circle before it could ignite the dry grass.

"If you want to get some sleep," he offered, "I can stay up and watch this until the water is finished boiling." He settled back down, this time choosing to sit slightly closer to her.

"No, that's alright. I don't mind staying up. It's kind of peaceful, here by the fire."

"Yeah," he agreed. He watched her as she traced designs in the ashes with her stick, not entirely comfortable with the silence between them, but he didn't know what else to say.

Suddenly she stopped and sat up straight, turning to him. "You don't have a sleeping bag," she said.

"No."

"How will you sleep tonight? You'll get cold."

"I'll be fine. I'll just use my fire suit."

"You're sure? Because I could share mine."

"Share your sleeping bag?" He asked, uncertain about what she was really offering. From the direction his mind took at her words, it seemed like an awfully bold offer coming from a woman who seemed pure as the driven snow, who prayed before bedtime and from whom he had yet to even hear a curse word. Was she really offering…?

"I could use it half the night while you watch the fire and then we'll switch."

No, she wasn't offering that. Was he relieved or disappointed? A little of both he thought.

"I'll be fine," he repeated.

Smoke from the fire shifted with the breeze and Brad leaned away from it, closer to Sky. Seemingly unaware of his closer proximity, she laid down in the grass cradling her head in her hands, elbows outstretched. Gazing upward she said, "There aren't as many stars tonight."

Brad stretched his long body and lay back as well, his head coming to rest not far from hers. "It's the smoke. The breeze is carrying the smoke from the fire our way. It makes it hard to see them." They stayed that way, gazing at the sky, each lost to their own thoughts, their bodies worn out from the hard day's hike, until Brad sat up and added more wood to the fire. The dry branches ignited quickly and the simmering flames jumped higher, adding more light and heat to the dark night.

"You know," Brad said, settling back down on the ground, gazing down on her, "Since we're going to be spending another day together, it seems only polite to find out a little more about you. Your last name for instance…?"

She sat up enough to see his face in the red glow, bracing herself with her elbows. She smiled at him then, adding to the glow of the fire. It didn't matter that her face was dirty, her hair unkempt, all he saw in that moment was her thousand watt smile with straight white teeth behind her full red lips. His heart skipped a beat as she introduced herself. "Thundering Sky Ryder," she said, holding out her hand to shake his.

"Seriously?"

"Seriously. I know, it sounds like something out of a Marvel comic, but it's the only one I've got."

"Can I call you Thunder?"

"Not if you want to live."

He grasped her small hand, not caring that it was covered in grit. His was too. He felt the softness of her hand, a few small calluses at the base of her long, slim fingers. "Nice to meet you, I'm Brad Stevenson." Then to reduce the tension he felt, he added humorously, "Do you come here often?"

"Only when I'm fleeing for my life at the heels of a mean forest fire." Her tone was equally light and suddenly the awkwardness dissipated. Instead of strangers, they were now friends in an impossibly obscure situation.

"Thundering Sky? You're Native American?"

It was more a statement than a question, but she confirmed it anyway. "Yes. My mother is a member of the Salish Kootenai tribe. I was born during a thunder storm, although my brothers claim I got my name because I'm such a loud mouth." She sat up next to him, folding her legs beneath her and holding her hands out to capture the heat of the fire. "And you're not Native American," she said matter-of-factly.

"No. I'm part of the Swedish American clan, with a little bit of German mixed in."

"Ah, I see. You're a mutt. You're lucky you aren't part of the English clan that came in and wiped out half of my ancestors or I'd have to pull out my tomahawk and scalp you."

He laughed at her obvious sense of humor. "It is lucky for me." He stared at her, studying her sharp features. "Do you scalp people often?"

"No, just the opposite, in fact. I stitch them up. I'm a nurse in Missoula. I also teach nursing at the college in Pablo.

"That must keep you busy."

"Yeah, it does, but I enjoy it. It's my way of giving back to my people."

"Your people? You mean your tribe?"

"Yes, and others as well. My great, great grandfather was Chief Charlo of the Salish tribe. My heritage is important to me so I do what I can for my people."

He assumed part of that heritage included religious rituals which would explain her need to pray so often. "I wasn't trying to offend you," he clarified. "I just don't know a lot about Native Americans. Even being born and raised in Montana, I've never had a lot of association with any of the tribes."

Rustling from the bushes made them both look over. Brad stared away from the fire, allowing his eyes to adjust, but it didn't help, he still couldn't see into the trees. He tossed a small rock in that direction, and whatever small animal had been there moved on into the darkness. Satisfied that they had scared it off, he turned back to the fire and Sky, warmed by more than just the flames.

"So, Native American nurse and Girl Scout leader as well?" he asked.

"Not Girl Scouts, just young women," she motioned with her head in the direction of the girls. "I was asked to be camp director for my church's youth group."

"Do you camp often?"

"Often enough, I guess. I enjoy camping, hiking, back packing. Anything outdoors really. This is definitely shaping up to be my greatest adventure so far. I've never had to run from fire before. What about you?" She asked, directing the conversation back to him. "Firefighter by day, superhero by night?"

"I work for the Kalispell Fire Department. I have experience with forest fires so I was sent in to help on this one. It's pretty big, lots of land to cover that's mostly all wilderness."

"I bet you had no idea just what you were getting yourself involved in."

The tone of her voice was wistful and Brad was quick to reassure her, "Hey, don't worry. We'll get out of this."

"I know. I just feel bad about the girls, is all. If it were just me it'd be different, but I worry about them. Their families must be worried sick by now."

"Yours too I imagine." He wasn't intentionally fishing for information but he was curious about her and the opportunity presented itself. He found it was pleasant sitting and talking with her. The night was so very still and quiet. "Your husband, kids…?"

"No, I'm not married—yet. I'm engaged to be married in October." Sky sighed and sat up, hugging her knees to her chest. "Tom's not going to like this."

"This? As in—"

"As in I was supposed to be home early tomorrow."

"Well it's not exactly your fault."

"I know," she acknowledged, sadly. "But we have plans. He didn't want me to come in the first place."

There was something about the way she said it that made Brad dislike the guy. He didn't even know him, but any guy that would be more concerned about his plans getting ruined than about the life and safety of his fiancé had to be a jerk in his opinion.

"I hope someone would have thought to contact him and my parents, although I hate for them to worry."

"Is it just you and your parents?"

"Oh, no. I've got siblings littered all over the place, but I doubt they'll worry about their little sister until I start making headlines, they're so busy with their families."

"So you aren't close to your family?"

"No, we are. Very close. We get together often, but they all have kids and are busy with jobs. Besides, they know I can take care of myself. What about you? Anyone keeping the home fires burning for you? No pun intended."

"Nope." For one brief moment he thought about London. Would she be worried about him if she knew where he was? That he was essentially missing? "No one special. I've got a sister who has a couple of kids, and my parents. They live in Polson." he confirmed.

Once again silence settled in around them, broken only by the gentle gurgling of the river and the occasional crackle of the fire.

"You're tired," said Brad. "Get some sleep and tomorrow this will all be a bad dream."

"You're right," she confirmed. "I should get to bed. You're sure you'll be okay?"

"My male ego wouldn't have it any other way."

"Okay, well..." Sky stood and stretched, reaching her arms above her head as she yawned. "If anything happens, don't hesitate to wake me."

He watched her disappear into the darkness, only yards away where he knew the girls were already sleeping.

Engaged.

So she was engaged. Big deal.

If it was no big deal, why was he so bothered by it? He thought back to those brief moments of staring into her dark eyes and the gut punch it had given him. He'd even thought of kissing her. Better not go there again, he told himself. Best to just focus on what needed to be done to get back.

Alone by the fire, he removed the last of the water containers, setting them aside where they could cool until morning. He banked the fire, hoping to reserve some coals that he could use to stoke it in the morning. Then he pulled the tattered map from his pocket and with a small pen light he studied the terrain, trying to decide the best course that would lead them out of there.

Chapter 14

Flushed and frustrated, Chief Charlie Carruthers shouted into his phone, "I guess you better get back here then. No sense in trying to look anymore tonight." He snapped the device closed, letting out a few expletives in the process. He wasn't the only one swearing. Tempers were running hot everywhere in camp since they'd gotten word about their missing man. Men stood ready to take on double shifts in the search effort.

"No sign yet?" asked Brett Fisher, Brad's friend and co-worker. After evacuating the campground earlier that day and seeing the small group of campers to safety, he'd worked a full shift, clearing lines in an attempt to halt the fire's progress. It was only when he returned to base that he'd learned Brad hadn't returned with the hikers and they'd had no word from him since. The fire in that area had been moving fast, making it nearly impossible to send a search party out. The few men that could be spared had been forced to retreat when they came too close to the flames. Taking another course, they'd made their way in the direction they hoped he'd gone, but there was no way to know for sure which way that was. The wilderness area covered hundreds of square miles in every direction.

"Not a trace."

"I'm ready to go out whenever you give the word, Chief," he offered.

"Can't risk it," Carruthers responded vehemently, quelling any further discussion. "Not in the dark. We'll try again at first light."

Discouraged and helpless, Brett accepted the older man's authority, "Yessir."

"We just can't seem to catch a break with this one." His voice was strained and tired. He rubbed his oversized hand down his face, scratching at the grey stubble that had accumulated on his jaw, talking to himself as much as to Brett. "Short on men as it is, trying to chase down this dragon, and now we're sending them out on search and rescue. Ground's as dry as the Mohave Desert, winds pushing this monster faster than the Indy 500…I'm getting too old for this."

Another fireman carrying two cups of coffee came up behind him. He handed one to Carruthers, "Too old for what, Sir?"

"Too old to be standing around drinking stale coffee in the woods like I'm at some Boy Scout camp," he answered gruffly to mask his concern. He took a drink of the strong brew and shaking his head added, "I sure hope they're alright."

The sentiment was mutual among all of the men and women at the base camp, Brett included. "Yessir," he said with more gusto than he felt.

"I guess I better make a statement for the families, although with the eleven o'clock news having aired the story already, they probably know as much as I do. I can't stand those press vultures."

London sat snuggled in the crook of Ammon's arm, and despite the fact it was August, she had a colorful afghan thrown over her lap. With Marty and Corkie already in bed, they were watching the late news. It had become a nightly ritual for them, one Ammon had begun when he lived in New York so he could keep abreast of any sudden changes to the world market and stock exchange. The local news in Kalispell wasn't quite the same; it was filled more with hunting accidents and land disputes than with extortion and price fixing. London had never been a big fan of watching the news mostly because she could never stay up that late, having had to get up early to deliver newspapers. Since that was no longer the case, she could enjoy these late night moments with her husband. They often talked after watching, sharing highlights about their day or discussing concerns about the children.

Tonight's broadcast seemed to be nothing special: A Missoula man sentenced to prison for cruelty to animals after being found guilty of starving his sixteen horses, the city council approving annexation of another neighborhood on the north end of town, continued thunder storms in the area with temperatures remaining high. Ammon picked up the remote control and pointed it at the large flat screen television, prepared to turn it off.

"News reporter Carly Rasmussen joins us now from Seeley Lake with breaking news," said the on-screen voiceover, while both newscasters turned to view the large studio screen.

"Wait," London protested before Ammon pushed the power button, "it's probably more about that big fire."

Reluctantly, Ammon set the remote back down. He'd heard a disturbing report on the car radio earlier and had been hoping to spare his wife the information. It was too late, she'd find out one way or another…

"…That's correct Mike. The fire continues to burn out of control. The situation has turned even more critical now with six hikers and one fireman reportedly missing. Evacuations took place earlier today of all campgrounds in the area, but one group of hikers has yet to return. Brad Stevenson of the Kalispell Fire Department was sent to rescue the group of Girl Scouts. According to one of the girls' leaders the group had been on an overnight hike in the Upper Holland Lake area. The group has not returned and firemen are very concerned about their safety in light of this fast moving fire. With me now is Chief Charlie Carruthers." The young, overly enthusiastic reporter turned to the bulky frame of Chief Carruthers and directed her question at him. "Are there plans to search the area, Chief Carruthers?"

"London…" Ammon interrupted. She had slid forward on the couch away from his protective embrace, her hand covering her mouth in shock. When he attempted to pull her back, she resisted. There was no way to protect her from this frightening news.

Chief Carruthers' loud, gravelly voice answered, "We've had to call off search efforts for the night, but will continue as it gets light."

"Can you tell us, were they in danger from the fire?"

"That area was evacuated early this morning as a precautionary measure. At the time there was no immediate threat from the fire," he lied smoothly to the camera, avoiding a PR nightmare for the forest service and fire departments. There was no way for the public to fully understand or appreciate the nature of fire and its unpredictability. The press had a way of pointing fingers and making it seem as if someone was responsible for putting them in danger.

"Will this affect your ability to gain control of the fire?"

"We are working around the clock to contain the blaze and will continue to do so. Search and Rescue efforts will not change that."

"Thank you Chief Carruthers." Turning back to the camera, microphone in hand, she went on, "We'll continue to bring you up to date information as this story unfolds. This is Carly Rasmussen for KSPL News. Back to you Mike."

The screen switched back to the studio and the newscasters began commenting on what they'd just learned. London didn't hear a word they said. Her mind kept replaying the words she'd heard earlier "...Brad Stevenson of the Kalispell Fire Department was sent to rescue the group of Girl Scouts...The group has not returned..."

Turning to her new husband, her voice quivering, she asked, "Did you know about this?"

He again reached to pull her close and this time she didn't resist. "I heard about it on the radio coming home from work this evening, but they didn't give any names. I'm sorry sweetheart."

She leaned into the comfort of his body, letting her fears loose in the form of big elephant tears. "I didn't even know he'd gone."

Ammon confessed, "I ran into him before he left. He mentioned going, but didn't want me to say anything to you. He just didn't want you to worry."

"How could I not? Last year there was a fire and he was called out to work on it. Three men got trapped and were killed. I heard all about it on the news. I was worried sick," she sniffled and wiped at her wet face. "In fact, I *was* sick." She told him about the previous summer, before she'd even met Ammon. Elsie, her friend and future mother-in-law had died that week as well. "I was laid up on the couch for a week with the flu watching all about it on the news and worrying that Brad was safe. I didn't want to lose him too."

Ammon knew she was referring to her first husband, Brock, who had died tragically in a car accident over four years ago. She had lost too many people in her life to tragedy. He hugged her closer, brushing back the dark curls surrounding her pale face. "Hey," he crooned gently, "you know Brad, he's a tough guy. If anyone can beat this thing, it's Brad. I've never met a guy more comfortable with the forest. He's like a regular mountain man. He's probably holed up somewhere keeping those other hikers safe from the fire and as soon as it's light, they'll come traipsing out of the woods." His words were comforting and spoken with confidence to hide his own worry. He didn't want anything to happen to Brad because he was a good friend, but more than that, he didn't want anything to happen to Brad because he worried what that might do to London.

"Tell you what," said Ammon, clicking off the television and pulling London up from the couch, "I'll check in with the fire station first thing tomorrow and see what else I can find out. But for now, we can say a prayer for him. Even if he doesn't believe in Heavenly Father, Heavenly Father believes in him."

Chapter 15

Exhausted, both physically and mentally, Sky quickly fell asleep. Though she should have slept deeply, her mind refused to settle. Her dreams were strange, disjointed thoughts, and always she was escaping, trying to run from danger. In her dreams her legs wouldn't move until just before she was about to be captured by monsters, or her feet would be stuck in heavy mud, deep in the jungle where she faced down snakes the size of a school bus. And the worst dream of all, she was in a furnace, flames licking at her, smoke filling her lungs…

She woke with a start. It wasn't a dream.

Smoke.

She could smell smoke everywhere. She looked to the fire, but it no longer glowed in the pre-dawn darkness. She couldn't tell exactly what time it was, but looking to the east there was barely a glow on the horizon. To the west the sky was pink and orange. A distant rumble shattered the solitude that should have been filled with the sound of birds chirping as they woke. Everything was wrong and it felt like waking on the edge of hell.

Scurrying out of her sleeping bag, she rushed to the edge of their make shift fire pit stumbling over branches and rocks. The fire that had burned so brightly the night before was now just glowing embers. She found Brad laying on the ground, his fireman coat pulled tightly around his shoulders for warmth. "Brad," she called, shaking him vigorously.

Instantly alert, he sat up. "What? What's wrong?"

"Look," she said, pointing in the direction of the unnatural orange glow. "Do you smell it?"

Taking a deep breath, he coughed as the acrid smell of burning forest filled his lungs. His coughing was answer enough. "Wake the girls," he instructed. "We've got to go."

Sky didn't need to be told twice. She knelt next to Emma, shaking her awake as she had Brad and calling her name before moving on to Laela and Annie. She tripped and landed on Heather's feet, jarring her from sleep while at the same time calling to Amanda. "Hurry girls! Get your things together. We've got to move!"

Dazed and half asleep still, the girls picked up on the panic in their leader's voice. They each obediently squirmed out of their sleeping bags, scrambling to find their shoes in the dark.

"What's wrong?" Laela asked, "Where are we going?"

"Look," Sky said, pointing at the horizon.

"Oh my gosh!" Heather cried. "What is that?"

"It's the fire," Brad said, racing up behind them to assist in tying up their sleeping bags.

"I thought we'd gotten away from the fire," said Emma, her voice calmer than the other girls'.

"I thought so too," he said without masking the discouragement in his voice.

"We must not have gone far enough," said Sky

"That or it's moved much faster throughout the night. The wind picked up after you went to bed." Brad finished securing Annie's bag to her pack and lifted it for her to slip her arms through the straps. As the other girls worked to get their packs secured, Brad gathered the water bottles and distributed them before tucking the small mess kit pans back into his pack.

As they packed up, small animals scurried past; squirrels and chipmunks in unusually high numbers. A large buck raced out of the forest foliage, unafraid of the humans present. They watched as he jumped lithely over obstacles in the opposite direction. A doe and her young fawn soon followed. Even the animals must have felt the impending danger.

"What about the campfire?" Amanda asked. "Shouldn't we pour some water on it to make sure it's out before we go?" She'd been taught well about the dangers of leaving a fire burning.

"Sweetheart," said Brad patiently, appreciating her conscientiousness, "this whole place is going to be one big campfire in about fifteen minutes and we're going to be burned marshmallows if we don't get out of here, and I mean fast." His point was made all the more clear by the loud crackling boom that vibrated from the western woods. "Make that ten minutes!"

Smoke filled the air and embers rained down around them similar to what they had experienced the day before. Through the haze the glowing light was coming closer and it wasn't from the sun. It was coming from the west, cutting off the route that Brad had spent outlining the previous night.

Forced to forget about his well-laid plans, Brad took the lead again for the small group, running north along the river bank. Behind him the girls did their best to keep up. At six feet four inches, his legs were long and carried him quickly, but there were no complaints about his speed. The pre-dawn darkness made it challenging to see and the smoke continued to thicken. The crackling and rumbling of burning pine trees compelled them forward. Forest animals scurried ahead of them, rabbits, squirrels, even deer ran past, oblivious to their presence, every creature seeking safety from the flames.

After twenty minutes of running, there was little distance between them and the fire. The terrain was simply too difficult to maneuver at any great speed. They would need to turn east and run directly away from it. But heading east would also put them further into the wilderness, higher up the mountains away from civilization and the possibility of rescue. It meant hiking uphill through deep forest and heavy undergrowth. Could they outrun the fire with those obstacles?

As red, angry embers showered the ground around them, Brad knew there was no other choice. He turned east and plunged into the river at his right hoping the water would act as a barrier between them and certain death. He didn't have time to find a narrow crossing or one that was also shallow. Even with the recent drought, the water came nearly to his waist. Brad stood in the rushing water, reaching for one girl after another as they took turns jumping to him, each of them gasping as their bodies hit the frigid water. At any other time the glacier-fed river would have caused squeals in the hardiest of swimmers, but there was no time to be squeamish. The current threatened to pull the lighter girls downstream and they struggled to stay upright in the rushing water. Sky was the last one in. She jumped and Brad held onto her, steadying her as she walked. Hand in hand, everyone held on tight trying to steady one another until one of them could get to the opposite bank and act as anchor to the others.

Even with the support of one another, it wasn't enough. Amanda lost her footing on the slippery rocks. Her legs shot out from under her and she was forced to let go of Laela's and Heather's hands or pull them under with her. She went down on her back, completely submerged in the icy darkness. Brad grabbed for her and missed as the current swiftly pulled her along. He plunged forward, using the length of his body to dive forward and catch her. Her head broke the surface and she screamed for help, but her garbled plea was cut short as the water pulled her under again.

With all of his strength, Brad swam forward, kicking desperately. He stretched his hand out and when he felt the nylon fibers of her backpack, he clamped his hand closed and held on. The water logged weight of her pack was making it impossible for her to get her feet underneath her body. Brad pulled on the pack to drag her back towards him. It wasn't easy with the force of the current determined to carry her away. Inch by inch Brad was able to pull her to him until finally he cradled her in his arms. He planted his feet and stood, bringing her with him.

"Are you okay?" Brad asked, relieved. He hugged her to him as his heart pumped adrenaline through his veins.

Amanda coughed, spitting out water. She nodded, still trying to expel anything in her lungs.

Though they had only gone about thirty yards downriver, it felt like more. Brad turned to see the others had stopped dead in their tracks, a chain of girls across the river. It was too dark to clearly see their expressions, but they appeared to be frozen in terror. "Come on, let's go. Move! Move!" He trudged back to them through the water carrying Amanda, both of them shivering and dripping.

For one brief moment they stood on the narrow eastern bank of the river, looking back at the inferno they had left behind. Yellow and orange flames danced through the trees. The river was only twenty feet across, much shorter than the Douglas Firs and Red Cedars around them. If one burning tree fell across, it would bridge the river and ignite the other side. They had to keep going.

Packs now heavy with water, they labored up the steep slope of the opposite bank. Water squished from their shoes leaving muddy footprints as they scrambled to get away from the danger. Heather and Laela were both visibly crying, gulping for air, fear pushed their legs to keep going.

"Come on girls," Sky encouraged, pushing them from behind. "You can do this!"

"I—I—I can't—breathe," Laela gasped.

"You've got to!"

Emma was the first to reach the ridge above the river followed by Annie. They were the oldest in the group and appeared to be in better control of their emotions. Amanda said nothing, but her small frame was so weighed down by her wet pack and clothes, it appeared to be all she could do to hoist one leg in front of the other. Brad did his best to pull her forward while trying to keep Heather in front of him as well. Sky brought up the rear, pushing Laela ahead of her.

Once again they all turned to see the enemy. The fire moved through the trees, propelled by the dry undergrowth. It was like dominoes falling, one tree igniting the next, until finally it stopped at the water's edge, unable to cross. But like any determined army giving chase, in time it would find a way. It seemed to roar up at them, angry at their escape. "Let's go," said Brad resolutely. "We've got to find some place safe."

Having outrun the immediate threat, they continued hiking east. The terrain was steep and rocky making every step difficult. The smoke filled air inhibited their breathing and made them all cough and wheeze as they demanded more from their exhausted lungs. When they encountered a slope too steep to climb, Brad would lead them north, following his own make-shift switchbacks that were more manageable to traverse than straight up the mountainside.

By midday they were totally spent. Intent on escaping the flames, they hadn't eaten since the night before. Their steps had been fueled purely by adrenaline, and it had all but run out.

"I don't think I can...go...anymore." Amanda fell to her knees. As she tried to push up, her limbs were visibly shaking. She hadn't the strength and fell back to the ground. "I—I'm sorry," she whispered.

Emma and Annie were quick to gather around their friend and offer assistance, but the strain on her face was enough to stop them from pulling her to her feet. Instead, Emma gently rubbed her neck and Annie lifted the pack off her shoulders. She removed a water bottle and held it to Amanda's lips.

Heather took the opportunity to sit. Tears welled in her eyes and she didn't try to blink them back. She had been crying off and on all morning. "Hey Mandy," she crooned, using the nickname that only she was allowed to call her twin. "It's okay, I'm tired too. We'll just rest for a while." She looked tentatively at Brad, seeking approval. He nodded consent and each girl removed her pack and sat on the forest floor.

As the girls rested and comforted one another, Brad pulled Sky aside to talk without the girls' hearing. "How are you doing?" he asked. "Are you holding up?"

"I'll be fine." Her words belied the exhaustion in her voice. "What about you?" She noted his face was tense and he had the same crease in his forehead that she'd glimpsed throughout the morning. She didn't know him well enough to read him. Was he angry? Concerned? He had spoken little except to direct them. She wished she knew what he was thinking.

"Yeah, I'm good," he confirmed.

"What do you think we should do?"

"The girls are obviously exhausted. I don't think I can push them much farther without having one of them collapse. We need to find some food and rest for a while."

"I have the few things left that we saved from last night, they might be a little soggy, but they're still edible."

"It won't be enough," he said. "We're going to need more. I think you should stay here with the girls. The six of you can eat whatever you have left and rest up. Have the girls drink lots of water. They're probably feeling the effects of dehydration. I'm going to see if I can find us a place to camp. If we can find another place by a river I can get us some fish. We're high enough now, I think we should be able to find some huckleberry bushes." Brad reached over to touch Sky's arm. He rubbed it gently, reassuringly. "Will you be alright while I'm gone?"

She appreciated his comforting touch and the unspoken concern in his voice. "We'll be fine. How long will you be gone?"

"I'm not sure. It depends on what I find up ahead. What time is it now?" He asked, checking his watch.

"I don't know," she answered as she checked her own wrist. "Looks like my watch quit after this morning's swim."

"Mine says it's twelve thirty. I'll walk for no more than one hour and if I haven't found anything then I'll head back. No more than two hours."

"And if something happens to you--"

"Nothing will happen to me," he was quick to say. "Everything'll be fine."

Sky took a few deep breaths and nodded her head. She hoped he meant more than just the next two hours. She hoped that they'd get out of this mess, that everything would be fine.

She just had to keep thinking that because the alternative was unthinkable. "Okay, two hours."

Brad squeezed her arm again and she looked up into his eyes. There was determination in them and something she couldn't quite give a name to—affection maybe? Whatever it was, it gave her a fluttering feeling in her stomach that was more than just hunger pains.

"Two hours," he repeated before walking away.

"I can't seem to stop shivering," Amanda said. She was sitting on the forest floor amid the dirt and grasses. Her body shook, almost seizure-like and her teeth chattered when she wasn't clenching them shut.

"I know." Sky rubbed her arms for her trying to increase her circulation. "It's because your clothes are still wet, particularly your shoes."

Now that they were sitting still they were all feeling chilled from having jumped in the river. The day was warming despite the grayness from a mixture of clouds and smoke, but it wasn't warm enough to counteract the shady forest and their soggy shoes. Even when daytime temperatures reached into the eighties, nights in the mountains could dip into the forties, sometimes even the thirties. It was a stark contrast and they were feeling the effects still from the cold water.

"We need to get moving again so we can dry out," said Annie.

"We will," Sky confirmed, "Just as soon as Brad gets back."

He's been gone forever," Laela noted. She and Heather sat huddled together for warmth.
Emma checked her watch. The waterproof timepiece was still working. "It's only been an hour."

"I wish I'd have chewed slower," said Heather. "That piece of granola tasted amazing."

Laela groaned. They were all hungry. They had split the last granola bar six ways, each of them getting one bite. "If you start talking about food again, I'm going to hit you."

"We have more water," Annie offered, holding a bottle out to the twosome.

"No thanks," Heather said. "I already have to use the bathroom, but I'm too tired to move."

"I—I'll take s-some." Amanda's words were stilted as she reached for the bottle.

"Let's play a game," Sky said suddenly, jumping to her feet and brushing off her bottom that was caked with dirt. Her efforts only turned it to mud as it mixed with water from her pants. Her smile and cheerful attitude belied the worry and fatigue she felt inside, but for the sake of the girls she mustered together as much enthusiasm as she could. "Come on, it'll keep our minds off of waiting."

"What are we going to play?" Laela asked.

"Something to get us moving so we warm up."

"How about twenty questions," said Emma.

"No, we need to get moving…I know!" Sky said as she pulled Emma to her feet, followed by Annie. "How about Mother-May-I or Red-Light-Green-Light."

Sky's feigned energy was infectious, and the girls began to quibble over who would get to be the 'stop light' first. Finally they decided Amanda could be it because she was still feeling weak and didn't want to stand yet.

It wasn't like the childhood game they'd played as kids, all running across an open field to reach the 'stop light' first. They all had to pick their way over rocks, tree stumps, logs, small trees and bushes until they were about twenty yards from where Amanda sat.

"Are you ready?" she called.

"Yes," Heather and Emma called back.

"If you're not going to turn around, you can't cheat by opening your eyes," Laela reminded her.

"What are we supposed to do now?" asked Annie.

"Haven't you ever played this before?" Sky asked, unable to believe that she could have missed playing the traditional children's game.

"Never," she answered.

In her usual blunt manner, Laela asked, "Gee, where did you grow up?"

Sky was quick to pick up on Annie's discomfort and rescue her from Laela's tactless and naïve questions. "When Amanda closes her eyes and yells 'green light,' you move forward, but when she opens them and says 'red light,' you have to stop. If she catches you moving, you have to go back to the beginning."

"Is everyone ready?" Amanda repeated. This time she didn't wait for a reply, she just closed her eyes and yelled, "Green light!"

It was comical, this rag-tag, dirty group of young girls picking their way through the rough forest terrain trying to be the first to reach their goal. They laughed at themselves, letting go of the anxiety that had gripped them all morning.

Emma was the first to reach Amanda, and seeing the good time they were having, she took her place among the ranks with renewed strength.

After several rounds, they were no longer thinking about how hungry they were or how wet and uncomfortable they felt. Still, Sky kept an anxious eye out for Brad. With her broken watch it was all she could do not to continually ask Emma what time it was. How long had he been gone? Was he able to find an area that would provide for their immediate needs? She certainly hoped so. She didn't want to imagine things getting any worse than they were right then.

Careful not to squish the delicate berry, Brad pulled it from the lower branch and added it to the pile. He used his shirt as a bowl to collect them. He'd been picking for nearly an hour but only those who had experience in picking the small huckleberries could appreciate the pile that had accumulated. It was no wonder they sold in town for over forty dollars a pound. Still, it was enough that everyone could have a handful. He glanced at his watch. He needed to get back. His two hour limit was nearly up.

After leaving the girls he'd only had to go another two miles before finding what he was looking for; water and a place to camp. He'd located a small clearing along a tributary. With the drought, the water level was low and had left a wide bank of small river rock and a patch of mountain grass. They could sleep on the grass and build a fire in the rocks. He'd also come across the huckleberry bushes and was excited to find the food source. It wasn't much, but it was better than nothing.

He retraced his steps through the dense woods, following the markers he'd set out earlier. He wasn't an experienced tracker, but he'd spent enough time hunting that he knew how to make a trail that he could follow back to the start. A few strategically placed branches and dislocated rocks could mean the difference between finding your way home and getting lost.

As he hiked back he thought about the girls and the precarious situation they were all in. If it weren't for the fire, he felt confident that they could find their way out just by continuing west. But they couldn't go west and if they continued east, they could end up crossing the entire continental divide before they found another road. So far, they seemed to be holding up, but he knew it was only a matter of time before things got bad. They were all hungry. If they couldn't get enough food, they'd start to weaken. And that was just physically, mental weakness was sure to come. They were scared and could be near hysteria soon. He just hoped it didn't come to that.

Playing out grim scenarios in his head, Brad wandered back to the girls expecting to find them huddled together disconsolately.

Laughter rang through the trees as Brad rounded the last corner. The girls were lined up fifty yards ahead of him, all except one. Sky stood only twenty yards ahead of him, her back to him.

"You may take three elephant steps forward," he heard her say.

Elephant steps? He stopped to watch as Laela bent over at the waist, held her arm to her nose and swung it back and forth in front of her as she took three giant steps forward.

"Mother, may I take five giant steps forward?" Emma called out.

"No, but you may take three bunny hops forward." Emma held her hands in front of her like rabbit paws before hopping exactly three times, landing unsteadily, and falling over. They all laughed, including Emma. She got to her feet again and waited patiently for the next girl to go.

Brad watched unseen from the trees as one by one they moved towards Sky following her directions to act like a variety of animals. These were not the frightened, cowering girls he expected to find. Amazing. He knew they were hungry and uncomfortable. They had to be. He certainly was. Who knew wet denim could chaff so badly? But they seemed to be taking it all in stride. Except for a few moments of panic and tears, they were making the best of a very bad situation. Either they were exceptional girls or they had an exceptional leader. Maybe it was a bit of both he thought, admiring the disheveled and dirty backside of Sky Ryder.

After the last girl in line had her turn, Brad called from behind, "Mother, may I take twenty steps forward?"

The sound of his deep voice startled her, and she turned to see him smiling. He was holding the edge of his shirt up to protect the precious berries, revealing a set of tanned and perfectly sculpted abs. He didn't wait for her to respond. "I brought lunch."

At the word lunch, the girls all came running toward him, their game forgotten.

"What is it?" Heather asked.

"What d'ya find?" Annie echoed.

In seconds they were on him like hungry wolves to a lone rabbit. He held open his shirt to show them the treasure he'd found. "Huckleberries," he said and began handing out fistfuls to each girl.

"You might want to savor those," said Sky to Heather. She was about to shove the entire handful into her mouth at once. "That might be it for a while."

I've never tasted anything so good before," Annie crooned. She picked another of the purple berries from her hand and placed it on her tongue. She closed her eyes and moaned her approval.

Her mouth full of berries, Amanda said nothing only nodded in agreement.

When they'd all received some, Brad tossed a few in his mouth and chewed slowly, wanting to prolong the sensation. They really were delicious, especially when you hadn't eaten in 24 hours.

"Any luck?" Sky asked between berries. She was eating them one at a time.

"I found a clearing by a river about two miles ahead if we keep to the northeast. Since we don't know how far the fire has reached, I think we should avoid going west. We've got to climb a ways to reach it, but I think it's the best spot. We can pick more berries on the way," he said as he watched her put the last of her share in her mouth. Strange, but even at a time like this when he should have been worrying about their next meal, he couldn't help but think about what it would be like to taste her lips and the lingering flavor of sweet berries.

"Sounds good," Sky said licking the last of the berry juice from her fingers. Brad's stomach clenched in pure male reaction. "We've got to get our gear dried before dark too. I think most of our sleeping bags are wet."

"Once we get there we can build a fire and lay everything out to dry."

Turning from Brad, Sky addressed the girls. No one was eager to hike more, but everyone understood the necessity. Within minutes they were ready.

"Before we go," Sky said, "I think we should say another prayer." She didn't wait for Brad's consent, just gathered the girls close. "Annie, would you mind offering it for us?"

Brad could have walked away, but he didn't. Something held him there. A force? A power? He couldn't name it, but he felt compelled to stay and listen this time. The girls were gathered in a circle, a circle that included him, and no matter his negative feelings about religion, there was strength in the circle. Who was he to break it?

Instead, he stood listening to the humble words of a young girl and his heart skipped a beat. A tingling sensation raced down his spine. No doubt he was just feeling the effects of wet clothes, he thought. Or maybe it was just part of the bond that develops between people when they share an intense situation. Either way it was…sweet.

As Annie closed the prayer they all said "amen," then looked to him to lead the way. He turned and began retracing his steps.

As he walked back through the forest, he thought about the words of the prayer. Annie had begun by giving thanks. She'd thanked God for keeping them safe that morning. Had it really been God that kept them from being burned alive? He didn't think so. More like good timing on their part. Sky had smelled the smoke early and that had given them enough time to get away. She'd also asked for a safe place to stay where they could get food and water. Well, hadn't he already found that for them? God didn't have anything to do with it by his calculations.

In the past few months, Brad felt like he was on religion overload. London was constantly pushing him to come to church, to meet with the missionaries, to read her Mormon Bible. Did he really have such animosity towards religion? Truthfully, no. He'd always had a strong belief in God. But he was also practical. God was busy running the universe. He didn't have time to listen to the prayers of everyone, the simple pleading of nobodies. Sure, maybe He listened to the Pope, to pastors and other leaders. But to him? To these girls? Highly unlikely he reasoned.

But he also couldn't deny that he'd felt something back there standing among those girls. He didn't know what their religion was, but they were obviously faithful to it. He hoped if God was going to listen to anyone today, it would be Annie. They could certainly use all the help they could get.

Chapter 16

The clearing was a peaceful retreat. Towering pines stood guard above the meandering path of a gently flowing crystal stream. Small rocks of every hue glistened beneath the surface. At one time the stream had been a raging river carving out its own path through the trees that stood like sentinels along its banks, felling any of them that got in its way. Constantly flowing, the water had smoothed and polished the rocks until they were round. What remained of the bank after the heavy spring run-off was covered in grass and wildflowers. The water had shrunk to no more than a stream, four feet wide, as it twisted and turned on its long journey to the sea.

"Well, this is it," said Brad as he shrugged off his heavy pack. It fell to the ground with a thud, stirring up a small cloud of dust on the dry forest floor. "It's not too smooth for sleeping, but at least it's fairly level. And we've got water."

There was a sense of relief all around to have found it at last. It had been a difficult two miles. They'd pushed uphill the entire way. At times the terrain had been so steep they'd had to practically crawl, pulling themselves forward by holding onto low branches and bushes. The smaller girls, Amanda and Heather, had an especially hard time and the others all tried to help by taking some of their things to lighten their load.

Sky nodded and turned to survey the surroundings. "It'll do for now," she said, resignation in her voice. She set her heavy pack down and rolled her shoulders to relieve the tension. Then she unfastened her sleeping bag from her pack and began spreading it out. Watching, the girls followed her example and started to do the same without having to be told. The late afternoon sun shone through the heavy foliage leaving only dappled light, but still it was warm enough to dry things out before sundown.

Within minutes the small clearing looked like a refugee camp as packs were emptied and belongings spread out on the ground. Clothes, socks, sleeping bags, flashlights; everything was damp.

Brad pulled his cell phone from the holster at his hip. There had been no service in any part of the mountains that they'd covered so far, but that didn't stop him from trying again. He flipped open the screen only to find it now had water bubbles behind it and a large crack down the center. Chances were it wouldn't work, but he turned it on anyway.

The screen remained black while a faint buzz hummed from the speaker. He punched the keypad, but it was no use. The buzzing stopped. "Worthless piece of junk!" he muttered. Next he attempted to unfold his map, but very little was salvageable. The ink had faded, the wet paper had stuck together, and where it had been folded and creased, it easily ripped apart.

His fireman's pack consisted of a small first aid kit, string, some wire, duct tape, some carabiner safety clips, a pocket knife, a fire retardant foil blanket, and a flare gun with two flares. The flares were soaked and ruined, but the other things were salvageable.

"Oh no," Emma moaned, "My journal is totally ruined." She held it up for no one in particular to see. The pages were glued together and came off in chunks when she tried prying them apart.

"You brought your journal?" Annie asked in disbelief.

"I always bring it. I write every night."

"What do you write? Was it important?" asked Heather.

"Nothing major," Emma answered sadly. "Just about my day and stuff. But it was important to me." She sounded like a small girl pouting.

"I could never do that," Laela said, pulling the last of her things from her pack. "Look what I found!" She held up a small plastic bag that contained a washcloth and a bar of soap. Both were still dry. "I am totally going to shower with these in the stream."

Still upset about her journal, Emma continued, "Did you know, President Wilford Woodruff wrote in his journal every night."

"So, you like want to be a prophet?" Annie asked sarcastically. She had emptied all of her belongings and was sitting on the ground trying to toss rocks into the stream—a distance of only twenty yards.

"No! But our prophets have always encouraged us to keep a journal."

"Just think," Amanda said, "You'll have tons of stuff to write about when we get back."

"That's why I don't keep one," Laela said. "Mine would say the same thing every day. My life is totally boring."

"This isn't boring," Amanda offered. "You could write about this."

"What—hiking until I'm dead?"

"No, just—you know, about the forest fire. This has been kind of exciting—scary but exciting." With her pack empty, Amanda lay back and closed her eyes against the glare of the bright sky.

I don't know how I'm ever going to remember all of this to write about it later," Emma sighed. She set the soggy book down and continued to pull items out of her pack.

"Not me," Laela groaned, "I don't know how I'm ever going to forget!"

"Hey you guys," Heather whispered conspiratorially. "Check it out." She motioned with her head to where Brad was standing in the stream. He had his shirt off, his back turned away, his well-worn jeans sat low on his hips just barely revealing the waistband of his navy blue briefs. The girls watched as he bent and scooped water onto his head, running his hands through his sandy hair, water flying off his shoulders and dripping down his muscular torso.

"He is so hot!" Laela breathed so that only her compatriots could hear.

"We're all hot." Amanda said, feigning to understand.

"Not hot like hot," Heather chided her sister. "Hot like yummy hot!"

"Seriously hunky," agreed Annie.

They continued to watch as Brad scooped another and another handful of water onto his head. Finally he stopped. He rubbed his wet hands down his face and then down his arms before bending to scoop up more of the stream for a makeshift shower.

Without taking her eyes off the show, Emma said, "Yeah, but he is way too old. He must be like thirty."

"Too old for us maybe," Laela confirmed, "But not too old for Sky." Like spectators at a tennis match, the girls' heads turned in unison to see what their leader was doing. She sat alone on the edge of the stream, resting.

"You know she's engaged, right?"

"So what. I like this guy."

"I like him too, but that's not the point." The girls continued to watch Brad. He had moved out of the water back to the bank where he seemed intent on inventorying the contents of his pack.

"Sister Ryder would never go for a guy that wasn't a member of the church," Amanda said to the others.

"You're right," Laela conceded. "But I still think he'd be totally perfect for her."

"Have any of you ever met her fiancé?" asked Annie

"I've seen him at the church with her before," said Heather.

Emma answered, "I met him once. He seemed okay."

"What do you mean he seemed 'okay'? Is he like totally geeky or something?"

"No. In fact, he's really good-looking. Like almost movie-star good looking. I just...I don't know." Emma shrugged her shoulders and twisted her lips trying to think of the right words. "I've known Sky—Sister Ryder—for a long time, forever. She's always been so open and fun. This guy just seemed kind of creepy almost. He wasn't rude or anything, he just wasn't the kind of guy I thought she would marry."

"Maybe he's just shy," Heather said.

"I think it's the opposite, like he knows how good looking he is and thinks everyone must admire him. He's probably really great though or she wouldn't have said yes."

"Well good, that will leave Brad the Fireman for me!"

"Laela!" the girls cried in unison, before falling into fits of laughter.

Sky sat on the edge of the stream. She had taken off her hiking boots and socks and was soaking them in the cool water. It felt amazing! Her body was tired, and she was mentally fatigued. She'd been worried about the girls all day. She'd done her best to keep their spirits up. She tried to stay positive and upbeat, but it was exhausting work. It was a relief to stop and rest. And, for now, at least, they would be alright.

She leaned back on her hands and gazed up. The sky was not blue, but even through the haze it was bright enough to make her squint. Pine trees rose up the mountain side as far as she could see. Majestic and mysterious, the mountains were forever changing. Thinking of home, she pictured the view from her apartment. The light could play behind the peaks making them appear at times far away and unobtainable, and at other times as though they were mere footsteps away. They reflected the world in shades of pink, purple, blue and gray. They were as moody as a teenager, yet aged with the wisdom of generations. She'd always thought of them as friends, but she was quickly learning that they could also be enemies.

Bringing her eyes back down to earth, she followed the flow of a leaf caught in the current until something better caught her attention.

Thirty yards downstream she watched Brad wade out into the stream. Unaware of his audience, he picked his way gingerly over the rocks in his bare feet, stopping at what must have been a deep spot. He squatted low and dipped his hand in the water. He stood again and stretched before grabbing the hem of his t-shirt and pulling it over his head.

Sky sucked in her breath, nearly gasping before she caught herself and quietly let it out. Mesmerized by his lean and muscular form, she couldn't look away. Repeatedly he washed his hair, his arms, his torso. Crystal clear water dripping from bronze sculpted muscle.

Behind her, the girls burst into a fit of unified giggles. Brad turned to see what the commotion was about. Quickly, Sky looked away before he caught her staring.

He went back to washing, and Sky stole another glance, keeping her head down. Within minutes he had finished, and as he walked back to the bank, she averted her eyes, faking a sudden interest in staring at her own toes.

"We need to get another fire going," Brad called out to her. She looked up just as he pulled his shirt back over his shoulders and she caught the last sight of his toned abs. "We need to boil some more water."

I think I need a cold shower she thought, feeling her cheeks blush. "Um…yeah," she stammered. "Just let me get my shoes back on and I'll help you."

What am I doing ogling over Brad that way, she thought, shoving her wet feet back into dirty socks. *I'm engaged!*

It's not like she'd never seen a guy with his shirt off before. She'd been swimming with Tom lots of times that summer. Tom was fit. Maybe he was a bit less fit, but he wasn't fat by any means. And really, she was a nurse. She was no stranger to the human body. Yet, the image of Brad standing in the stream would be one she knew she'd remember for a long time, maybe for the rest of her life.

As she pulled on her boots and began to lace them up again, she tried to erase the image of Brad and replace it with Tom. He'd probably only done it to show off. He probably liked women looking at him, the big—big hunk. She couldn't seem to come up with anything derogatory enough to mask the perfection she'd seen. But really, he didn't seem like the kind of guy to parade around in front of girls just so they could check him out. He was probably just feeling gritty and dirty. After all, they'd been hiking and sleeping in the dirt for nearly three days, longer if one considered that she and the girls had arrived at the campground on Monday and it was now Saturday. She scratched at her head, noting the dirt under her nails afterward. No, he didn't seem like the show off type.

She looked over and saw Brad had gotten a few of the girls to start building a fire ring out of river rock. She couldn't hear what they were saying but Laela and Heather were smiling, attentive to whatever he was telling them. For a minute she wondered how Tom would act in this situation. Tom liked an audience, or at least, he liked having lots of people around. Tom was often a flirt, but that was just his personality. He was just really friendly. So what if that friendliness overstepped the boundaries into flirting sometimes. She'd gotten over being hurt by his attention to other girls. Sky knew it didn't mean anything. *Did it?* No. Absolutely not. He'd told her that over and over. She trusted him. It wasn't like it was his fault that girls were drawn to his amazing good looks.

And he was just as good looking as Brad. In a different way maybe, but certainly just as handsome. Tom was fastidious about his appearance. He wore the best clothes, the best shoes. He had a standing appointment to get his hair cut every three weeks. He liked things clean and orderly just like Sky. She liked things to be neat too--only that was hard to do when you were camping, or hiking, or had been working for twenty-four hours straight at the hospital and you were too utterly exhausted to wash the dishes in your apartment. And punctual—Tom was a stickler for punctuality. He could get downright angry when his schedule was interrupted. Truthfully, Tom was a contradiction that often astounded her—carefree and fun one minute, obsessive compulsive the next.

Ah, Tom! She thought, missing him and wondering how much he was missing her.

"The floor creaked as he stepped forward into the dark hallway. Creak! Creak!" Brad softly screeched. His voice held the girls mesmerized as they sat around the fire. Each stared at him, anticipating his next words, "Until a loud roar from behind blew out his candle—" Just then, as though it had been scripted, Brad's stomach growled loudly enough that everyone heard it. He laughed, breaking the stone faced stare he'd held while telling them a ridiculous ghost story. The girls laughed with him, but only at the timing, not the fact that they were all starving.

"So what happened next?" asked Amanda. She had been completely drawn into the story, as were they all.

"Yeah, did he ever find the gold?" asked Heather.

"Nope," Brad resumed.

"So where was it?"

"Nobody knows. Nobody has ever dared to look long enough in the house. There's always the ghost there that scares them off."

"No way." Emma stated. "I don't believe you. There's no such place."

Sure there is. I've seen it—from the outside anyway."

"I'd love to find a long lost treasure, even if it's guarded by a ghost," Laela decided. "I could use a new car, some new clothes, a trip to Paris—"

"After you pay your tithing, of course," supplied Sky.

Laela looked at her and smiled sweetly like a Primary child answering, "Of course."

Tithing? Brad had heard that word before. He remembered London talking about it and suddenly it dawned on him, these girls were Mormon. He laughed out loud at the irony of it, surprising the girls when he couldn't stop. Wouldn't London love to see him now, he thought, stuck out in the wilderness with a bunch of Mormons.

"What's so funny?" Sky asked.

"You're Mormon."

"And that's funny how?" Her tone was defensive.

Brad quickly sobered, not wanting to offend her. "It's not."

"Then why are you laughing?" she questioned him.

"It's a long story." Avoiding any further questions, he quickly changed the subject. "I'll take some help fishing tomorrow. The more lines in the water, the more we eat."

They had caught three small fish for dinner. It wasn't nearly enough to satisfy their appetites. At first some of the girls had been squeamish, claiming they didn't like fish. But watching the others enjoy the small bit of food was enough to make them change their mind.

"This isn't so bad," Laela claimed after pulling off a tiny morsel and gingerly chewing it. She reached for another piece from the pan.

"There's nothing quite like eating trout fresh from the stream over a campfire," Brad claimed.

"Oh, I could think of at least a hundred," Annie quipped.

"Spoilsport!" he teased. A familiarity had developed among the group that now included Brad. The girls had said very little to him for the past two days on the trail. Suddenly, that evening they were surrounding him, conversing, joking, asking questions. He'd come to know them a little better, understand their personalities. He found them all to be nice girls. Typical girls, if there was such a thing. They talked about boys, about clothes. They all complained in one way or another about being hungry and wanting to get home, but not one of them caused any problems.

He rather enjoyed teasing them. They kind of reminded him of his sister, and heaven knows he had always loved to tease her. Even at thirty three, two years his junior, he loved to poke fun of her. They'd always been close, even after she got married. When he had moved to Washington after college and later traveled around the west with the Forest Service, his sister, Jenna, had called regularly. Now she had children of her own, bickering and fighting just as they had when they were kids. He loved his niece and nephew. The thought occurred to him that they might be worried if they'd heard he was missing. But he couldn't do anything about that and worrying about it wouldn't get him home.

"I used to fish with my dad when I was a kid," Brad continued talking. With nothing more to eat and little to do, storytelling had become their only diversion from their situation. "He was a logger so he spent a lot of time in the mountains and forest. He'd find the perfect fishing hole and then he'd bring me with him when he had some time off. We ate a lot of fish together," he finished. "What about you?" he asked, turning to Sky. "What do you think of this gourmet meal we've got here?"

"It's not bad. It could use some lemon," she answered drily.

"Lemon? Only sissy girls would eat mountain trout with lemon." Sky looked at him and smiled demurely, matching his teasing tone. "Then it's a good thing we don't have any, because we are no group of sissies, right girls?" She looked around the fire for confirmation. They concurred, grunting hardily and showing stern faces to prove their leader's words.

"There isn't a tougher group of girls anywhere," Sky confirmed. She looked at them, meeting each one's eyes as she scanned their faces. Her own eyes filled with tears as she continued, "You couldn't ask for a braver, more wonderful group of young women anywhere in the world." Two small tears fell down her cheeks.

Around the campfire, Brad heard sniffles and knew some of the girls were tearing up, but it was difficult to take his eyes off Sky. She was dirty, her hair wasn't brushed, yet she looked beautiful. He watched as she quickly wiped the tears away. She glanced at him as if embarrassed that he had noticed. He admired her strength, keeping her cool under this stressful situation. She hadn't lost it or fallen apart. In fact, she had been instrumental in keeping everyone's mood positive. She had a dry wit that often surprised him, but which he found completely endearing and comical. It was just too bad she was engaged.

And Mormon, he reminded himself.

Emotions around the fire were suddenly fragile. Everyone was undoubtedly thinking about home. Bringing the conversation back to a happier, lighter tone, he met Sky's eyes, held them for another brief moment before grinning broadly, "You're right, I'm sure there isn't a tougher, meaner--dirtier group of girls on the planet!"

"Dirty! Heather yelled, "Who are you calling dirty?"

"Yeah, I'll have you know I smell like Irish Spring," Laela informed them. "I am so glad I brought that bar of soap."

"When are you going to use it?" he asked innocently, knowing full well the girls had all walked downstream to bathe earlier.

"You---You!" She pushed him over, not able to think of a better comeback. Brad just laughed.

They were lost in the wilderness, and had been on the run from a forest fire for two days. They had little food, no real shelter besides the trees. They were exhausted and worried. Who knew when they would get home and be reunited with their families? It could be days. There seemed to be no end to their problems, Brad surmised.

Around him, the girls continued joking, making the best of a bad situation. Sometimes laughter was the only solution.

"Okay, so who's next?" He asked, tossing another stick on the fire. "Who's got a ghost story for us? Laela? Emma?"

"I've got one," said Heather. She scooted closer to the fire making her face glow brighter. She glared at the faces staring back at her own as though sizing them up, preparing them for her tale of terror. "Our dad told me this one." She looked at her twin for confirmation, but Amanda said nothing."

Heather continued, "He works for the city as an engineer. Last year someone donated a piece of property that they thought might make a good museum. It's really old, like a hundred years or more. Anyway, it was his job to go in and do some inspection stuff on it. So he goes in and he's in the basement, right. And there's like junk everywhere, like whoever lived there never threw anything away. He's making his way through the junk when he hears someone behind him, and he thinks it's his friend who was supposed to be working upstairs. But when he turns, there's no one there. So he calls out and his friend answers. He's still upstairs."

Heather paused, rearranged her legs.

"That's it? That's your ghost story?" Annie asks.

"No, my legs were falling asleep."

Laela yawned. "I think your story is putting me to sleep."

"You guys!" Heather crooned, making the word sound like two syllables instead of one.

"Really, it gets better," Amanda piped up. "I was there when my dad told it. It's totally real. Just wait."

"So, as I was saying," Heather smirked at Laela and tossed a small pinecone at her friend, "He calls out and his friend or co-worker, or whoever, is still upstairs. Since there's nobody there he keeps going, trying to find the right piping or whatever in the basement. But there's so much junk he can hardly walk. A few minutes later, he hears someone again, but there's still no one there. A third time he hears it, and this time he feels someone tap him on the shoulder."

In the dark, Brad reached around Sky's shoulders and tapped Laela. She screamed and jumped. "That's not funny!" She cries in mock anger as the group began laughing.

Brad innocently held both of his hands up "I don't know what you're talking about." But he couldn't hold back the grunt when Sky elbowed him in the ribs.

"You're ruining the story," she said.

Leaning over he whispered to her loud enough so that all of them could hear, "I thought I was helping it."

"Just be quiet and listen. Go on Heather," she encouraged.

"So anyway, he feels someone—or something—tap him and he turns around to look. As he turns around his flashlight blinks out and a wind rushes past his face."

"A wind?" Annie asks.

"You know, like when someone walks past you really fast."

"Did he see anything?" asked Emma.

"No, he just felt it. And it was dark so he couldn't see. He said he shook his flashlight and it came back on, but there was nothing there."

"That doesn't mean it was a ghost," Laela said, glaring over at Brad. He winked at her with a lopsided grin.

"No, but the really creepy part is that when they cleared all the junk out of the basement they found parts of a skeleton. Like someone had died down there."

"They're still investigating," said Amanda. "My dad said he thinks it might have been the ghost trying to tell him something."

"Or maybe, your dad was just pulling your leg," said Annie.

Above the group the wind stirred the trees and an owl hooted in the silence. As if on cue, they all looked towards the sound, seeing nothing but darkness. Then, turning back to the fire they looked at each other and burst into laughter.

Yes, laughter was definitely the best medicine.

Chapter 17

"Gather round folks, gather round." Chief Charlie Carruthers was sweating profusely as he stood in the dusty field at twilight. Surrounding him were the worried faces of mothers and fathers anxious for news about their missing daughters. News reporters from all over Montana, Idaho, Wyoming, Utah, and even some from as far away as Oregon, Washington and Colorado were among the throng of people that had gathered to hear the latest update about the lost hikers. The burly man wiped at his brow with a red and white bandana, but it didn't stop the droplets of sweat from trickling down his neck and back.

"We've halted the search for the night," he reported. "There's not enough light to send up another helicopter, but we'll begin again at first light tomorrow."

"What about the ground search?" someone from the crowd shouted. Like opening the flood gates on a dam, everyone began tossing questions to the chief. Mothers began crying again, husbands holding them by the shoulders to offer comfort.

"Have you seen any evidence?"

"Are they alive?"

"Were they burned?"

"What area are you searching?"

Carruthers held up his hand to silence the crowd. "The bad news is we've seen no trace of them, but the good news is we haven't seen any bodies either. Now that the fire is somewhat under containment—"

"What do you mean by 'somewhat'?" a reporter interrupted.

"We've got the blaze at least thirty percent contained." The wind had died down early in the afternoon, allowing the firefighters to make some progress towards putting it out. The camp had been notified by forecasters that heavy clouds would be rolling in towards midnight and would likely bring some rain. That news had been welcomed by everyone. Now, if they could just avoid any more lightning strikes, the fire crews might all be able to go home before the next weekend. But that was counting chickens, the blaze was still burning strong in several locations and they had seven missing people to find before anyone would leave.

The chief continued, "Now that the fire has moved on, we've been able to send search and rescue teams to the area where the campers were reported to be. The ground is still hot, and dangerous so only limited numbers have been allowed in, but they found no sign of them, no bodies, no gear. Nothing."

"So what does that mean?" Jake Cordin called out. "I've got two daughters out there somewhere. They can't have just disappeared."

"No. The fact the search teams found nothing would suggest they fled the area when the fire got too close. We're basing our search on that assumption, and widening it. But you've got to understand, we're talking miles of wilderness here."

"Do you know if the fireman that's missing is with the girls?" another reporter asked. The cameraman behind him readjusted his hold on the camera and zoomed his lens in on the faces of the distraught parents.

"I can't confirm that. But he was sent to find them when the campground was evacuated."

"So you don't know if you're looking for a group and a single man, or just one group? Is that correct?"

"That's correct—"

"So who are you trying to find first?" It was an insensitive question thrown out by a tabloid reporter. "Who has priority?

"Everyone that's missing is a priority," emphasized Carruthers in a tone of disgust.

"So, you're telling us they could be anywhere? They could be alone and…and…" Shayla Knudson cried hysterically, unable to even finish her sentence.

"Ma'am," Chief Carruthers said patiently, "I know this is upsetting—"

"Upsetting! You have no idea—" Jake Cordin shouted again, pointing an accusatory finger at the older man. Next to him, his wife put her hand on his arm, pulling it back down.

"Jake, it's not his fault," she tearfully reminded him.

Tension in the gathering was palpable. Even the reporters had gone strangely quiet as though they could feel the pain and sorrow these parents were experiencing. Again, the chief wiped at his brow. Taking his time to fold the cloth and replace it in his pocket, they waited for him to speak.

"I know this is upsetting," he repeated compassionately. "I've three daughters of my own. In addition, every one of these men and women that put their lives on the line each day are like my family. I'm in charge of their safety, their well-being. It is my responsibility to see that they make it out of here alive. I've made that commitment to them and their families. And I promise you," he paused, looking at each of them for emphasis, "I will do everything in my power to find your loved ones."

"Sir," Timothy Stone spoke up, acting as spokesman for the parents. He was calm and his words had an air of authority to them. "We appreciate all that you're doing. We just feel helpless. Is there something we can be doing to help?"

"We can't allow civilians to go searching through these mountains, not with a fire like this causing such a threat. We're employing as many trained search and rescue teams as we can get, plus two helicopters. The smoke is making it difficult for spotter planes to see much below, but we've got volunteers to go up as soon as it clears some." Chief Carruthers took off his glasses and rubbed the lenses on the hem of his shirt. He placed them back on his face and while looking directly at Timothy Stone, he said, "Now I'm not a religious man by any means, but I never underestimate the power of prayer."

London picked up the remote control and clicked the power button. The television went mute, cutting off the sports announcer in mid-sentence. Tossing aside the controller, she picked up the portable phone that was ringing from the end table.

"Hi, Sister Huish," Ammon heard her say as he walked into the family room, the garage door swinging shut behind him.

"Of course, we'd be happy to...Oh wow, that's awful...I know—I've been watching all day." There was silence for several seconds before she began again, "He's a friend of mine actually...You're right...I appreciate that...I'll be sure to let them know. Thanks for calling."

Sighing heavily, London flopped back into the overstuffed cushions, and tossed the phone next to the remote control she'd discarded moments earlier. Behind her, Ammon reached down and rubbed consolingly at her shoulders. "Well, it's not good news, but it could be worse," he said, referring to the television and the news reports he knew she'd been listening to all day.

"I know," she capitulated. "I just hate not knowing." She had spent most of the day glued to the television, waiting for updates or breaking news reports about Brad and the missing girls. Ammon had done his best to coax her away, but he was unable to persuade his wife to leave for long. Worry was still written across her face.

Ammon was similarly worried, and though he tried to stay busy by getting some yard work done and helping Corkie with his Cub Scout project, he kept a radio on in the garage tuned to a talk station with frequent news reports. "What was that call from Sister Huish about?"

"She was calling to tell us about a special stake fast that they're holding tomorrow."

"Really?" Ammon said, surprised. "They don't usually hold a fast for something like this, but—"

Cutting him off, London spoke up, "Turns out the girls that are missing are part of the Missoula Stake. They're a group of young women from Missoula who were attending their ward girls' camp. When the Forest Service came to evacuate, five of them and one leader were on an overnight hike."

"So Brad was sent up to bring them back." Ammon guessed at the rest of the story, based on the news they'd heard the night before.

"I guess so."

Ammon came around the side of the couch and sat down next to London. She leaned her head on his shoulder as he wrapped his arm around hers. "It makes sense. If the fire has been as out of control as we've been hearing, they might have been forced to go a different direction."

"I've got to phone the sisters that I visit and let them know about the fast."

"Well, one thing's for certain," Ammon said.

"What's that?

"Brad will have the strength of the church behind him whether he wants it or not."

Chapter 18

Brad felt something fall on his cheek. He reached up and wiped it away, only semi-conscious. He stuck his arm back under his heavy fireman's coat and pulled it more snuggly around his shoulders. It was the second night in a row he'd used it to stay warm while he curled up under the open sky. It didn't seem to be working nearly as well tonight, probably because it was still damp. Even though he'd let it sit out all afternoon, the heavy, fire resistant material was slow to dry.

Another drop hit his cheek and he pulled the substitute sleeping bag over his face. He wasn't sure which was worse, whatever kept hitting him in the face, or the smell of his own coat. Neither would allow him to sleep peacefully. He rolled over, adjusting his hip to fit between rocks. Within minutes he was almost back to sleep. Suddenly several drops landed on his exposed forehead, his legs were cold and—wet?

He sat up just as the deluge began.

At last, the rain they'd hoped for all summer poured down.

The girls hastily came awake.

"What in the—"

"I'm getting wet!"

"Aaarrgghhhh!"

The sound of heavy droplets splashing into the stream broke the night's silence. Brad called out to them, "Hurry, hurry! Let's get under the trees."

"It's too dark," Laela cried. "I can't see where I'm going."

"Here, hold my hand," Sky offered, reaching into the darkness. The light of their small campfire had long since died.

Brad turned on one of the two flashlights that still worked. The others had apparently gotten too wet and refused to shine any longer. "Everybody grab hands. We'll have to play follow the leader." With the dim light, he saw the girls had linked up, all hunching over instinctively to avoid getting wet, a task that was proving impossible as the heavy rain fell like buckets dumping all around them. He grabbed Sky's hand and headed for the shelter of the trees.

"What about our stuff?" She sputtered.

"I'll come back for it." They didn't have to go far before the canopy of the trees afforded some protection. He searched the base of the trees, trying to find one that looked fairly dry, a place where they could wait out the storm. When he discovered one that looked promising, he said, "Wait here."

Leaving them all dripping under the large coniferous branches, he headed back to the clearing and gathered six soggy sleeping bags in his arms.

They hadn't gone far into the woods, but in the dark, even with his flashlight, it was difficult to find his way back.

"We're over here," he heard Sky shout. She must have seen his light searching around. He followed her voice back to find them huddled together under the tree. The ring of dry earth was quickly shrinking as the water penetrated its way down from the tree tops.

"It's fr-freezing." Heather was chattering and so was Annie.

"We'll have to use your sleeping bags to keep warm and keep some of the water off of us. We can make a canopy of sorts," instructed Brad. Handing the sleeping bags out to the girls, he kept one and began unzipping it all the way. The girls watched and did the same.

Soon Emma had spread hers out on the ground, making an area large enough for all five of the girls to huddle. Laela and Heather who were in the middle shared a sleeping bag, pulling it over them and covering as much of themselves as they could. Amanda and Annie did the same. Emma was on the end so she took one bag and draped it over one of her shoulders and extended it as far as it would reach over the head and shoulders of the others. At the opposite end of the group, Brad spread a sleeping bag next to the girls where he and Sky could sit down. The last bag, he draped over their head and shoulders as Emma had done. It wasn't the most waterproof of tents, but it was better than nothing.

The rain pelted down steadily. They all watched in uncomfortable silence, waiting for it to end. But it didn't. Water dripped from the pine boughs onto their makeshift tent. It sounded like dull thuds as it hit the nylon sleeping bags.

This was the second night in a row that their sleep had been interrupted. They had hiked what felt like endless miles with nothing to sustain them but fear and adrenaline. They were hungry and cold. There seemed to be no end to the misery.

After twenty minutes of heavy rain, the downpour finally eased to a steady drizzle. It was evidently not going to end any time soon.

Heather leaned over and put her head on Laela's lap. "I'm so tired," she murmured. "Can I lay on you?"

Laela, barely awake herself, was already leaning on Emma's shoulder. "Sure, go ahead," she mumbled. Emma was braced against the tree trunk, leaning her head on top of Laela's. Her eyes were already closed, and though she still held the end of the sleeping bag they were using as a tarp, her arm had dropped to her side causing it to pull down more tightly over their heads. Amanda too leaned over and rested on her sister. Annie was the last to give in, but before long she had dozed off, slumping against the others.

Brad leaned back against the tree, preparing himself for a long, wet night. Next to him, he could feel Sky struggling against the need for sleep, her head nodding forward before jerking upright again.

"Come here," he said, rearranging his arm so that he could wrap it around her shoulders. "Lean your head on me."

He felt her hesitate, but then she welcomed the invitation and leaned her head against his chest.

"I think the girls have fallen asleep," she whispered.

"Yeah, I think you're right. They're probably pretty tired."

"It's been a rough two days," she confirmed. With her head on his chest, tucked under his chin, he could faintly smell her hair, a combination of strawberry scented shampoo and smoke. She had left it down before going to bed and it hung down her back and over her arm. His hand absently played with it, gently combing his fingers through, and feeling the silky strands.

Brad closed his eyes and listened to the forest. It was still and quiet except for the drip of water and trickling of the stream in the distance. Despite being damp he felt almost peaceful. There was an unfamiliar feeling of contentment holding Sky in the darkness.

"Are you asleep?" Her voice was barely audible above the rain.

"No. Are you?"

"No." She waited another minute before continuing, "Can I ask you something?"

"Go ahead, I'm an open book."

"Earlier, when we were talking around the fire and you figured out that we're Mormon, why'd you laugh?"

It wasn't what he'd been expecting. Maybe something to do with the fire, or about their predicament, or—anything but that. Surprised, he had to think just how much he would share before answering. "I'm sorry, I didn't mean to laugh."

"You don't like Mormons?" she asked.

"I just thought it was really ironic, that's all."

Sky adjusted her weight so she could sit up better. Lifting her head from his side, she looked up at him. "Ironic? How so?"

He could barely see her face in the darkness. She had high cheekbones and an angular jaw. He studied her, wanting to run his finger down her flawlessly smooth skin. She gazed up at him and he felt her eyes piercing him. "It's a long story," he finally answered.

"I could use a good story right about now." She tucked her head under his chin again. He felt her shivering and pulled her more tightly into his side.

"I didn't say it was a good story, just a long one."

"It's okay, I'm listening." She pulled both arms in close and tucked them between their bodies. Loving the feel of her snuggling close, Brad couldn't resist laying his cheek on her head.

"Last summer I met someone and we started dating. She's a young widow with a couple of kids."

"What's her name?"

"London." He tried to say it indifferently, but even he caught the hint of longing in his voice. "We dated all summer. She was terrific. I asked her to marry me. I really thought she'd say yes, too, you know. I really thought we were right for each other."

"She said no?" Sky's voice showed her surprise.

"She said no," he confirmed. "She said she just didn't feel like she could be the kind of wife I deserved."

"That sounds kind of corny," said Sky, "especially after dating all summer."

"You have to understand, I was the first guy she'd dated since her husband was killed," said Brad, unconsciously coming to London's defense. "She wasn't mean about it or anything. I just figured she wasn't ready."

"Makes sense."

"Yeah, well, the very next day she finds out she has inherited some money from a friend who had died. Only this friend had a son that she hadn't talked to and didn't know where he was. So London doesn't feel right about taking the money. Instead, she gets this crazy idea to drive across the country and find him so she can give him his mom's money."

"She drove across the country? Like how far?"

"To New York."

"New York!" She gasped loudly, pulling away and looking at him as though she'd misunderstood. The sudden movement caused Annie to stir beside her. She lowered her voice and carefully moved back into the safety of his arm. "What, was she crazy?"

"I thought so. But I tried to be supportive. She'd had a rough childhood, gotten pregnant in high school and never really had the opportunity to do much or go anywhere. I figured she'd go and when she came back, she'd change her mind about us." He stopped talking, remembering the heartache of those summer days without her. He had missed her terribly.

"So what happened?"

"She left. She drove to New York. She had this package she was taking to him from his mom. Turns out it was some kind of book of scripture. She ended up reading it and learning about your church."

"The Book of Mormon?"

"I guess."

"Did she find him?"

"Yeah, she found him alright. They got married about two months ago." There was no derision in his voice, just acceptance.

"I'm sorry," Sky offered. She put her hand on his chest consolingly. "That must be really difficult."

Was it difficult? How could he begrudge them a happy marriage? They were his friends and he was happy for them. Truly happy. There was a time when it had been difficult. It had nearly torn his heart out. But as he thought about it now, talked about it, there was no more pain. Time really had healed his wounds.

"It was hard. But it's all good now. They're happy and he's a good guy. We've actually gotten to be pretty good friends."

"Did she join the church?"

"Yeah. Ammon was already a Mormon, although he didn't practice it for a time. London is always trying to get me to listen to missionaries."

"And you don't want to?" Sky said it already knowing the answer.

"No!" His arm around her tightened with the vehemence of his statement.

As the night pushed towards dawn, the rain slowed until it was barely discernible through the blackness. The girls were sleeping soundly under soggy sleeping bags. Next to them, Sky was only slightly cold thanks to Brad's body heat. They had talked for over an hour, but after asking about the missionaries, he had gone quiet. She hadn't asked any more questions and he hadn't offered any more explanations.

She had enjoyed their conversation. She felt sympathy for this big, strong man. She could feel his strength all around her, keeping her safe and almost dry through this miserable night. Obviously, the size of his heart matched the size of his biceps. She had heard it in his voice. He'd been hurt.

She thought about what he said and it seemed obvious to her that his feelings about the church were tied up in his feelings for this woman.

"Brad?" she whispered. He had been silent for a long time and she wasn't sure if he had fallen asleep.

"Yeah?"

"Did I wake you?"

"No, I wish. That would mean I'd actually fallen asleep." He shifted his back against the tree emphasizing the fact that it wasn't the most comfortable place to try to rest.

"Am I hurting you?" Aside from her backside getting sore, she was quite comfortable in the crook of his arm. Strange that she should feel so at ease sitting with him like this, but she did. She felt safe. She felt protected. She also felt aware of him, his very heartbeat as it thumped beneath her cheek. She couldn't help remembering him as he'd washed in the stream, the size of his pectoral muscles and the sprinkling of blond chest hair across them. They made for a nice pillow she decided.

"You're fine. Are you warm enough?"

"Yeah. You're like a heater." She looked over at the girls, all curled up together. "I hope they're warm enough." They didn't move even though none of them looked comfortable.

Putting her head back against Brad she kept talking, "So let me ask you...are you really not interested in the church or are you just refusing to be interested because it became one more wedge between you and London?"

Instead of answering, he changed the subject. "So tell me about this fiancé of yours."

"Okay, I guess we're not going there," she said with a sigh. When he didn't respond she continued by answering his question. "His name is Tom Allred. He's from California, but his family moved here to Montana when he was on a mission."

"So he's Mormon."

"Yes—"

"Do all Mormons marry only Mormons?"

"Well, no. Not always. It's not like a rule or anything. But you have to admit, if you plan to spend eternity with someone, it would be much more enjoyable if you share the same beliefs." Having grown up in the church, Sky had never considered the possibility of marrying someone of a different faith. She'd been taught for as long as she could remember about the importance of temple marriage and eternal families. She'd never given it a second thought—until now. Could she marry someone outside of her church? Someone like—like Brad? He seemed like a great guy. He was kind, funny, responsible. He was certainly good looking. And as much as she hated to admit it—she was engaged for heaven's sake—she felt an undeniable attraction to Brad. But she knew all of those things were only secondary to sharing a love of the gospel of Jesus Christ.

Brad started fingering her hair again sending shivers down her back. He didn't directly answer her, but she guessed by his silence that he was at least contemplating what she'd said. Finally, after several minutes he spoke again, "Anyway, you were saying?"

"Saying?"

"About Tom…?"

Was that a sneer in his voice or was she just imagining it? Either way she didn't let it get to her. "Oh yeah, let's see…His dad is a retired lawyer and is hoping Tom will go into law as well. He hasn't really decided though. He's taking some time off—"

"What does he do?" Brad interrupted.

"He's been going to school since he returned from his mission."

"So, let me see if I understand you, you're marrying a guy who doesn't even know what he wants to do with his life. A guy who's going to school and who you may end up supporting while he finishes—if he finishes—school. But it's all good because he's a member of your church?"

"No, that's not—you make him sound like…like—"

"Like a jerk? A spoiled kid?"

"You don't even know him!" Sky said, trying her best not to shout. She pushed away from him so she could see his face. The sky was getting lighter as the morning edged towards sunrise and she could more clearly make out his features. His jaw was set and his eyes held judgment. "And you certainly don't know me!"

"I know your type, Thunder," he said with a hint of cockiness, using her given name as a way of getting at her. Without her near, he folded his arms, all the while meeting her furious eyes.

"My type?" Sky was angry now.

"Sure. You're a mother hen. You like to take care of everybody. You make sure everyone else is happy, even if it means you're miserable. Guys like him love girls like you. They need someone to take care of them so they can go on being selfish little boys."

"You're wrong! Tom's not like that. And neither am I!" She stood, too angry to sit so close to him any longer. She took a few steps before turning around to face him again. "You have some nerve! Judging me—us—like that."

"I'm not judging you, Sky. I'm just telling it like I see it. It'd be a shame for you to wake up one day and discover that your perfect little world isn't so perfect. That all your so-called beliefs," he used his fingers to make quotation marks in the air, "can't make you happy."

She folded her arms defensively across her chest. "I never said my life was perfect, but my *beliefs*," she said, emphasizing the word, "Do make me happy. I don't know what happened to make you such a cynic, but I feel sorry for you. I really do," she finished and turned to walk away.

"Where are you going?" he called.

"None of your business!" she yelled without turning around.

Chapter 19

As the sun rose over the tree tops, the clouds that had plagued them through the night began to burn off. One by one the girls started to stir, all of them stiff and sore from their awkward sleeping positions.

"I think my neck is broken," complained Laela. Slowly she sat up, nudging Heather away from her side.

Annie stretched her arms over her head and twisted her neck side to side, wincing at the sound of her bones cracking. "I'm awake, but my left leg is still asleep." Gingerly, she unfolded it from beneath her and began rubbing life back into it.

On the end, Emma untangled herself from the sleeping bag she'd held onto all night and stood. "My whole side is wet," she noted, surveying her darkened clothes. "And I think my tailbone will never be the same." She rubbed her bottom where the pressure of having sat on the hard ground all night had left it sore and aching.

"Hey, where's Sky?" Amanda asked, looking around.

Brad was still leaning against the tree, a sleeping bag draped around his wide shoulders. His head was tilted back unnaturally far, his mouth open, snoring softly.

"Should we wake him?" Annie asked, ready to shake him with her foot.

"No, let him sleep. He probably didn't get much last night," answered Emma. She looked around too, trying to see where their leader had gone. "Sky?" She called out softly. When there was no reply, she turned back to her friends, "She must be back at the clearing. Let's go find her."

"Come on, get up!" Laela tugged at Heather, the only girl to still be lying on top of the bag they had spread out under them. Next to her, Annie pulled at the corner, urging her to move so they could carry it back to the clearing with them.

"I can't," she said weakly.

"Come on," repeated Laela, taking hold of Heather's hand and pulling. "It's morning. We need to find some more food."

"Please don't say—" she swallowed loudly, "food."

"Heather?" Emma knelt next to her, sensing something more than just not wanting to wake up. "Heather, are you alright?"

"I—I don't feel so good." She looked apologetically up at her friends and then vomited at their feet—all over the sleeping bag. They jumped back, surprised, each of them groaning at the mess.

Their whispered stirrings and jostling hadn't been enough to wake Brad, but at the sound of Heather's violent retching, his head shot forward. "Ah man!" he said, coming to her side and holding her as her body continued to convulse in dry heaves. When the spasm finally ended she slumped against him, wiping at her mouth with the back of her hand. Tears streamed down her face, which was red and splotchy from the involuntary strain. Obviously embarrassed, she looked up, her eyes pleading for understanding from her friends, "I'm s-s-sorry," she managed to say before her breath was stolen by racking sobs.

"Hey, hey, it's okay," Brad soothed, his hand rubbing up and down on her arm. He looked at the others, meeting Emma's eyes. There seemed to be an unspoken agreement among the girls that in the absence of Sky, she was their leader.

"Yeah, Heather. It's okay. We can wash this out," said Emma. The others joined in with their own words of support.

Carefully avoiding the soiled sleeping bag, Amanda sat next to her sister and put her arm around her. At the comfort of her sister's familiar touch, Heather shifted from Brad's shoulder to Amanda's. "Do you feel better now?" she asked her sister.

"Not—Not really," she said in between sniffles. "My stomach still hurts."

"Do you think you can walk back to the clearing?" asked Brad.

"I'm so w-w-weak. I'm n-not sure." She continued crying, unable to control the tears.

Now the girls were all looking at Brad, silently asking him what to do. "Come on, then," he said, putting one hand under her knees, the other around her shoulders, and scooping her off the ground. "Let's find you some place more comfortable to rest." He started to walk away but turned back to the remaining four. "The rest of you, bring the sleeping bags so we can get them dry again. We'll wash that one out in the river. I hope you've got some Irish Spring left, Laela."

Sky was already busy in the clearing, laying out the wet gear—again—that had dried in the sun only the day before. Hearing voices, she turned to see Brad carrying Heather, followed by the others.

Amanda rushed forward and spread one of the less wet bags on the ground where they had started sleeping before the rain forced them into the trees. Brad gently laid Heather down and she curled into a ball, pulling her knees tight to her chest. She had stopped sobbing, but her face was still streaked with tears.

Ignoring Brad, Sky rushed over. "Heather, what's wrong?" she asked, kneeling beside her. Sky stroked the girl's long blond hair away from her cheeks and wiped away the remaining tears.

"I threw up," she said matter-of-factly.

Sky looked up at the others as though to confirm her story with them. In answer, Emma and Annie held up the soiled sleeping bag, both grimacing at the unpleasant task of having carried it even though they'd only touched the clean corners.

Heather noticed the look on their faces and apologized again, "I'm s-sorry," she hiccupped. "I know it's totally gross."

"Don't you worry about it," Sky soothed, continuing to stroke her hair. Looking back to Annie and Emma she said quietly, "Why don't you just put that in the water. The current should take care of most of it.

"I'll get my soap," Laela offered, running to retrieve it.

Amanda, acting as spokesman for her twin said to Sky, "She says her stomach still hurts, and she's really weak."

Sky looked at Brad. His face showed concern. Between the two of them they had a lot of medical training. Their eyes shared a brief consult, their mouths not saying a word. Sky turned back to Heather. "Heather, did you eat anything that the rest of us didn't eat? Any berries or plants?"

"No, just the fish last night." She groaned and clutched at her stomach as a spasm of pain ripped through her middle again. Sky waited for it to pass before asking, "What did you drink? Did you drink from the river?"

"Just a little," she confessed. "I didn't have any water left in my bottle yesterday. I was so thirsty and I didn't want to wait for more to boil and cool so I took some handfuls when we were washing up last night. The water is so clear, I figured it was okay."

"It's okay sweetie. You just lie here and rest." Sky stood and addressed Amanda, "We'll find the driest sleeping bag we have and keep her warm. I'll get you some clean water. You're going to have make her drink so she doesn't get dehydrated."

Amanda nodded at the instructions and took Sky's place next to her sister. The two faces of the young girls were almost identical, but one was considerably paler now.

Brad followed Sky unbidden a short distance away, out of earshot from the girls. "You think it's giardia?" he asked.

"I can't be sure, but it seems the most likely."

"There wasn't a lot in her stomach, mostly bile."

"Well, none of us have had much in our stomachs lately." It was true that the small amount of fish they'd had the night before wasn't nearly enough to satisfy their gnawing hunger. "I'm worried about dehydration. That's the main concern with giardia cases. Although," she said, sounding discouraged, "that's when we can get them on antibiotics quickly. Unless you've got some hiding away in your pack, she could experience high fever as well."

"'Afraid not. It's not life threatening, is it?"

"No, not usually. As long as she doesn't get too dehydrated, her body can fight it, but she's going to be mighty uncomfortable. And weak."

"Yeah, I get that." Brad put his hands on his hips and hung his head down. He exhaled on a sigh, obviously contemplating what to do. He was tired, not just physically, but mentally. It seemed like they kept incurring one hardship after another, like they were jinxed or something. "Look," he said, meeting Sky's eyes, "I don't think it's a good idea to move."

"But—"

"No, just listen a minute. We're all exhausted. The girls may have gotten some sleep last night, but I know you and I didn't. We're hungry and our strength is nonexistent. Now one of us is sick. We can't expect her to hike today, and none of us have the stamina to carry her. Besides, there's no way we can get her enough fluids if we're on the move. Better to just stay put."

"But we've got to get home!"

"Sky, think about it. We're lost." She started to protest, but he kept going. "Yeah we have some idea where we are, but we don't know for sure where any marked trails are. Our map is ruined. We have no food except what we can catch or gather. It doesn't make sense to push further into the wilderness. I'm sure they're looking for us, and with the rain last night, the fire is probably better controlled so they can put more manpower into the search. We'll be better off to stay where we are and let them find us."

"What if they think we're dead already, burned in the fire."

"They don't," he said with conviction. "It's only been three days. Don't worry, they'll keep looking."

She silently nodded, acknowledging all he'd said. He was right and she knew it. It was just so hard to accept. They had no choice if they wanted to survive.

Brad pulled her to him for a quick hug. Then, with a hand on each of her shoulders he looked her in the eyes. "It's going to be okay."

"Yeah, okay," she said, taking a deep cleansing breath and blowing it out slowly to regain her composure. "You're right. We better find some more food." She attempted to walk away but he held tight to her shoulders.

"Sky, I'm sorry."

She looked up at him, into the depths of his blue eyes. He wasn't apologizing for their situation. That was beyond any of their control. No, he was apologizing for having upset her earlier. But she wasn't ready to accept his apology. Not yet. Not when she was still hurt and angry and just a little bit annoyed that he had pegged her so closely. Was she that transparent? There'd be plenty of time to think about what he'd said, mull it over and decide. They had a long, boring day ahead of them. Maybe several long, boring days.

She didn't say anything, and eventually he let her go.

By midmorning the clearing was dry and the day promised, luckily, to be hot. Once again their gear was spread over rocks to dry, making the area look like they were hosting a yard sale of camping materials.

After agreeing on the necessity of staying put, Sky had called the girls together for morning prayer. They knelt in a circle next to Heather and Amanda offered a heartfelt plea to heaven that they would soon be rescued. She also included a prayer that her sister would get well. Brad didn't join them, but Amanda's innocent voice carried to him across the clearing.

Heather, still sick and uncomfortable, managed to fall back to sleep. Her sister keeping an ever watchful eye on her, ready to offer clean water should she wake up.

The rest of the group divided out the necessary tasks for survival. Brad rigged as many fishing lines as he could with the small amount of string and wire they had remaining while Sky took Emma with her to look for more berries. Laela and Annie helped Brad man the fishing lines, occasionally stopping to gather firewood because, despite the heat, they had to keep the fire burning hot enough to boil water. There was no shortage of things to do, but each one quickly became tedious.

To pass the time, the girls chatted about school, who was dating who, which boy liked which girl, and what classes they hoped to have in the coming year. Brad listened, getting a whole new education.

"So what you're saying," Brad drawled as he flicked a line back into the water, "Is that guys don't really ask girls out anymore?"

Annie and Laela sat next to him, each holding a stick with a string dangling into the gently flowing stream. The sun was high, not a cloud in the sky, so they kept cool by dangling their feet in as well. "Yeah, it's not like in the olden days," Laela acknowledged.

"Olden days?" Brad laughed. At thirty three he didn't consider his high school experience could be classified as 'olden days,' but to a fifteen year old, it probably seemed like ancient history. "You mean back when we chased dinosaurs and lived in caves?" he teased.

"Well, you know what I mean," she sputtered, just a little bit embarrassed at having made the social faux pas of calling him old. "We just kind of hang out together."

"So how do you know if a boy likes you?" he asked.

"He hangs out with you more than other girls. Oh, and he calls sometimes."

"Does he do anything special?"

"Well, he might ask you to a dance. I haven't actually been to a school dance yet because I'm not sixteen and my parents won't let me date until then."

"School dances are lame," Annie stated. "Everyone just stands around most of the time anyway. It's more about the dress you wear than actually dancing. At my last school, it was like a fashion show."

"Oh yeah, I hear it's like that at ours too. It's hard to find a modest prom dress." Laela wiggled her toes in the water and looked over at Annie. "Where were you before?"

"Seattle."

"No way! How'd you end up here?" Laela asked, lifting her eyebrows in astonishment as though living in Montana was akin to outer space.

Annie didn't answer immediately, just let the cool water run over her feet. She jiggled the fishing line, but nothing seemed to be biting. After what seemed like an uncomfortably long wait, she looked up at Laela, "My parents just got divorced." Her voice was soft and held the remnants of pain and sadness. "My mom left us. We—my dad and I—wanted a fresh start, some place completely different."

"Gosh, I'm sorry. That totally stinks."

"Yeah, I guess." Again they were quiet. Only the humming of bees stirred the air until Annie spoke again. "It's not so bad now. They fought all the time. My mom had lots of problems." She didn't elaborate and her companions, Brad and Laela, didn't push, just listened.

The atmosphere had gone tense so Brad tried to lighten the mood by changing the subject. "I used to live in Seattle. I hated it. Too many cars. So what do you think of Montana?"

"It's alright. I like the mountains, but I miss the ocean. I can get my driver's license sooner now though. And I wish we had a Krispy Kreme donut store in town."

"I could go for a donut or two myself." Just then Brad's line went taught and the stick nearly slid from his loosened grip. He tightened his hold and began pulling back, winding the string around the end to help drag his catch in closer before it could swim free. Next to him, Laela and Annie cheered him on and before long there was a wriggling, twelve inch trout on the rocky bank. Brad grabbed it, slapping it quickly on the rocks to end its misery.

He held the shiny fish in the air by its tail. "Well, it's not donuts, but at least we won't starve."

Emma traipsed behind Sky, following her back the way they had come the day before to the patch of huckleberries. The forest was thick and offered shady relief from the heat. The ground was still wet under the heavy foliage and the small rivulets of standing water were a testament to the heavy rain they had received in the night. It smelled like damp, warm pine trees, a kind of mustiness that was not so much refreshing as it was cloying.

They walked slowly, taking their time. For the first time in days there was no need to hurry. Neither had the energy to rush.

"I hope we can find lots more," Emma said. Sky held a branch back to let her pass.

"We will," Sky assured her. Short on words, she said no more, just kept walking, picking her way through the fallen logs and underbrush that covered the forest floor. Her mind kept going back to the conversation she'd shared with Brad and the things he'd said about Tom.

Was he right? Was Tom selfish? There'd been times in their short relationship when she had thought his actions were insensitive, but that didn't mean he was selfish. He was a guy. All guys were apt to think about themselves—weren't they? Her brothers did, or had growing up. They were older now and married with families of their own. They were good husbands and fathers.

And of course, there was her own father. He was a big man, his face roughened with the weather, his hands callused from ranching, but he was also the first to cry when something touched his tender heart like the death of one of his herd, hearing the Star Spangled Banner sung, or just the spirit in any given Sunday School meeting. It seemed like he was almost always working, but he never complained about the long hours. And when he wasn't working he was helping someone else. He never missed one of her volleyball games or her brothers' football games when they were in school. He'd been their loudest cheerleader. Everyone in town knew and loved August Ryder. He had wholeheartedly supported the Native American traditions of his wife and encouraged his children to embrace them. No, there was nothing selfish about her father.

She had been swept off her feet by Tom in a whirlwind courtship, but that hadn't stopped her from considering whether he'd make a good husband, a good father. He would. She'd prayed about it. He could. She knew he could when…

Wait! Stop! Go back.

No when.

Just now. Was he those things now? Was she marrying his potential? Or him? The questions startled her and she stopped.

"Are you okay?" Emma asked, nearly bumping into her from behind.

Lost in her own thoughts, she looked at Emma, confused. "What?"

"Are you okay? Are we there yet?"

"Oh—Oh, no. Sorry. I was just—just taking a break."

"Sounds good. I'm tired too." Emma sat on a fallen log. She rolled her shoulders back, trying to release some of the kinks that had developed overnight from sleeping upright against a tree. Sky was still standing, staring into the distance, her eyebrows puckered. "You sure you're okay?" Emma asked again. "You look a little upset."

Hearing the concern in the young girl's voice, Sky turned and smiled at Emma. "No, really I'm fine. Just tired. I didn't get much sleep last night." Her explanation seemed to settle any concerns.

"Is Heather going to be okay?" Sky hadn't told any of the girls about the diagnosis for Heather. She hadn't wanted to alarm them or make Heather feel like she needed to be quarantined as a health risk. Giardia was contagious, but as long as they didn't share a water bottle, the others had little chance of contracting the bacteria.

"She'll be fine. She'll probably be pretty uncomfortable until we can get her to a doctor though."

"A doctor? What do you think she has?" The word 'doctor' was a sure indicator that something more than a twenty four hour stomach virus was the culprit.

"She may have a bacterial infection from drinking contaminated water."

"But we've all been drinking the same water. Are we all going to get it?" Emma asked, a tinge of panic in her voice.

"No we won't get it. We've been careful to boil our drinking water so that we don't get sick, but Heather took a drink from the stream yesterday."

"Oh," she said, clearly relieved.

"Come on." Sky stretched her hand out to pull Emma up. "We better get going if we want to eat today."

It took them another half hour to find the patch of huckleberries. They skipped over the area they'd picked from the day before, knowing that those berries were already gone. The small, low-lying bushes spread out, growing in clusters, and they were able to find more berries as they searched the area. The pea-sized purple berries weren't always easy to spot, hiding under leaves. They didn't grow in bunches. Sometimes one bush would harbor only a single berry.

Two hours later they had scoured the site, picking every berry they could find within a quarter mile radius until there were none remaining, at least none they could find. It was tempting to eat as they picked. Their stomachs were empty and cramping with hunger pains. But thinking of the others back at camp stopped them from indulging. To be fair, they needed to take back all that they found and divide it equally among the group. Everyone was hungry.

"It'll have to do." Sky looked at the containers now filled with fruit. They were full, but they were hardly a feast. "We better get back and see if they caught any fish."

They headed back in the direction they'd come, picking their way along a path that was becoming all too familiar to them. "You know," said Emma, stepping over a moss covered rock the size of a microwave, "it's a good thing we have Brad with us."

Taken aback by the sudden insight, Sky stammered, "Uh…yeah. Yeah, I guess it is."

"I mean, if we'd just been on our own and had to run from the fire, we might have gotten trapped or even burned alive. And he knows how to catch fish. We might starve if he didn't know how to catch fish."

"I fish."

"Yeah, but he knows how to make a fishing pole with a stick and string."

"And you don't think your trusty girls' camp leader could do that if she had to?" There was a lighthearted challenge in her words. It was easy to tease Emma. She'd known her since she was little.

"It's not that—"

"No, I get what you're saying." Sky said with mock offense, "I'm hurt Emma. You don't trust my survival skills."

"Sky, I—"

"Don't try to deny it now." She sniffled, pretending to cry.

"Oh come on, you have to admit, it's kind of nice having a big strong guy around to help us."

"Well…Okay, maybe."

"And he knows lots of stuff."

"Stuff?"

"Yeah, you know, like survival stuff. Like how to follow a map and how to build a fire."

"Emma, those are all things I've been teaching you girls to do," Sky pointed out. "You have those skills too."

"I guess. I never thought I'd have to use them to survive though. I thought they were just for camping and fun, you know. I just feel better knowing there's someone here to help us."

Sky recalled all the things they'd been through in the last three days. She was glad she hadn't had to do it all on her own, that there had been another adult to share the burden. "You're right. It is nice to have a man around."

"It doesn't hurt that he's a total hunk too."

"Emma Knudson! You are way too young to be noticing hunks."

"Hello! I'm almost eighteen. And besides, he may be too old for me, but he's not too old for you…" She raised her eyebrows and gave Sky a mischievous grin.

"I'm already engaged, in case you've forgotten."

"I know. But I saw you looking yesterday when Brad was washing with his shirt off." Sky's face went instantly red at the knowledge that the girls had witnessed her staring. "It's okay," Emma assured her. "We were all looking. You have to admit, he is pretty nicely built."

Utterly embarrassed, Sky just shook her head. It was a good thing the girls couldn't know how her heart had raced when he'd looked at her the first time, or how much she'd enjoyed his arm around her in the night. It was a good thing they'd be home soon and Brad would be out of her life, that Tom was waiting for her and would be there to welcome her back.

Emma wouldn't let it go, "Come on, just admit it."

"Emma—" Sky was laughing now, shaking her head. "You're going to make me spill these!"

"Just say it!"

"Fine. If it'll make you stop, I'll admit…" They were just steps away from the camp and they could hear voices from the clearing. Sky turned and smiled sweetly at Emma. She had a smirk on her face, obviously thinking she'd gotten the best of her leader, but Sky was not to be outsmarted. She took a few steps backwards into the clearing before finishing her sentence. Calling loudly she continued, "…that I am really looking forward to eating these berries!" Then she turned and ran the remaining distance. Laughing aloud, Emma chased after her.

Chapter 19

Once again there was not enough food to satisfy their hunger, but at least there was food. They didn't wait for it to be evening before eating their meager dinner. Annie, Laela and Brad had managed to catch seven fish by early afternoon. Two of them were so small they could hardly pick the meat away from the bones, but still they fried them up. It wasn't a feast, but the berries and fish went a long way to improving everyone's mood, except Heather, who declined any food at all.

"Heather, you've got to try and eat," Sky encouraged.

"I can't. I'll just throw up again," she complained. She was lying near the fire, not because she was cold in the sunny clearing, but because she was tired of sleeping and being bored. Had she been at home, she'd be plunked down in front of the television to convalesce, but that wasn't an option here. At home her mother would have waited on her, bringing her popsicles and ginger ale to calm her stomach and keep her hydrated. Amanda was doing her best to help her sister, but there was only so much she could do to keep her entertained. It was nice to have everyone back from their tasks just to have more conversation. "Besides, my stomach is so nauseated, it all looks disgusting."

"Have you been drinking water?"

"Yes."

"But not enough," Amanda threw in. "I've been making her take a drink every fifteen minutes, but it doesn't always stay down."

"That's good, Amanda. Thank you for helping." Sky sat on the ground next to Heather and pulled her head onto her lap. She brushed at her hair with her hand and tried to comfort her. "I know you feel awful, sweetheart. I wish there was something more I could do for you."

Heather seemed to appreciate the sympathy and the gentle, soothing hands. "It's okay. How much longer do you think we'll be here?"

It was the number one question on everyone's mind. When would they be found? Everyone was thinking it, but they had thus far avoided talking about it for fear the answer would be too depressing to contemplate. "I don't know." She looked around the circle, at the faces of her young charges and wished she had a better answer. "I just really don't know."

Brad piped up, "They're looking for us now. I'm sure it won't be much longer until they find us." His words sounded certain, spoken with confidence, and it gave them all some hope.

As day dragged into evening, no one was anxious to get back to the monotony of gathering wood and food. Instead, they sat around the small fire watching water boil and making small talk.

"The sun feels good," said Sky laying back and pillowing her head in her hands.

"Yeah, but I think I'm sunburned from sitting for so long trying to catch fish," Laela countered.

"Your nose does look pretty red," observed Annie. "How's mine?"

No longer able to keep her eyes open, Sky closed them, shutting out the bright blue expanse above her. Within minutes she was asleep.

"Girls," Brad said, following Sky's example and making himself comfortable on the rocky ground. "Will you keep an eye on the fishing poles? I think I'll take a short nap too."

"You go ahead," Emma answered. "We'll take care of it."

And they did. While the adults slept the girls gathered wood. They made a substantial pile from which they could keep the fire going for hours. They dragged large branches out of the undergrowth, breaking them into smaller pieces when they could or leaving them whole when they couldn't. At least with their fire built on the delta of river rocks, there was little danger of it spreading to the forest if they burned the larger wood one end at a time.

Annie and Laela went back to fishing since they were considered the experts after having done it all day.

The sleeping bags had all dried in the hot sun, including the one that had been soiled. It was now the cleanest bag they had, having been scrubbed with the remaining soap. Emma zipped them back together in preparation for the coming night. It seemed they would be sleeping out under the stars again.

Finally, when there was nothing left to do, Emma sat with Amanda and Heather, talking about anything they could think of that they hadn't already covered. Would this day never end?

It didn't take Brad any time at all to fall asleep. Even with the girls talking and stacking wood only feet from where he lay, he quickly fell into a deep and dream-filled sleep of exhaustion. His dreams were random, mostly about food.

In one dream he was a small child again, sitting around the dining table with his family. It was Thanksgiving and his mom had prepared her usual holiday fare; stuffed roasted turkey with cranberry sauce, golden mashed potatoes drenched in thick, creamy gravy, fluffy rolls dripping with butter, corn on the cob, and pies. The table was lined with pies in every flavor. He reached out to sneak a bite, but his mother slapped his hand. "Those aren't for you!" she scolded. With his mouth watering, tears came to his eyes. "Please! Please Mom!" he begged. "I'm so hungry!"

The dream faded into another. This time he was standing on the pier in Seattle, a place he had frequented when he had lived and worked in the city. It was crowded with people as usual. He stood in line to order fish and chips from his favorite vendor. The world around him moved as if in slow motion; people walking and talking slowly. Slowly. The line inched forward. His stomach growled as he anticipated biting into the flavorful, crispy crust of the halibut. Finally he was at the front of the line. But before he could order, the man reached for the rolling door above the counter. "We're closed," he said, his words low and drawn out. Then he slammed the door down.

Brad turned over, his mind still roiling with disappointment at not getting any food. His body was uncomfortable on the rocky ground, but still he slept.

He could feel the sun on his face, both real and dreamlike. He was standing on the shore of an aqua blue lake. Above him pine dressed hills rose up to an azure blue sky dotted with white cotton clouds. There was laughter around him. Corkie? Marty? He recognized this place. They'd been here before to swim. They'd roasted hot dogs and marshmallows. It was a wonderful dream. London was there laughing too.

"Come in, the water feels great," she called to him. He dove in taking several strokes beneath the surface to reach her in the water. When he surfaced, she was gone.

No, not gone, he realized. Just further out. Then she was calling for him, her head barely above the water. Her arms were flailing. "Brad! Help me!" She called. "Brad! Where are you?" And he saw her disappear beneath the water.

In his dream he dove again, swimming with strong, powerful kicks. He had to reach her, to save her. At last he felt her under the water. He reached down, pulling her up to the surface. Then he kissed her. Long and passionately. He was so relieved that he had saved her.

"Thank you Brad," she whispered between kisses. "Thank you for saving me."

He stopped kissing her and looked in her eyes. They were dark and brown. London? He wondered. But London's eyes are blue. Drawing back to see her more clearly he was stunned to see it wasn't London.

It was Sky.

And he was glad.

He woke with a smile on his face.

For once there wasn't water to boil as they sat around the fire that night. They had filled every container they had. There was also nothing to eat. Laela and Annie had caught three more fish in the late evening hours, sitting on the bank of the stream, getting eaten alive by hungry mosquitoes. But they all agreed it would be better to save them for breakfast, so Brad fashioned a pool with rocks where the water could keep them cold until morning. Hopefully they would still be there and not get stolen by a woodland creature looking for a free meal.

"We could sing," Sky suggested. She had slept fitfully for two hours until the cooling temperature woke her. The nap had done much to revive her energy, but there was no place to use it now. "How about some camp songs?"

There was little enthusiasm among the girls to begin with. Boredom, not to mention hunger, was making them grouchy. But as Sky started with a round of "The Princess

Pat," the girls joined in on the repeats and were soon laughing at Sky's exaggerated actions.

"The Princess Pat lived in a tree, she sailed across the seven seas." Sky moved her arm across her body making pretend waves. "She sailed across the channel too, and brought with her a rig-a-bamboo." On the final word she wiggled her hips, twisting and turning to the ground and back up again.

"Okay girls, faster!" she called. In unison the girls sang the silly song faster, each of them mimicking Sky.

"Let's sing "Noah's Ark"," suggested Emma when they had finished. They were starting to get into the spirit of things, much as they had done on their first night of Girls' Camp--minus the s'mores and banana boats.

"Yeah, I like that one," Annie grinned.

The six females stood around the small fire singing at the top of their lungs.

So rise and shine
And give God his glory, glory
Rise and shine and give God his glory, glory,
Rise and shine and give God his glory, glory,
Children of the Lord.

"You call these camp songs?" Brad listened through all six verses followed by the chorus. He laughed at their actions and at the ridiculous words. "Whatever happened to '99 Bottles of Beer on the Wall?' That's what we use to sing at scout camp." He didn't mention that Jimmy Bezos had snuck a few of his dad's beers into his bag and they'd taken turns passing around the bottle after each verse until they all had a nice buzz going. They'd had the time of their lives until they were caught. None of them were singing when they had to scrub the latrine floor with a toothbrush.

"That would be '99 Bottles of *Root Beer* on the Wall'," interjected Sky. "Besides, that one is way over done. Sophisticated women like us prefer to be a little more original." She batted her eyelashes at him, looking anything but sophisticated. Her clothes were a mess, her long hair hadn't seen a brush in four days and her face was smudged with dirt. Still, there was something beautiful about her that was more than skin deep.

"This is fun, what should we sing next?" Though small and quiet, Amanda had a strong, lyrical voice and she loved to sing. "How about a round?"

"My favorite is the spider web song. It's not really a round, but it has two parts," said Laela.

"Okay, let's try it. Does everyone remember the words?" Sky asked. It was a song she had taught them the first night of camp. They stood on one side of the fire, their arms linked. As they sang it now the sweet flowing melody and innocent lyrics floated out into the still night where none but the heavens could hear the longing for home in their voices.

It's a web like a spider's web
Made with silver light and shadow
Spun by the moon in my room at night
It's a web made to catch a dream
Hold it fast 'til I awaken
As if to tell me my dream is of you.

Sky thought about Tom. Was he missing her? Was he dreaming of her? She longed to have him put his arms around her and make everything right again.

The mood had grown more somber with the last song. There was a kind of reverence in the air as the darkness closed in around their tiny circle of light.

"That was nice," complimented Brad. "I liked that one." His lean body was stretched on the ground in front of the fire where he could watch and listen. The girls' melodic voices were lulling him into a lazy calm he hadn't experienced since he'd set out to find them.

Sensing the feelings of the girls, Sky quietly began one of her favorite hymns. "I am a child of God," she sang. "And he has sent me here..."

With no further urging, the girls joined her, matching their voices in perfect harmony to the familiar children's song. When they finished, someone began another Primary song. The familiarity of the words was as comforting as the message they delivered.

As they sang, dusk turned to complete darkness with nothing but the fire to give them light. It was still and quiet in the forest without even a breeze to stir the trees. The forest animals, though surely there, were not yet prowling around. Not even the song of crickets or hum of mosquitoes disturbed the silence.

When their voices finally stopped, Heather commented on the eerie stillness, "It kind of creeps me out when it's so still and quiet like this. It reminds me of a horror movie when you know something bad is about to happen and then something jumps out and makes you scream."

"I don't think we have to worry about that," said Sky. "It's so quiet that nothing could sneak up on us before we heard it." She got up and grabbed two more pieces of wood to add to the dying fire. "How are you feeling?" she asked, referring back to Heather.

"Tired, drained, and generally miserable for having done nothing all day."

"I'm sorry. I wish I had something that would make you feel better. I wish there were someone here who could give you a Priesthood blessing."

The girls all looked at Brad. He was still laying stretched in front of the fire, his eyes closed as though he was asleep. He was the only one who could hold the priesthood, yet he knew nothing about it. It wasn't his fault. He wasn't a member of their church. Still, as they looked at him there was an unspoken yearning from each of them that things were different. If only…

Brad opened his eyes to see them all staring at him. "What? What'd I do?" he pushed up on one elbow looking from girl to girl. It was obvious by their expressions that something was wrong.

"Nothing," Sky confirmed. "It's nothing." The priesthood had always been a part of her life. There were countless times growing up that she'd received a priesthood blessing at the hands of her father; when she had strep throat, when she broke her arm, when she had to have her tonsils out just to name a few. And those were only for healing. She'd received other blessings as well; at the beginning of every new school year and when she had gone away to college. Her father had always been there to place his hands on her head and offer her comfort and wisdom from her Heavenly Father.

She had always been grateful for that blessing in her life, but never more than now. She hadn't taken it for granted then, but the absence of it now was so keenly felt, she wanted to cry. She didn't doubt that her Heavenly Father was aware of their current struggles, but it was still hard to endure them.

Hadn't the early pioneers of the church endured worse? She thought about the saints who crossed the plains in handcarts. They were hungry. They were cold. They were following the commandment to gather to Zion. Heavenly Father had not stopped their suffering. Her suffering and that of the girls did not even come close to what they went through. Would he stop their suffering? Would they ever be rescued? Or was this all a part of some greater plan? "We were just saying how it's kind of spooky out here if you think about it," she finally said to Brad.

"Oh." He seemed placated by her explanation. "I guess it can be. But don't worry girls, there's no such thing as a Sasquatch or a Yeti. No Big Foots out here."

"There are bears." Always the practical one, Emma pointed out the one monster they couldn't deny roamed the woods.

"And wolves," added Laela.

"True," he responded. "But wolves are afraid of people, unless they're mad with disease. And bears only like people if they have food. Since we don't qualify, we shouldn't have any problems." He stood and stretched, yawning widely. Reaching his hands high above his head he linked his fingers and extended them even more. The silence was filled with the sound of cracking knuckles like small popping fireworks. "If it'll make you feel any better, I don't mind staying up and keeping the fire going. That way we'll still have some light and if you get scared in the night at least it won't be so dark."

"You didn't get much sleep last night," Sky pointed out. Her tone sounded motherly and concerned at his generous offer.

"No, but I got a couple of naps in today. Don't worry, I'll be fine."

"Well it doesn't matter to me, I'm going to bed," Annie claimed. "And I plan to sleep all night. I don't care if there is a forest fire coming, or it rains cats and dogs in the night. Nobody wake me up!" She left the warmth of the fire and walked to where they had put the now dry sleeping bags. The rest of the group listened to the rustle of nylon as she slid into her bag and pulled up the zipper.

"I think I'll join her," Emma said. "My neck is still sore from sleeping against the tree last night. It think it's giving me a headache." She leaned over and gave Sky a hug, "Good night."

Sky put her arms around her in return. "Good night. Sleep tight."

One by one the remaining girls hugged their leader and gave a nod towards Brad as they too moved off to try and get some sleep. Hopefully it would be the last night they had to sleep on the hard ground under the stars. What had been a once in a lifetime event for some of them that first night of their hike had become a necessary evil, the novelty having long since worn away.

"Looks like it's just you and me again." Brad stirred the fire with the end of a stick, pushing the wood pieces together causing it to burn brighter.

"Looks like it."

"You're still mad at me." It was made as a statement, but there was just a hint of questioning in his voice.

She stared at him across the flames. His tanned face glowed orange in the fire's light. His blond hair picked up the reflection as well, making it appear lighter than it actually was. His face was scruffy with four day's growth of beard, the same color as his hair. It was a handsome face, and when he broke into a smile, it was a face no woman could resist. The smile reached his eyes as he stared back at her. What was a girl to do with a face like that?

"Yes, I'm very mad at you," she said trying not to smile in return. She looked away to hide her face before he could catch her in the lie.

"I really am sorry that what I said upset you."

"You're sorry it upset me, but not for what you said?" she clarified.

"It really is beautiful out here tonight, isn't it?"

"Smooth. Really smooth." She squinted her eyes and smirked at his obvious tactic to change the subject.

"I thought so." He shifted his body, dodging the smoke as the slight breeze changed direction. When it didn't change back, he scooted closer to Sky. Twenty yards away he heard rocks hitting together in the water. He turned and could just make out the shape. "Only a deer," he said.

There was no good to be had by arguing with him over points they disagreed on. She wasn't going to argue religion with him, and since he hadn't ever met Tom, it wouldn't do any good to try and convince him he wasn't some kind of mama's boy. Better just to let it go, no matter how his words from the night before had stung.

"So what do we talk about now?" she asked. He didn't answer immediately so she went on, "I'm so sick of this." She angrily hurled a stick into the darkness. It splashed as it landed in the water. "I mean, I like camping. I like hiking and being outdoors. But this is—this is more than that."

He could appreciate her wanting to throw something. They were helpless here and it frustrated him beyond words. But he wasn't ready to give up either. They'd get out of this so long as he kept his head straight and kept the girls from losing theirs. "Hey, have I told you about my most embarrassing moment?" He asked. He knew he hadn't, but he needed a segue back to pleasant fireside conversation and away from the mess they were in.

"I imagine a guy like you is never embarrassed."

"A guy like me?"

"Yeah, you know…" She waved her hand at him, gesturing from his head to toe, but was too embarrassed to finish what she had started. She didn't want to tell him that she thought he looked amazing, all fit and strong, or that he was cool, calm and collected. He was like MacGeyver meets James Bond. Her cheeks burned and she hoped it was too dark for him to notice. His eyebrows only puckered in confusion so she cleared her throat and continued. "Anyway, you were saying?"

Brad shifted his body so he was lying on one hip, his torso propped up by one elbow. It took him a minute to find just the right spot, one that didn't have a sharp stone poking into his backside. When he was finally settled he began, "My most embarrassing moment was in high school. I was a junior. I played football for two years, ran track--"

Sky interrupted "Yeah, yeah. You were Mr. Popularity."

"No, that's just it, I wasn't. I mean, I wasn't a total geek, but I didn't run with the really popular kids either. That's why I was kinda shocked when Carli Symes asked me to the girls' formal—"

"That's your most embarrassing moment?"

"If you'll quit interrupting, I'll get to it. I'm just giving you the background."

"Sorry," Sky apologized. She used her fingers to pull an imaginary zipper across her lips. Her eyes dancing with laughter, she twisted an imaginary lock at the corner of her mouth and pretended to toss it over her shoulders.

"That's better," he said before continuing with his tale. "Carli was a total babe, not to mention a senior. She was pretty popular too. It was a big deal, you know." He looked at her to confirm that she understood what he was getting at. Still consigned to silence, she kept her lips pursed and nodded vigorously, her eyebrows raised. "Fine, go ahead and mock me, but for my junior-wanna-be-cool-ego, it was huge. I was psyched for the dance. I rented a tux, I ordered a corsage—the works. I was determined to really impress her."

Sky raised her hand like a fifth grader hoping to be called on. Brad laughed. "Okay, what?" he consented.

"Didn't it occur to you that she was already impressed with you or she wouldn't have asked you to the dance?"

"That's not how high school boys' minds work," he informed her.

"How do—"

"That's not the point! You're doing it again."

"Oh, sorry." He watched as she repeated her previous actions of zipping her lips closed and locking them.

"So it's the night of the dance and she comes to pick me up. We were doubling with another couple that I didn't know. We drive to the restaurant and they are all talking and laughing, obviously friends, right. And I'm feeling kind of left out. I'm nervous and not sure what to say really. We get seated and make our selections from the menu. The waiter comes to take our order and then he leaves and we're all just sitting there. It's quiet and no one is talking, and I'm feeling like a total moron because I haven't had more than a few words to say so far."

Brad looked at Sky. Her eyes were still bright with amusement and now anticipation. He could tell she was dying to say something, but she kept her mouth shut and patiently waited for him to go on.

"She had on this dress that was kind of low in front. Not totally revealing but not like a nun, if you know what I mean." It was meant as a rhetorical statement so he didn't give her time to respond. He used his free hand to outline on his own chest just exactly what he meant. "And where the dress came together in front, she had a big pin with rhinestones. Really fancy, you know. It kind of drew your eyes there."

Sky put her hands over her mouth to keep from laughing out loud at his awkward description of her dress and cleavage.

He ignored her and kept talking. "I wanted to say something nice, kinda break the ice, you know. Make myself sound like a cool guy." He paused for effect. "So I turned to her and I said, 'That's a beautiful brassiere you have on, Carli'."

Sky couldn't help it, her hands weren't enough to hold it back, and she burst out laughing. She couldn't stop as he tried to explain himself. "I meant to say brooch—her shiny pin—but I got the word wrong." His explanation only made her laugh harder until tears were leaking from her eyes.

Brad kept talking, "Of course, she was shocked. She just looked at me with these huge eyes, and the other couple busted up laughing at me. I felt so stupid. I tried to cover my butt by asking about it—are those real crystal?--that kind of thing, but it only made them laugh harder. I think the worst part was I didn't realize I'd used the wrong word in the first place. I told my mom about it later and she had to explain it to me. When I went to school the next week, I completely avoided her. Needless to say, we never went out on another date."

Sky wiped at the tears that continued to roll down her cheeks. "You're right, that's pretty embarrassing," she said between fits of giggling. Her stomach was hurting from laughing so hard, and she was sure she must have woken the girls. "Brassiere…I can't believe you thought—"

"Anybody could have made that mistake," Brad defended.

"Yeah, sure," she took a deep breath, finally managing to get some control. "Any boy in high school."

He watched her in the dying light of the fire. The flames reflected off her hair making it look like long streaks of onyx. A stray piece graced her cheek and he reached up to brush it away, his hand lingering long enough to enjoy the smooth texture of her skin before falling back to his side. "So what about you?" he asked casually. "Any moments of complete humiliation?"

"I once snorted water out my nose at my date."

"That's the best you can do? Water? We've all buck snorted before. Be glad it wasn't Coke. That really burns. Come on, you can do better than that," he encouraged.

Sky pulled her legs closer, hugging her knees for warmth. She looked up, noting the clear sky and the millions of stars that twinkled above her. With her arms still around her knees, she held her hands out to catch the heat from the fire. The diamond on her left hand caught a flicker of light and glimmered back at her.

"Most embarrassing, huh?" She continued to stare at the ring as she spoke. With disappointment in her voice she said, "The night Tom proposed, he took me to dinner at a nice restaurant on Flathead Lake. Afterwards, we went to the theater in Big Fork. It was a Saturday, totally crowded with Canadian tourists. They were doing My Fair Lady, so it was popular. I doubt there was an empty seat in the whole place. At the beginning of each show, they have an actor come out on stage and give a spiel about cell phones and taking crying babies out. Sometimes they make announcements about people, anniversaries, birthdays, that kind of thing."

Brad nodded his head. He had been there several times and knew just what she was talking about.

"So they finish all that, and then the guy calls me up on stage. I didn't know what was going on and I didn't want to go, but Tom made me. We were in the center so I had to crawl over all these people trying to get out of the row without stepping on their toes and walk up to the stage. Meanwhile people are clapping for me and I don't even know why." She stopped talking as though letting Brad listen to the applause she could still hear in her head. And all the while she looked at her engagement ring, twisting it between her fingers. It still felt foreign there.

When the silence dragged on, Brad encouraged her, "So what happened?"

"I got up on stage and they sat me in a chair right in the middle. Then these dancers come out as music starts playing and I hear Tom's voice singing *You Light Up My Life*. He's not that great a singer, but he comes out on stage with a microphone and he's singing this ridiculous song to me while these people are all dancing around me. The audience is laughing and cheering. He's loving it and he starts to egg them on by making himself sound more ridiculous. And I'm sitting there wishing some kind of trap door would open up so I could fall through it and get away because I'm so embarrassed, not just for me, but for him because he's making such a fool of himself. And then the song ends and he gets down on one knee and he pulls a ring box out of his pocket and asks me to marry him. And I'm stuck. I mean, what could I say after he's made such a fool of me? No?" Water was leaking from her eyes again, but it wasn't because of laughter this time. Brad didn't answer. He just watched and waited. "So I said yes as quickly as I could so I could get off that stupid stage and away from everyone."

"That sounds awful," he said gently.

"The thing is, I'm not a real showy person. I like to be in the background, behind the scenes, so to speak. I just wasn't expecting it—him proposing. Especially like that. But he's fun and outgoing and likes to do crazy things." Her words sounded like she was trying to defend him, to somehow justify his actions even though they had obviously hurt her.

"Sky, if a guy's going to propose, it should be special."

"Oh, it was special alright!" She forced a smile and looked at him. "I definitely won't forget it. Our kids will get a good laugh out of it, I'm sure. It won't be anything boring like those guys that take you to a secluded spot, some place with special meaning, and they tell you how much they love you and quietly, humbly ask you to marry them."

"Some place with candles and firelight..." Brad prompted. They stared at each other, now just silhouettes in the dying flames. He leaned closer.

"Some place," she faltered, leaning unconsciously towards Brad until their lips were just a whisper apart, "where it's just the two of you, sharing one of life's most important moments."

Frozen, she couldn't move, couldn't breathe, couldn't think.

From above, an owl hooted, breaking the silence, shattering the moment. Sky sat back and looked up into the darkness, uselessly searching for the source and silently thanking it. Her heart pounded in her chest.

That was close. Too close.

He was too close.

She stood and grabbed some more wood for the fire. It was nearly out so she had to bend down and blow on the glowing embers. She used it as an excuse to sit further from Brad.

"So that's it. I think you win for most embarrassing moment," she said as though nothing had happened. "Pretty much anything that happened in high school was embarrassing."

"Yeah, you couldn't pay me enough to go back," agreed Brad. He had rolled over and was on his back, his forearm thrown over his eyes.

"Kids now have got it a lot worse than we had, and it was pretty bad fifteen years ago." Sky looked in the direction of the girls. She couldn't see them, but knew they were there. "I am amazed at these girls and what they have to put up with. Drugs, alcohol, sex. Yet, it doesn't seem to faze them. It's all around them, but it's not a part of them. I've watched and listened to them for over a week now. They're incredibly strong. I feel bad for teenagers and kids who don't have the teachings of the church in their lives to help them," said Sky.

"Do you really think it's because of your church that they're strong?" Brad sounded incredulous at her statement. "There are a lot of good people out there who don't go to your church, you know. The rest of us aren't heathens."

"I know that. That's not what I meant. It's just good that they have a moral compass to help them."

"Moral compass?" he quipped. "What, like not drinking and going to church every Sunday is going to keep you from having problems? It sounds to me like you follow a bunch of rules and spend a lot of time at church just for some kind of mythical eternal reward. Don't get me wrong, I'm not an atheist or anything. I believe in God. He's a good guy. He created the earth and all. But the buck stops there. We're on our own here and it's up to us to make the most of our life." He sat up on his elbows and looked directly at her, challenging her with his words.

Across the fire, Sky recognized his goading tone. He wanted her to get angry, to argue with him. She'd seen it before on her mission, people wanting to dispute the gospel.

But it never worked. You couldn't. It was indisputable. Your best defense was humility. He couldn't dispute her feelings, her testimony. No one could when it was given sincerely.

"Look Brad, I won't argue with you. We obviously have some major differences of opinion when it comes to religion. All I'm saying is that I'm glad I have the gospel. That they do," she said, gesturing towards where her young women slept. "It's not just some list of rules. It's not just casually going to church on Sundays. It's more than that. It's who we are inside. It's knowing where we came from, why we're here, and what will happen when we die. The church isn't just an organization. It's people and programs. Sometimes they aren't perfect. But the gospel is. The way we choose to live isn't just someone's suggestion for a healthy lifestyle. It's God's law. And if we live by that law, He has promised us eternal glory. To me, that's worth whatever it takes. And the beauty of it is that it's my *choice*. We all have a choice. *You* have a choice," she said pointing dramatically at him. "Most people just don't know there *is* a choice so they go on in their unhappy, hum drum lives asking themselves, 'Is this it? Is this all there is?' when the truth is, there is so much more." She spoke openly, from her heart, and when she finished, she was tired. It had drained her.

Brad sat, stunned at her impassioned speech and the vehemence with which she delivered it. She was like a boxer, battering him with two right punches and a quick left jab. For all her tiny frame, there was a lot of power inside.

"I'm tired," she said. "I think I'll try to get some sleep. Wake me when you want me to tend the fire."

For the second time since they'd met she walked away with the last word.

Chapter 21

The historic clock that hung outside Seeley Lake's town hall finished striking seven as Chief Charlie Carruthers entered the local restaurant. Despite it being prime hours, the place was nearly deserted, just like the rest of town. Though there had been no formal evacuation, residents had been warned to be prepared for one if the fire shifted direction. Summer tourists that were the town's livelihood had fled the area seeking less smoky adventures. Looking across the large, near-empty dining area, it wasn't hard to spot who he was meeting. Five men and one woman surrounded a table in the center, maps and charts spread out in every direction. They were loudly discussing the material. The party had apparently already begun.

"Oh good, you're here," said Miles Connely, head of the National Forest Services in Montana. With him were his two assistants, James Hansen and Zane McLeod along with Chris Jacobs and Bud Calder from the Flathead Search and Rescue team. Allison Porter, a no-nonsense, no frills woman from the Montana Department of Land Management looked over and nodded curtly in acknowledgement.

"Sorry I'm late. I had a heck of a time getting down the mountain."

"Not a problem," said Chris. "You want a beer or something?" As he spoke, a waiter in baggy shorts and a Montana Grizzlies t-shirt walked over.

"I'll have whatever's on tap, the biggest burger you've got, and an order of onion rings," Carruthers told him before turning back to the business at hand. "Boys," he started, then looked at Allison, "and girls, we've got a major problem here."

It was an understatement to be sure. For six days they had sent out teams searching for the missing hikers and fireman. So far, they hadn't recovered a thing. There was no trace of them. They'd searched the burn areas that had been cleared as safe, but hadn't recovered any evidence that they'd even been there. Nothing but ash. The fire had either incinerated them, or they hadn't been there at all. And if that was the case, where the heck were they? Tempers were running as hot as the fire they'd yet to put out.

"There's just too much land to cover," claimed Bud Calder. "We don't have the resources or the man power we need."

"I hate to sound like the grim reaper, but we don't even know they're alive still. We're spending thousands, maybe even millions of dollars here and there's no guarantee we'll find anything more than a bunch of bodies," Miles pointed out.

"I agree with you Miles," James interjected. "We can't keep searching like this when we've got a major fire to concentrate on."

"Reports are coming in that they've got fires over in Glacier now." Zane tapped the map that included Glacier National Park. We're going to lose some men to them. Our crews are already feeling overworked. You all know the National Park is going to take precedence if it comes to that."

Carruthers listened to the men, his anger barely controlled. "You want me to quit looking for one of my own, not to mention six women--six young women--just to save a bunch of protected trees?"

"That's not what we're saying Charlie," Allison said, placing her hand on his arm as a warning to keep his cool. "We're just saying, things are looking bad all over the place. We've got to make some decisions here. Hard decisions."

He looked at the men around the table. Two of them were still young enough that there was no gray in their hair. The others were seasoned with age and experience. All of them were nodding in agreement with what the older woman had said.

"We don't like it any better than you do," confirmed Miles.

Chief Carruthers sighed loudly and sank into a chair. His actions indicated his feeling of defeat. The waiter came and without a word placed his order in front of him. The burly man grabbed the mug of foaming beer and took a long swig. Setting the sweating mug on the table, he ran his arm across his lips, "Rock and a hard place," he said more to himself than the others.

No one spoke to him, they just watched him bite into a burger—the most he'd had in days—before turning back to discuss the maps surrounding them.

"We need to focus on getting this fire out," Miles said to no one in particular. "The rain helped some, but not enough. I've been talking to my counterparts all over the country, asking for men and advice. They've had a lot of success up in Alaska by starting back burns--controlled fires to draw the main fire to where they want it. Essentially by starting fires of their own, they limit the fuel that's left to burn. When the main draft runs out of fuel, it dies."

"We've been studying these maps for days now," continued James. "We've got three main branches to worry about, but we think if we start another burn here," he said pointing at the map, "we'll draw the fire from the other directions and bring it back into one main fire. Once the flames quit moving in three different directions and start heading back to a main focus point, we'll be able to get a handle on it. It won't require as many men running over the mountains, just waiting in a central area for the fire to come to them."

"Alaska has land to burn, figuratively speaking," said Carruthers. "We don't. We can't afford to lose any more of this wilderness area. If we start our own burn, we could lose a lot more than we already have."

"I don't think so," said Zane, setting his bottle of beer aside and pulling one of the maps closer. "This area between the branches is already threatened. Chances are we'll lose it anyway, but at least we won't continue losing acres around the periphery. I think it's our best bet."

The group continued planning, discussing the details late into the night. The seriousness of what they were about to undertake was not lost on any of them. Nor was the fact that it was going to take every man and woman they could get to keep it under control, men and women that were currently scouting the mountain for one man and six women. The hardest part wasn't going to be setting more of the forest on fire. The hardest part would be telling seven families they were scaling back the search for their loved ones.

All around the cultural hall faces were solemn. Many had tears, and despite the anger and frustration that hovered in the air, there was no shouting, no loud arguments. The quiet voices and hushed tones only added to the feeling of desperation in everyone's heart.

The gathering, an impromptu meeting, was well attended, not just by the families of the missing girls, but by friends and fellow ward members. All of them reeling at the thought of not finding the six women.

Among them was Mr. and Mrs. Stevenson and their daughter, Jenna. Brad's parents had retired to Polson, not far from the town where the missing girls lived. Though they weren't members of the LDS church, it was a small community and many of them were already acquaintances.

Among the strangers in the group were Ammon and London Moffatt. When the early morning news released the decision to suspend search efforts, London had called Brad's parents to talk with them about what was being done and asked to be kept in the loop. In the afternoon they'd received word that one of the girl's fathers had arranged a meeting with someone from Flathead Search and Rescue for that night. Ammon and London had hurried to make it in time.

People mingled around, waiting for word, munching on cookies that some of the ward members had provided, and offering hugs of support to one another. London shook hands with Hayden Marquardt, Annie's dad. Having come straight from work, he still wore his uniform and his face was haggard.

A man wearing a starched polo shirt and looking more like a well-to-do golf pro than a local citizen stood next to Ammon sipping punch from a Dixie cup.

Ammon turned and introduced himself. "I'm Ammon Moffatt. Are you one of the family members?"

"Judd Allred. My son's fiancé is missing up there," he said pumping Ammon's outstretched hand. "He couldn't be here so I wanted to find out what was going on.

"I'm so sorry," offered Ammon. "We're friends of Brad Stevenson. He's the missing fireman."

The gold and diamond ring on the man's pinky flashed as he took another sip. Judd Allred was a man used to getting his way. He'd fought courtroom battles for years as a successful lawyer, staring down judges and juries alike. "This is all a bunch of hogwash if you ask me. Bunch of government bureaucrats calling the shots while we stand here like we're at a church social."

Ammon had dealt with his share of lawyers and officials. He knew yelling and getting nasty was no way to win friends and influence people when what you really needed was a little sugar to sweeten the deal in your favor. "You strike me as the type of guy who can get things done," Ammon noted.

"I like to think so," Judd responded, not quite sure what the man beside him was getting at.

"I've just been wondering about getting together some funding for our own search and rescue, if that's what it comes to—" He was cut off before he could finish. Both men turned forward to listen.

"Folks!" Bud Calder yelled for attention. It only took a minute for the conversations to stop and soon there was total silence in the hall. "I know you are all upset at the news. I want to express my deepest sympathy to all of the families here. Also, I want to make it clear that we aren't suspending search efforts as was stated on the news. We are, however, scaling back the search."

"It's only been six days. You can't give up already. Surely you can look longer," said Timothy Stone.

"It's not a matter of giving up. But you've got to look at it from a different perspective. We've only got so many people. We've still got a major fire burning out there. More fires have started in Glacier and we're already losing manpower. If we don't get this fire under control it will threaten homes and more lives.

"The only perspective I've got is seeing my daughter's empty bed each night. Let the rest of the forest burn to the ground for all I care, just as long as she comes home safe."

Bud was doing his best to keep this from becoming another shouting match. He had agreed to the meeting because he felt like the families deserved more of an explanation about what was happening. With a heavy sigh he said, "Sir, I understand. But the decision has been made. I'm just the messenger."

Brad's father, Carl Stevenson, raised his hand and waited patiently for Bud to recognize him. All eyes turned to him as he asked, "So what is the plan? What does scaling down mean?"

"Good question, thank you." Bud was all business again. This is what he had wanted to share with them. "We've been sending up helicopters three times a day in two hour shifts. We've also had teams on the ground. The ground teams are obviously slow, but more thorough. We use ATV's where we can, but because this is wilderness area, there aren't a lot of places we can use them. The ground teams have also been hampered by the fire zones. Once the fire has burned through an area, it has to be cleared by the firemen before we can get in. The firemen have been helping as much as they can, but I'm telling you..." he paused and looked around at the group to see whose attention he had. All eyes were focused on him. "Those men and women are beat. They're pulling four, maybe five hours of sleep a day. When they aren't on duty, they're volunteering their time to search. You're not alone in this folks. There's a lot of good people up in those mountains that are determined to find them."

"Okay, so we send out our own search teams. We can get volunteers from the community," suggested Shayla Knudson, Emma's mother.

"Well, it's not that easy. I realize there are a lot of experienced hikers in the area who would probably be willing to help us look. The problem is that the Forest Service has authorized what's called a back burn to try and stop the blaze we've got going. It's a little dangerous, but if all goes well, it will help get the three spurs back together and make things more manageable for the man power that we've got. We just can't have a bunch of hikers roaming around up there. It would put more lives at stake."

"What if this back burn endangers the missing hikers?" asked Carl Stevenson.

"We've already searched the area planned for the burn. There was no sign of them."

"What about the helicopters? Are they still sending up the helicopters?" Carl's wife asked. She was trying not to be emotional, but it was difficult to hold her emotions in check. Her only son was out there somewhere, and though she knew he was a capable man, she couldn't help but worry about him.

"The good news is we will continue to send up helicopters." Bud Calder wiped at the sweat that had formed on his upper lip. Looking out at the faces in the crowd he saw hope ignite, but he knew his next sentence would extinguish it. "The bad news is, we've been authorized to send only one a day."

Voices instantly called out, questions ringing left and right wondering why there would be so little air support. Sometimes he really hated his job, thought Bud.

He put his hands in the air to silence the building noise, waving at them all to be quiet. "I'm sorry, but the ugly truth is, we simply don't have the funds."

Again voices erupted, everyone talking at once. The hall sounded like a beehive humming.

In the back of the room, Ammon looked down at his wife. She was crying openly, wiping at the unstoppable tears with a wad of well-used tissues. He held her hand tightly and squeezed it reassuringly. He looked over at Judd Allred. The two men nodded at each other in silent agreement. Then Ammon raised his hand and without waiting to be acknowledged, he called out, “How much do you need?”

Chapter 22

The days felt wretchedly long. After six days of surviving in the wilderness, everyone was desperately short on optimism. They tried to think of games to play to keep them occupied. One day the girls made up a game of throwing stones—something they had plenty of. They picked a target and tried for hours to hit it. As their aim improved they picked more difficult targets, and ones further away. Of course, Brad often won those with his muscular arm that could out distance them all. Heather was still not well, so often one of the others would sit and play less active games with her, drawing a tic-tac-toe board in the dirt with a stick or twenty questions. That particular game was also a favorite around the fire at night when it was too dark to do anything else.

Games filled in the gaps between gathering and fishing for food. They spent long hours every day sitting at the river's edge waiting for fish to nibble on the lures made from wire and anything else they could think of. Sky had found some biscuit root plants and dug them up. The bitter flavor of the bulbs didn't deter them all from trying them. The lack of food was beginning to show in their faces with sharper bones and sunken cheeks.

It was late afternoon and all the girls including Sky were gathered together talking. It was the hottest time of day, no one having the energy to do much of anything. Brad had rigged up a sleeping bag into a small awning that provided a few feet of shade. It mostly covered Heather, but the others crowded in around her.

"At least I know I'll have no problem fitting into my skinny jeans when school starts," Laela commented. She held the waistband of her shorts out showing the three inch gap that had developed over the week.

"No kidding," agreed Emma. "I might be able to wear the clothes that got too tight last year after I quit running cross country and joined the debate team."

Heather's face was gaunt. She had eaten the least of anyone despite the constant urging from her sister and Sky. Little of what she did eat stayed in her system for long. "I wouldn't recommend this as a diet strategy," she said trying to make light of her illness. The others laughed at her joke even as they saw their friend shrinking away day by day.

"I'm so sorry, sweetheart," Sky said. She was sitting, holding Heather's head in her lap, smoothing her hair, at a loss for anything that would relieve her suffering. "I wish I had something—"

"It's not your fault," Annie cut in. "None of this is your fault Sister Ryder." For someone who had been distant and quiet to begin with, Annie was quick to defend her leader, showing an inner strength that hadn't been there before.

Brad who had been at the river fishing, walked up to the group. His t-shirt was wet and clung to his body. Though still muscular, the lack of food had taken its toll on him as well, his ribcage more prominent, his jeans riding lower on his hip bones. He looked at the girls, six pairs of sunken eyes stared back. "I hate to ask, but is anyone going out for berries today?"

There was a unified groan and then Sky spoke up, "I'll go." It was said with little enthusiasm, but there wasn't much of an option. "Anyone else want to join me?"

"I would, but—"

"It's okay, Amanda. I think it's probably best if you stay with Heather," said Sky. It wasn't the same as having her mother there, but the two sisters were close, and Heather seemed to appreciate having her twin near. "What about you, Annie? Are you up for a walk?"

"Sure, I'll go if Emma wants to trade me jobs," she said referring to the fact that she had become one of the fishermen for the group.

"Gladly!" Emma conceded. "I'm tired of traipsing around in the bushes looking for berries. My legs are so scraped up it'll be weeks before I dare wear a skirt again." She stood up and brushed the dirt from her shorts that revealed red welts and scratches covering her shins. "If you show me what to do with that, I'll put it to work" she said, nodding at the makeshift fishing pole in Brad's hand.

"Deal," he said then turned to Sky and Annie. "Maybe you'll have more luck if you go the other direction. I'd guess things are getting pretty picked over that way." He pointed to the south with his pole. It was the direction they had come from five days ago. Sky and Emma, the designated berry hunters, had been back and forth over the area so many times, they'd worn a visible trail through the brush. There wasn't a huckleberry or wild strawberry bush that they hadn't touched hoping to find even the tiniest bit of fruit.

Sky looked to the north where the thick forest trees closed in, blocking the sunlight and making it appear dark and forbidding. "You're probably right," she said turning back to him. There was sympathy in his eyes as he looked at her, as if he knew and understood just how much she didn't want to forge another trail. "We'll go that way and hope we find a bunch."

Sky and Annie picked their way through the trees. The terrain was difficult, garbled by hidden holes, sticks, bushes, ant hills, and rocks. They could move slowly at best. Sky took the lead trying to find the best way through. When they came to a fallen tree they scrambled over the top instead of choosing to go around it. And though it wasn't steep, there was a gradual uphill slope.

Conversation was interspersed with caution warnings as Sky alerted her young charge to the dangerous footing. "Watch your step, there's a hole under that leaf."

"Thanks," said Annie. They continued forward, Sky holding back the branch of a low hanging limb so it didn't flip back and hit Annie in the face. "So when are you getting married?" she asked.

"October twelfth."

"How long have you been engaged?"

"One month is all. We haven't known each other all that long really." Sky wondered if she should be sharing that bit of information with her. It wasn't something she would recommend if she were giving a lesson in church, but it had worked for her and Tom. He was the kind of guy to make things happen. He was also the one that had wanted to do it right away, but Sky had felt they needed more time to plan the wedding—and get to know each other more.

"Where's he from?"

"He grew up in California, but his family moved to Montana recently. Here, give me your hand, I'll pull you up," she said climbing over a three foot boulder that was surrounded by some kind of thorny bush. "This stuff is terrible. I wonder what it is."

"Do you—do you love him?" Annie hesitated. "I'm sorry, I shouldn't be asking you so many questions."

"Hey, it's okay, I don't mind," Sky assured her. She stopped and turned around to look at her, noting the hesitancy in which she'd asked. "And yes, I do love him or I wouldn't marry him."

"But people sometimes say that and don't really mean it." Sky hadn't been present when Annie shared her story with Brad and Laela, but she knew from talk around the ward that Annie's dad was recently divorced. She didn't know the circumstances behind it, but she didn't need to. It was obvious from Annie's words and tone that she was hurting. She reached for Annie's hand and giving it a squeeze she said, "It's hard to understand relationships. Love can be very complicated. People do things for reasons we may not ever understand."

"I guess," Annie murmured.

"Come on, I think I see some over there." Sky turned to her left, still holding Annie's hand to drag her along behind.

Their conversation distracted them both from the large, four footed creature that had quietly ambled into the area, munching on wild berries, separated by just a handful of yards. The dappled forest light created shadows, making it impossible to see the black shiny fur until it was too late. Sky had her eye on the berries when suddenly she was face to face with the largest black bear she had ever seen.

Surprised, she screamed like someone had just jumped around the corner and yelled, "Boo!" The sudden shriek startled—and angered—the bear. It rose up on its hind legs, stretching to its full and impressive height. Sky's small frame looked childlike compared to the bear.

Looking back on it later, Sky would remember thinking how soft the bear's underbelly looked for that was all she could see as he stood before her, his giant paws edged with razor sharp claws shaking in the air as he roared, his jaws dripping with saliva and unswallowed berries. Like a slow motion movie clip she would forever be able to see the bear lunge forward, swiping at the arm she instinctively held in front of her body for protection. She would recall the mind-numbing sting as its claws sliced through the flesh of her forearm, the force knocking her to her back, her head slamming on the rocks below. She would remember the horrible stench of his breath as he stood over her on all four paws before swiping again at her stomach. She would bear scars for a lifetime as four inch claws carved lines across her abdomen. She wouldn't forget hearing the shrill and courageous shouts of the young woman frantically trying to scare away her tormenter. And she would always be grateful that it wasn't her time to die.

Annie shouted again, hollering nonsense at the terrifying beast while she waved her arms. "Back! Get back!" She shoved her arms forward to push it away from Sky. The bear roared again, stood to height again. Adrenaline fueled Annie's movement, filled her lungs as she roared in return. She was powerful. More powerful than she'd have ever imagined she could be. And though she was more scared than she had ever been, she fought on.

The bear fell back to the ground on all four paws. It stopped roaring, closed its mouth with its thick black lips, and took a step backward. Annie stepped over Sky and toward the bear, never taking her eyes from it. Somehow, in the midst of the terror, her subconscious pulled out the facts about black bears that Sky had gone over with them in their many pre-camp meetings. Black bears could be intimidated, stared down. If running wasn't an option, you had to show them who was boss. Grizzlies were different; you had to slink away and hope they didn't follow. But with a black bear, she just needed to show him who was the alpha. She couldn't—wouldn't—back down. She continued to shout and push at the bear's hulking form. "I HATE YOU! GO AWAY!" She was the alpha, using all the strength she could muster, showing up the bear until, like a coward, it turned and ran.

"I've never liked fishing," Emma commented as she sat next to Brad on the river bank. "My dad likes to fish, but I never go with him."

"I've spent a lot of time fishing with my ol' man," said Brad. It was something they'd both enjoyed and often the only time when they could really talk. There was something about being in the outdoors that had always relaxed him, centered him.

"But there's something about knowing I won't eat tonight if I don't do this that makes me think it's not so bad."

"Well, there is that," Brad laughed. He liked Emma. She was a nice girl and had proven that she had a good head on her shoulders. He was starting to see each of the girls like a little sister. Each of them, that is, except for Sky. There was nothing brotherly in his thoughts about Sky. Every day he spent with her proved more and more tempting. Her long black hair, her dark eyes, her hundred watt smile. And that was only on the outside. The inside—who she really was at heart—was just as beautiful. They had argued several times, proving to him that she was no withering daisy. There was passion under that skin, well hidden by a calm and compassionate nature.

And she was engaged to be married.

"Do you think—" Emma broke off as a blood curdling scream pierced the air. "What was that?"

But Brad didn't hear her. He was already running.

He wasn't sure who had screamed first, but he could hear Annie clearly as he bounded over the fallen tree, over the boulder, and past whatever obstacles got in his way. He hurled himself through the forest towards the sound of her shouts, and though it felt like he'd never get there, in reality it was only minutes until he reached her just in time to see a black bear turn and run.

For one brief minute he thought everything was fine. Then Annie turned and fell to the ground, hidden by the bushes that stood between them until he could no longer see her and all he heard was, "Oh, Sky!" His heart sank.

Ten feet in front of him Sky lay on the ground. He leaped forward and saw her bloodied body shaking with shock. There was so much blood!

Shoving aside his emotions, he forced the paramedic in him to the surface. He needed to help her and he couldn't do that if he allowed his feelings to get in the way. Kneeling behind her head he spoke gruffly, professionally, "Sky? Sky can you hear me?"

Through her tears and moans of pain she acknowledged him. Both of her arms were cradled over her stomach, making it impossible to tell where the source of the blood came from. "Where are you hurt?" he asked as he whipped off his shirt and began using it to mop at the blood.

"Arm," she squeaked. She moved her arm, revealing the inside of her forearm where the bear's claws had left four deep cuts. The one closest to her wrist gushed dark red liquid. With no thought about being gentle, he grabbed her arm and lifted it above her head, at the same time wrapping his t-shirt around it as tight as he could. She flinched at the pain and cried out, but he ignored her, refusing to let her bleed out. The bear had obviously nicked an artery, perhaps sliced right through it.

He continued to hold her arm tightly, checking her pulse at her neck with his free hand. As he did so, he saw the blood on her shredded shirt continue to spread, red seeping into the pink fabric. It stuck to her much like his wet shirt had done earlier. "Hold this!" he commanded Annie. He was already moving to a better position as Annie came around to the other side where she could hold Sky's arm and apply life-saving pressure. She was crying now too, shaking with fear and adrenaline.

Brad knelt at Sky's side and carefully peeled her shirt up exposing four more deep cuts. Without her shirt to soak up the blood, it simply pooled on top of her belly until enough had gathered and it began to drip down her sides to the ground. It wasn't the most gruesome wound he had seen, but it wasn't pretty. It reminded him of the fake wounds Hollywood could create in horror movies. Only this wasn't Hollywood, and it definitely wasn't fake.

With his only shirt wrapped around her arm, he had nothing else to press against the wound and slow the bleeding. "Argh! I need—I need something to…"

Annie didn't need to be asked. She let go of Sky's arm and lifted off her own shirt, revealing the white sports bra she wore beneath. She wasn't thinking about modesty, only the life of her friend. She tossed it to Brad then picked up Sky's arm again and squeezed.

Brad used the shirt to press at the diagonal wound that ran across her smoothed and narrow abdomen. After holding it in place for several seconds, he lifted it to get a better view of the cuts. Once the pressure was released, the cuts began to seep blood and he had to press down again. He continued, carefully examining each red line. All the while, Sky cried, trying not to writhe in pain. "I've got to get you back to camp." Without another word, he scooped her up, one arm beneath her shoulders, the other under her knees. As he lifted, her abdomen was squeezed together and she cried out involuntarily. "Sorry," Brad acknowledged. "I know it hurts."

Annie kept her grip on Sky's arm as he lifted, but the uneven terrain made it nearly impossible to keep holding it while trying to walk after Brad's enormous steps. "Just keep it up," he admonished Sky. "You can lean it against my head. Annie run ahead of me. Gather all the clean water we've got and anything that can be used to wrap the wounds, shirts, sweatshirts, anything! And make a place for her to lie down. Hurry, run!"

With no further urging, Annie bolted back through the forest. Brad was moving swiftly behind her, but she soon outdistanced him. He was trying to carry Sky as gently as he could without further jarring her sore and bleeding body, but with every move she moaned, biting her lip to keep from screaming. Her blood was now smeared across his chest, the fine blond hairs matted with sticky red liquid. Her arm, which she tried to keep in the air, waved and bounced against his head, wiping smudges of blood that had soaked through the shirt against his face with each contact.

Laela, Emma, and Amanda stood watching from the clearing as Annie came racing out of the trees wearing her shorts and bra. Breathless she called, "Quick! Quick, help me!"

"What's wrong? What's happened?" asked Emma, tamping down on her own panic. Brad had moved so swiftly when they heard the scream, she'd hardly had time to register what it was they'd heard. Unsure of what to do, she hadn't followed him, but waited anxiously next to her friends.

"Water! Get all the water! Make a bed!" Annie fell to her knees, smoothing out one of the sleeping bags that still lay on the ground, throwing aside the few personal articles that were lying on top. The others, moving swiftly but still not knowing why, ran to the fire pit to collect water bottles. Heather, too weak to get up and help, pushed to a sitting position. "What's going on?" she asked, but no one heard her.

Turning around, they were just in time to see Brad emerge from the trees. "Oh my gosh!" Laela exclaimed. The water bottle dropped from her hand as she stood, too stunned to pick it up. The macabre sight of the bloody figures coming out of the forest scared them all.

"Sky?" Emma croaked.

"Bear." It was all Annie needed to say.

Brad carried Sky to the sleeping bag and placed her on top as carefully as he could. As he pulled back his arms, her body flattened, pulling apart the cuts on her abdomen, reopening the wounds. She screamed, flinched, and tensed, sending more blood oozing out.

Brad saw what was happening and the idea struck him that it would be better to keep her bent rather than flat. It might just hold the cuts together and stop some of the bleeding. "Amanda, push the backpacks under her body," he directed, pulling Sky's shoulders up. The girl was shaking with fear, still unsure of what had happened, but she did as she was told. Together they propped Sky's feet so they'd be higher than her heart and one pack behind her back kept her abdomen closed.

"Emma, we need a fire. Boil water! Laela, we need cloth. Anything that can be spared rip into strips!"

Sky's strength was gone. She could no longer hold her arm in the air, and it rested at her side. Brad grabbed it, holding it in the air again, above her heart. "Annie, hold her arm, squeeze it as tight as you can. If you get too tired, trade Amanda, but don't let the pressure off!" If they were going to save her, they had to get the bleeding under control.

Laela rushed over with a small wash cloth, the one they had used for washing, and handed it to Brad. "Good, we'll need more," he said, taking it from her. He reached for the water bottle Amanda had dropped by his side and poured it over the cloth.

Rushing off to find more, Laela called behind her, "I'm on it!"

"And sleeping bags, grab some to cover her," he said. Her body continued to tremble. "Stay with me Sky," Brad spoke calmly but firmly to her as he continued to administer aid. "I know it hurts, but I've got to see how bad it is and I can't do that if I don't stop the bleeding." He continued dabbing at her stomach. The girls kept him supplied with the remaining clean water. Finally, after what seemed an eternity he said, "They don't go all the way through, but the cuts are deep into the muscle. We don't have what we need to stitch them up. All I can do is bind them with rags until they come for us. Sky, it's very important that you hold as still as possible. The bleeding has nearly stopped, but if you move, it'll start again. Sky? Sky, do you understand?"

Her body felt as weightless as a ragdoll's, yet at the same time heavy. She knew it was her body, but her mind couldn't move it, couldn't connect to it. All she could do was feel it, the mind numbing pain that consumed her whole body. Excruciating. Head aching. Arm stinging, core throbbing. Move? No she wouldn't—couldn't—move. "No," she croaked. "Don't move."

"That's right," he repeated back to her. "Don't move." His voice sounded far away, like it was coming at her from the far end of a tunnel. There was movement and sound around her, distorted voices and fuzzy images.

She closed her eyes, shutting it all out. Perhaps if she closed them tight enough the pain would stop too. If she could just close her eyes and sink into oblivion. Suddenly there was water on her lips, trickling into her mouth. She swallowed. It was cold and tasted sublime. More. She hadn't even known she was thirsty, but she wanted more. The water revived her enough to open her eyes. And there he was.

His bronzed face was rough, a straw colored beard on his chin. His blue eyes were warm and tender as he watched her. His hair was shaggy and fell over his forehead. There was blood on his face. She followed the streak down to his chest. It too had blood on it. Lots of blood. Through it she could see the hardened plains of muscle. "Not like Tom at all," she murmured.

"What?" Her words were so soft he had to bend close to her mouth to hear. "What was that?"

"You," she whispered. "You're not like him at all."

What was she talking about? He wondered. She was becoming delirious from the shock. If only he had some decent medical supplies with him. Some bandages, some pain killer, anything to help. Like a helicopter and a medevac team, he thought ruefully.

He pressed his fingers against her throat. Her pulse beat faintly, but it was steady. She was calm and drifting towards sleep. Perhaps that was the best thing for her. Annie was still gripping her arm, holding it above her head. He hated the idea of having to put a tourniquet on for fear she might lose her hand. If they could just keep the pressure tight, maybe he wouldn't have to. He'd have to keep pushing fluids into her to replace the blood loss, but so long as she didn't go into severe shock, sleep would slow her body systems and keep her still. She certainly wasn't going to hike out of here now. Where were those rescue crews? It felt like they had already waited a lifetime.

With his hand at her throat, he caressed her cheek. "You're going to be okay, Sky. I'm not going to let anything happen to you," he promised. "You just rest now." He kept his hand there, feeling the smoothness of her skin, grateful that it was still warm. Her eyes fluttered close. How on earth, he wondered, was he going to keep his promise?

Chapter 23

For a long time no one spoke. There were too many questions to ask, but nothing to say in response. Fear hung like a heavy cloud over the small mountain clearing. The crystal water of the river continued to flow. The trees swayed with the evening breeze. Nothing had changed, but everything was different.

Brad kept his fingers at Sky's pulse. Her breathing was shallow. He feared she would slip away and he wouldn't even know.

The girls kept quiet, tiptoeing around as though any sound would cause Sky more pain. And though they all had shed tears at least once that afternoon, none had shied away from the gruesome sight of blood. They had silently done their part to save their leader.

"How's the fire, Emma?" Brad asked, not taking his eyes from Sky's face.

"Good." She had kept it burning for over three hours now, tending to it as though doing so would keep Sky alive. "I'm taking Amanda with me for more wood before it gets dark."

"Good thinking. We'll need to keep it going throughout the night. You girls may have to double up and share sleeping bags. We have to keep her warm." Her body was no longer shaking, but he knew it didn't have the strength to keep her warm, especially with all the blood loss. "And the water?"

Laela had taken it upon herself to fill and re-fill every available container with boiled water as though doing so would somehow keep Sky alive. "We're full," she reported.

"Heather—How is Heather doing?" he asked unaware that she was within hearing distance.

"I'm fine," she answered. Feeling lousy with a stomach ache seemed trivial at the moment.

The fishing poles lay unused, the containers empty of berries, yet there was no mention of food by any of them. Who could think of food at a time like this?

The evening darkened into night. Brad kept his vigil at Sky's side urging her to drink even in her semiconscious state. The girls moved mechanically around camp, finding tasks to fill the hours until they could cross this day off as finished. Worry, fear, hopelessness, and despair were the only things on the menu.

When they could stand it no longer, Laela and Amanda cuddled up close to Heather and fell asleep. Annie, still holding tight to Sky's injured arm, had fallen asleep as well. Emma continued to sit at the fire, but her head kept nodding forward. Finally she relented and pulled up her knees, folded her arms on top and laid her head down.

Brad couldn't sleep. Though he was exhausted both physically and mentally, he wouldn't allow himself the luxury of sleep. Instead, he sat in the dark, feeling the steady movement of Sky's body rising and falling with each breath, her pulse beating in her neck. He worried that she would be too cold in the night, for though the day was hot, the nights were always cold in the mountains. He was still shirtless and Laela had brought him his fireman's coat for warmth. The girls were sharing two sleeping bags between the five of them. The remaining four were given to cover Sky.

In the darkness, he could no longer see her face. It didn't matter. He had stared at it all evening, memorizing it so completely that her image burned behind his eyelids. She had looked so still and peaceful, he could almost imagine she was taking a nap on a pleasant summer afternoon. And then she would grimace, her face twisting with twinges of pain and he would remember the grizzly sight of her lying in the woods, soaked in blood and screaming in agony.

It ate at him, this helplessness. There was nothing more he could think to do, nothing that would fix her. It was against his nature to do nothing. He was a paramedic. A man. That's what men do. They fix things. But try as he might, he just couldn't fix this, not without the proper tools anyway. Medicine, bandages, they had none of those things.

A basic first aid kit was all. It would take a thousand Band-Aids to cover her wounds.

Frustrated, he sat thinking when he felt her fingers brush his leg. "Sky? Hey Thunder it's me, Brad. What do you need?" he whispered into the dark.

"Drink," she croaked. Her throat was dry and raspy. Within seconds he offered the cool relief of water at her lips. She drank deeply as Brad held the bottle to her mouth, tipping it further and further as she drained the water. "Better," she said quietly after he pulled it away empty. "I'm too weak to get you for that," she added, referring to his use of her name.

"What can I do for you? Are you cold? Can I get you anything?" He fired questions at her, not allowing her time to answer.

"I could use—ah—a doctor if you've--got one--handy." She attempted to make light of the situation, but her words were stilted with involuntary gasps from the pain. They both knew this was no joking matter. There was no denying her life was at stake.

"Would you settle for a paramedic with no supplies?"

"And no shirt?" In the dark, she reached up with her good arm and felt his bare chest. She let her hand linger for just a minute above his heart before dropping it back to her side. "Thank you," she added.

His skin tingled where she had touched him, something so simple sending vibrations throughout his body. He wanted to pull her hand back and hold it against him so she could feel how her touch made his heart race, but he couldn't—didn't dare. He grinned, so happy was he to have her awake and talking like herself again. "You're welcome. I wouldn't give away my favorite Tim McGraw concert t-shirt for just anybody." He, too, wanted to keep things light, but he couldn't. He added in a more serious tone, "She'd have to be someone pretty special." He made as though to feel for her pulse again, but used the opportunity to trace his thumb across her cheek in a gesture that was as innocent as it was intimate. For just a split second he felt her head turn into the warmth of his palm.

"The girls? Are they okay?" she asked through the pain. "How long have I slept?"

"The girls are fine. They're worried about you. We're all worried. You've been asleep since around four. I'd guess it's close to one o'clock."

Sheepishly she said, "I'm sorry."

"You're sorry?" He couldn't believe she was apologizing. But then again, he knew that's just who she was. "Did you tell that to the bear who tried to kill you too?" There was a touch of anger in his words. "Sky, you don't have anything to be sorry for. Just rest and don't worry about anything."

"I know you don't believe like I do, but would you…" she hesitated then finally asked, "would you say a prayer with me?"

"Of course." There was no way he could deny such a simple request, even one that he thought would do no good. He felt for her hand and finding it, he held on while she whispered a prayer.

"Dear Father, I thank you for saving me. I'm thankful for Annie and all the girls and—and Brad. I'm thankful for Thy son who has felt what I am feeling. Please, if it be Thy will, help me to live through this. And if not, please let them find the girls so they can go home. In the name of Jesus Christ, amen." Her humble words faded with her strength.

"Amen," Brad repeated, gently squeezing her fingers.

"Brad? Brad, I—I hurt." Nothing unnerved him more than those few words as he heard tears in her voice and could do nothing to stop them.

"I know, love. I know you do."

By morning she was burning with fever.

The sky was light long before the sun rose over the granite peaks. Pink clouds streaked across the blue in rippled lines. Dew dripped from the trees and ran in rivulets down the nylon backpacks in the clearing. Four of the five girls were huddled together next to the dead fire, one sleeping bag covering them all. The fifth lay at Sky's head, still holding her arm, tucking it under her chin as though it was a teddy bear to snuggle.

Sometime in the night when Brad could no longer keep upright, he had laid on the ground next to Sky. He was like a first-time parent, coming awake with every sound he heard that could possibly be her. But she had slept, or pretended to, throughout the night.

She moaned, rolling her head side to side. Instantly, Brad was up. "No, no, no," she mumbled, getting louder and louder with every word until finally shouting, "Nooo!" She couldn't move, but her eyes flew open looking panicked and wild.

"Sky, it's okay," Brad crooned. "It was just a nightmare. You're safe now."

"The bear…I saw the bear." She was only half conscious, remembering the horrible events of the previous day.

Brad noted the beads of perspiration on her forehead. He soothingly placed his hand on her head. She was hot. Too hot. At the coolness of his touch she closed her eyes but her countenance was troubled.

Seeing her like this, he knew he had to act. He couldn't wait any longer for rescue teams to find them. If they waited any longer, Sky would die of infection if not blood loss.

Looking around the clearing, he took note of what he needed to do before leaving. He would need water, but he didn't want to take time to eat. They had nothing on hand, no catch from the day before. Fishing would only take precious time away, time that Sky might not have.

For the first time in over twelve hours he left Sky's side and walked over to the fire pit. The four girls held each other in sleep, likely trying to stay warm. He watched them. He hated to leave them, especially under these circumstances, but he had no choice. He had grown to care for them. He had also grown to trust them. They had done their best to pull their weight, to share the burden of survival. They had shown amazing courage. They would be alright, he told himself. They had to be.

Amanda was the first to stir. She looked up at him, his shadow blocking them from the rising sun. "Is she…Is she—" She couldn't say it, couldn't name the fear they'd all slept with.

"No, she's not," Brad answered, reading her thoughts. "But she's far from okay."

Amanda wiggled her way out of the group, gently pushing aside the others. She stood up, hugging her arms around her body to replace the warmth she'd left behind. "You're leaving." It wasn't a question. His face said it all.

He pulled her close to his side, her small frame only reaching his chest. He rubbed her blond hair against his scraggly cheek. "I have to. It's our only chance to save her."

She nodded, sniffled. He placed both hands on her shoulders, turned her to face him, and looked into her eyes. They were large and round and swimming with tears. "I'm coming back for you kiddo, I promise." She nodded again. Elephant tears rolled down her cheeks. "Everything's going to be okay," he tried to assure her.

The other girls were coming awake now and seeing the two of them standing there, Amanda crying, caused them all alarm. Emma jumped up. "Is it Sky?" she demanded.

Brad reached for her hand and gave it a squeeze. "No, she's asleep." Kneeling down on one knee, he said, "Come here, we need to talk." Anxiously Laela, Heather, Amanda and Emma all joined him. To his surprise, Annie called over. "Hey, talk louder, I want to know what's going on but I don't want to let go," she said in a loud whisper, still holding onto Sky's arm.

Turning his body slightly he addressed them, "Sky's in trouble--obviously. She's developed a fever, probably from infection setting in. If she's going to make it, she's got to get to a hospital quickly. We've been waiting for them to find us, but we can't wait any longer. I'm going for help. I'll be able to move fast. If things go right, this will all be over soon."

"Shouldn't one of us go with you?" Emma asked.

"No, I need you here taking care of Sky. You've got to keep the fire going, keep clean water on hand. Someone's got to help her drink it. A couple of you need to fish. It's been too long since you ate."

"What about you?" Heather asked feebly. "You haven't eaten."

"It'll take too long now. I'll be fine."

"What if something happens? What if there's another bear, or Sky…you know…dies?" Laela whispered the last word as though it was forbidden to say.

"Nothing's going to happen. You guys can do this. I know you can." It was a weak pep talk, but it was the best he could do. "I'm depending on you," he emphasized. Brad looked over at the woman laying on the ground, the woman that had become embedded in his heart in just one week. "Sky's depending on you."

Preparations began immediately and thirty minutes later he was ready to leave. He had pulled anything that might be useful out of his pack and stuffed it in his pockets. He wanted to travel fast and light. He had one small pocket knife, some string, his broken compass—with the hope that he could get it to work again, a flashlight, a water bottle, and four matches. He still had no shirt to wear. He didn't dare remove it from Sky's wrist for fear it would begin bleeding again. Opting not to take his coat because of its weight, he left it with the girls. They could use it for warmth. Besides, he wasn't planning on stopping to rest. Speed was of the utmost importance.

The girls had gathered around Sky, to see for themselves that she was still among the living. Eventually the whispered voices and stilted movements were enough to wake her. "Good morning," she mumbled, trying to force a smile to her mouth. It never reached her eyes. They only reflected her pain and misery.

"It's not good, but it's morning," quipped Laela.

"Can we get you anything?" Heather asked. Her long blond hair that had shown like sunlight at the beginning of girls' camp hung in stringy clumps around her sunken cheeks. Her pallor was gray and ghostlike.

"No." She hadn't the strength to say more.

"Okay girls," Brad said coming up behind them. "The fish are probably biting." The four of them took the hint and left him at her side alone, moving off to allow them some privacy.

Kneeling beside Annie he took Sky's arm and checked her pulse. Her fingers were cold and slightly blue indicating the circulation in that hand was poor. "I think you'd better let go for a while, Annie. We don't want her losing her hand."

"You sure? What if it bleeds more?"

"I want you to check it every thirty minutes. If it looks like more blood is seeping through the shirt, you hold it again," he instructed. "Can you do that?"

She nodded solemnly.

"Go on and help the others."

Brad gently moved Sky's arm, lying it across her upper body and tucking it beneath the sleeping bag. Sky's eyes fluttered and slowly opened. "Hey," she managed.

"Hey yourself." He put his hand behind her head, holding it up enough to allow her to drink some water. She swallowed slowly, taking in only a few sips. "Better?" he asked.

"Hmmm." He held his hand behind her head, gently lowering it back to the ground. She tried to take a deep breath and winced at the pain. "How long--do you think it w--will take you?" she asked through labored breaths.

He hadn't told her he was going for help, but she obviously knew. "I figure if I move fast, I can make it back to the campground by dark. From there I can get on the road and flag down anyone I see driving. I assume the evacuation is still in effect."

"And the fire?"

"We haven't been getting nearly as much smoke, the sky has been getting clearer. I don't think it will be an issue." He put his hand on her forehead. He wanted to touch her. To be close to her. To say goodbye.

"Infection," she whispered. One word, but it was enough to make his heart jump.

"I'll be back with help by morning. Just hang on," he begged, caressing his hand down her cheek.

"Umm, try."

"The girls are going to help. They know what to do."

"Pray."

"Yeah, I know they know how to do that."

She rolled her head slightly from side to side, the barest movement. "No, you."

"I don't think God would listen to me if I tried. Too much bad blood between us."

"Always listens." Her words were weak, but her conviction was strong. "Brad, if I— "

He put his finger over her lips, cutting off her words. "You won't, Sky. You can't. These girls need you." *And so do I,* he added silently. "I better go."

Sky closed her eyes in consent.

He'd had all night to think, to ponder in the dark. So much had happened in so short a time. He'd experienced numerous emotions over the past week; anger, resentment, sadness, a little fear and even some jealousy. But love—he hadn't expected to ever feel that again. Looking at Sky he didn't see just her hair, her lips, her nose—that was only a part of who she was. He saw a caring, gentle, funny, brave woman and knew that he loved her. There was nothing he wouldn't sacrifice for her if it would save her life. Even knowing she belonged to another man—would never belong to him—didn't matter. So long as she lived, that would be enough, he told himself.

With her eyes closed, he bent and kissed her. The touch of her fevered lips burned deep into his soul. He lingered, not wanting to pull away, yet knowing he had to. When he pulled back, her eyes were open, surprised. "What—Why?"

"Because I may never get another chance."

Before she could say anything, he disappeared into the trees.

"Thank you," Sky murmured as Annie pulled back the water bottle she held to her lips. The cold liquid slid down her throat adding to the shivers she already felt. The sun was high, the day warm, yet Sky lay beneath three sleeping bags and still felt chilled. The fever was relentless. To add to her misery, her bladder was full but she couldn't move. The pain in her injured abdominal muscles was excruciating. There was no way she could stand. The idea of soiling herself was humiliating, but as a nurse, she knew it was inevitable.

She tried to focus on other things, other thoughts, feelings…kisses. Brad had kissed her. His lips had been soft and cool. They'd left an impression that not even her pain could shake. She lay there, concentrating, trying to put feelings into words. But she couldn't. He had made her feel…feel…cherished? No, that wasn't right. Important? That wasn't it either. How could one kiss—and at a time like this—make her feel so…so loved? But it did. That one kiss had made her want to fight, to hang on for dear life. Her life.

It would be so easy to give in—give up. Just let the infection, the fever consume her. The fire they had run from hadn't burned her, but now there was fire inside her that she couldn't escape. The wounds in her belly burned, her arm felt the stinging singe of bear claws. If only she could melt back into the earth, turn to ash, stop the pain.

But for that kiss…

Chapter 24

Sweat dripped, running in rivulets down Brad's chest as he ran. Ducking, dodging branches, he moved swiftly, knowing that every step he took was a step closer to saving Sky. He retraced their earlier steps through the forest as best as he could, trying to remember every rock, every bush and tree, low spots, high spots and fallen logs. It had only been a week, but the forest was like a maze. Around every corner the scenery was the same, disorienting him until he wasn't positive he was even running in the right direction. He thought about an article he had read in a magazine once. It said that when people are lost, they generally end up walking in circles, coming right back to where they had started. Using the sun as his compass point, he moved towards what he hoped was the west.

With the sun at its zenith, he stopped and drank. The water was cool and refreshing. He felt it hit his empty stomach. Gosh, he was hungry. What he wouldn't give for a Power Bar! He couldn't remember the last time he'd been fully satisfied, but one thing was for sure, he wouldn't take time to enjoy food until he knew Sky and the girls were safe. The water would have to be enough.

Ahead he could see brighter light, like the forest was thinning. He didn't remember coming through any meadows once they had gone off trail, but it was possible they skirted around one. Emerging from the trees, he stopped. Shocked and awed, he stood looking at the devastation. Nothing but black stretched out before him. What was once trees; giant conifers of western red cedar, lodge pole pine, and douglas fir were nothing but charred spikes pointing towards a blue sky. The ground that had been covered in underbrush, pine needles, fallen trees, stumps, wild flowers, and ferns was a barren waste land. This was the monster they had escaped—barely. In the distance, small wisps of smoke rose to show that even now, the ashes were still smoldering. He'd seen the after-effects of hundreds of fires throughout his career. It never ceased to amaze him how thorough fire could be. It left nothing. Not even a trace of the trail.

Looking through the trees now was like peeking through tooth picks. He could see the cliffs that rose up at the far end of the narrow valley. The sun was starting to dip towards them, a good sign that he was headed in the right direction. If he was right, those cliffs were part of the Swan Mountain Range. On the other side would be the highway.

All he had to do now was reach them, climb them, and he was home free.

With the ground cleared of underbrush it was easier to see safe footing and he took off at a run. In little time he reached the base where he began to ascend the eastern side of the mountains. Greenery started appearing again. Trees that had escaped the meandering path of the fire grew in clumps amidst large rock slides. He scrambled up the rocks, sometimes slipping as the chosen foot hold loosened from the pile and went tumbling down the hill. His hands were scratched and raw from pulling himself up and over boulders, his shins bloody with scratches. But it didn't matter. They were small in comparison to what Sky was feeling, he reminded himself.

He was so close, so close to reaching the top. He stood balanced on two rocks looking for the next best place to step and noticed that in less than twenty feet the rock slide ended at a stone plateau. Surely that had to be the top and he could begin his descent. Relieved, he reached high and jammed his left hand between two boulders, using the space as a wedge for better grip and stability. To his right was a sheer faced stone just taller than himself. With his left hand secured, he found a small knot on the face that he grabbed with his right. There was another knot three feet from his right boot. Placing his foot on the boulder, he pushed up.

In this precarious position, he studied the rock looking for a place to step with his left foot. When he'd located the best option, he shifted more of his weight forward, ready to move.

Just then, the rocks used to wedge his left hand, broke free. A small boulder the size of a basketball came rolling, hitting him in the head and knocking him backwards. The momentum of his fall sent him rolling head over heels down the rocky slope. He stretched out his arm looking for something to hold on to. He kicked his leg out and felt his shin snap as the weight of his body and the torque of his hold was too much for the bone. He cried out in pain, finally coming to a stop at the base of a small tree, the impact at his side breaking a few ribs.

Brad could see stars dancing around his head. It throbbed and so did his side and leg. He lay back, not quite sure he ever wanted to—or could--move again. Dazed, he tried to get his bearings but the sunlight was suddenly too bright. Instead, he kept his eyes closed, breathed deep and tried to take mental note of everything that was hurting. He felt like he'd been hit by a bus.

When next he opened his eyes, the sun was gone. The sky was blue but the sun was no longer overhead. In fact, it was no longer visible. It had slipped behind the rocky cliff that rose up in front of him like a towering wall.

"I must have passed out," he enunciated, making sure he was actually awake and could talk. With much effort he pushed himself to a sitting position, using the tree as leverage. "Agghh, Holy—" He bit back an expletive as the sharp pain from his ribs made moving torturous. Once he was upright, he used his good leg to scoot himself back where he could lean against the tree. The effort winded him, but he could only take shallow breaths. His ribs felt like they were bursting!

He knew without looking that his leg was broken. He had heard it—felt it—snap as he fell. There was a tear at the hem of his jeans so he grabbed both sides and tried to rip them apart, but the action made his ribs scream with pain so he stopped. Instead, he inched his pant leg up, pulling at the fabric above his knee until it would go no further. It was enough to expose a portion of his shin. It was already blue with pooling blood, but the break had not punctured the skin. A small lump surrounded by masses of swelling confirmed that at least one bone was broken. He looked around him, but there was nothing to splint it with, no sticks, no branches, just rocks.

"Great! Just Great!" He howled. No one could hear him anyway. What difference did it make if he screamed and cursed for all the world to hear?

If only they could.

If only they would.

"What am I going to do now?" His thoughts turned immediately to Sky and the girls. He had left them, promising he would bring back help. They trusted him. He had been their only hope. "God, what am I going to do?"

The question had no more than slipped from his lips when tears pooled at his eyes and were soon streaming down his cheeks and he realized he was powerless to do anything but pray.

"She's going to die out there. Dear God, she's going to die, and there's nothing I can do! I don't know what to do. Please don't let her die," he cried.

Life had shown Brad some pretty ugly things, terrible things, gruesome things. He'd witnessed countless accidents and injuries. He'd seen the evidence of inhuman cruelty and the aftermath of catastrophic events. He'd gotten hurt so many times himself, he'd lost count. He'd even found love and lost it. But nothing brought him so low, made him feel so hopeless, as the prospect of this one woman dying. Not even his own injuries hurt as bad or cut as deeply. Always before he had found a solution within himself to deal with anything that came his way. He prided himself on his ability to cope.

Always, until now.

Ever so slowly a melody began forming. He wondered briefly if he was losing it, starting to hear voices. But no, he knew this song. The music grew louder in his head and he began humming the tune. It had stuck in his head ever since he'd heard the girls sing it around the campfire. But what were the words?

"Hmm Hmm…Hmm Hmm…walk beside me," he mumbled until suddenly, the words were clear. Quietly, he rested his head against the tree and let the words fill him, "Lead me, guide me, walk beside me. Help me find the way…" He stopped. The answer was there, not just in the words, but in the calm assurance that washed over him as he sang.

Speaking with more confidence, Brad's voice grew loud again, "Dear God, please help me. I can't save her now, but I know you can. I know I probably don't deserve your help, but she does. They all do."

Exhausted and completely spent, Brad closed his eyes and waited. Warmth filled him. Peace and serenity enveloped him until he was sure death must be near. And in the quiet stillness he thought he heard a voice whisper, "Yes, my son, you do."

Chapter 25

"We're going to take one more pass, do you copy?" The helicopter pilot shouted into the radio. A scratchy reply crackled through Ammon's earphones, "Roger, copy that." Beside him, the pilot pulled the control stick to the right and the helicopter swung nimbly in a one hundred eighty degree turn.

It was getting late, the shadows longer, making visibility from the helicopter difficult. Ammon searched out his window from the co-pilot's seat, looking for anything that might lead them to the whereabouts of the missing hikers.

The pilot, Everett Graves, was an experienced veteran who had flown missions during the Gulf War. Now, semi-retired, he flew for a sightseeing venture out of West Glacier, taking tourists up and over the mountains of Glacier National Park. Ammon, along with Judd Allred had hired him among several others to continue flying search and rescue operations.

The weather had been favorable all day. Winds were light and moving east, carrying away the smoke from fires that still burned to the south. When arrangements had been made to continue searching by helicopter, they had agreed to move their efforts further north to avoid the hot spots as fire crews worked to put out the last remnants of fire. The back burn had proved successful and the fire was now considered eighty percent contained.

From high above, both occupants could see the remaining devastation left by the fire. It had burned through the area a week ago, leaving a wide path of destruction through narrow valleys and up over the tops of cliffs. It would be decades before the natural beauty of the forest returned.

"Didn't leave much behind, did it?" Everett spoke into his mouthpiece. "Must have been one helluva fire down there."

"I imagine it looks like a war zone," Ammon commented.

"None that I ever saw. Of course, the desert doesn't have quite as much to burn."

"Let's head up that direction towards the mountains," Ammon directed, pointing west.

Everett made slight adjustments to the mechanical bird, aiming for a visible rock slide at the base of a cliff.

"Did you see that?" Ammon shouted, sitting forward in his seat.

"Where?"

"To your left, there." Ammon pointed towards a group of trees growing out of the rocks. "There it is again. Another flash."

"Yeah, I saw it. Could be nothing..." He broke off as they both saw the repeated flashing of light below.

"That's more than nothing!"

Keeping the position of the flash in his mind, Everett Graves looked for a place to set the chopper down.

"Brad! Wake up, Brad!"

He could hear someone calling, calling him from a distance, sounding like they were at the far end of a wind tunnel. Voices were indistinguishable, only his name came clearly through the loud reverberations of wind whipping through the air. He opened his eyes. His focus was blurry. Was he dead? Was that an angel standing before him? If he could just focus...

"Brad? It's me, Ammon."

"Ammon?" Was it possible? "How did you..."

"Where are you hurt?" Everett asked. Many of Brad's injuries were visible as bruising, swelling, and scraping. His ribs on the left side of his body were purple. But there was no way to see the internal injuries. The fact that he wasn't completely coherent didn't bode well either.

"Head—concussion I think. Broken leg, ribs too," Brad answered, slowly coming out of the fog. This was real, these men were real. He was still alive. Immediately he thought of

Sky. He recognized the sound of rotating chopper blades a short distance away. There would be time for explanations later. Right now, there was something more important to do. Adrenaline surged through his body. "Quick, help me up!"

Chapter 26

The room was bright with afternoon sun shining through the sheer curtains that hung in room 341 at Missoula Regional Medical Center. Brad could see rays of light between his eyelashes as he slowly regained consciousness after what seemed like days of much needed sleep. In reality he had slept for only six hours, but it was amazing how much better he could sleep in a bed—even a hospital bed—versus on the hard rocky ground of the Bob Marshall Wilderness without a blanket or pillow. There had been little time for sleep immediately following the miraculous rescue that was still making headlines across the intermountain west.

After being picked up by the helicopter, Brad directed the pilot to the spot where Sky and the girls were camped.

The trees were thick in that area, but the small opening around the river was just large enough in which to maneuver the helicopter. Everett's military expertise was put to use as he landed the chopper on the delta of rocks that had been home to the lost hikers for five days. Immediately he radioed his position and requested more air assistance.

The girls cried tears of joy and relief at the sight of their rescuers. Unfortunately, their ordeal was not quite over. There was not enough room in the chopper to take them all. The first priority was to get those in need of medical attention to a hospital.

The two able bodied men carefully lifted Sky into the helicopter and set her next to Brad. She was so weak and fevered that she barely acknowledged the movement.

In the front seat, Heather was strapped in next to the pilot. Ammon remained behind with the others until another chopper arrived.

Brad, Sky and Heather were flown to Missoula where emergency personnel were standing ready to meet them.

It seemed like chaos upon their arrival. People rushed everywhere calling out instructions as one by one they were whisked off the landing pad on gurneys, pushed by nurses in white lab coats and orderlies in surgical scrubs.

Word of the rescue had spread like the fire that had chased them into the wilderness. Even as a medical team rushed Brad through the hallways, taking his vital statistics and assessing his injuries, reporters thronged him for answers. Microphones were shoved in his face and flashbulbs erupted, until they reached the double doors of the emergency room.

Two hours later he was moved to his own room. His ribs were taped and his head was bandaged. Fortunately, he had sustained no internal injuries from his fall. He had suffered a concussion that doctors would continue to monitor. An orthopedic surgeon had been called in to study the x-rays of his leg. It would require surgery to pin the bones back together, as soon as the swelling subsided. He was given intravenous pain killer and a dish of Jell-O. It wasn't the steak and potatoes he had been hoping for, but having eaten so little, and with so much trauma, the doctor was concerned that his system couldn't tolerate heavy foods yet. It was by far the best thing he had tasted in a week, pure ambrosia to his deprived taste buds.

Inside his room came a steady stream of visitors. His parents and sister, who had driven the eighty miles to Missoula as soon as they'd gotten word, were the first ones admitted. His mother hugged him—gently to spare his ribs—crying in gratitude that he was safe.

"You've lost weight, son," his father noted, putting his hand on his shoulder and squeezing.

"It's a new diet plan called survival," he joked. He'd looked up at his father and smiled. "Thanks for teaching me to fish, Dad." Brad didn't know what they would have done without the small fish they'd been able to catch. All joking aside, the reality of his son's ordeal stared him in the face and the older man covered his emotions with a cough.

Brad's sister, Jenna, had thrown her arms around his neck, "I thought we'd lost you, you big oaf!"

He groaned, "You still might if you don't let go." She pulled back, wiping at tears. "You'll never be rid of me,

Squirt," he said, using the nickname he'd called her since she was five.

After his family came he spoke to police, search and rescue, the forest service, and even Chief Fitch. He allowed reporters to filter in, answering the same questions repeatedly until he felt he'd told his story a million times. He wanted to push them all aside, but he knew they were just doing their job.

Brad had a few questions himself that no one seemed to be able to answer satisfactorily: How was Sky? And how in the world had they ever found him?

When they reached the hospital, Sky had barely been hanging on to life. He had held her as best he could on the helicopter ride, but with her in his arms, he felt her slipping away. Her breathing had been so shallow he could hardly feel her next to him. She was hot with fever, but her body no longer shook with chills, it had given up the fight. She wasn't completely unconscious, but she wasn't coherent. He wasn't even sure if she knew that she was being rescued. She mumbled and groaned, half dreaming, half crying. It was just before they'd reached the hospital that she had gone completely quiet, and that had scared him more than anything.

She was the first victim out of the chopper and within seconds she was gone. Though reporters had mentioned how anxious they were to talk to her about her experience, they confided to him that no one had been admitted to see her. Her diagnosis, they'd been told, was listed as critical, and she remained isolated in the hospital's intensive care unit.

Through the hours of medical attention and questioning, Brad pondered how it was that Ammon and the chopper pilot had found him. He knew he'd been hidden from above by the branches of the trees. He remembered the events of the morning; running through the forest, the burn zone, climbing the rock slide, and falling. He remembered pulling himself up and resting against the tree. He remembered his prayer—if it could be called that—pleading for help. And he remembered the warmth and a feeling of total and complete peace that washed over him. He imagined it was a sign that he was close to death, and so he'd sat back, prepared to die.

The next thing he knew, Ammon was calling him. He wasn't dead. The pain was back and he'd almost wished he was dead, but he'd remembered Sky and the girls. They were waiting for him, depending on him to bring back help. Help had come to him, but how it had come was still unclear to him. Ammon mentioned a flashing light that had directed them to the clump of trees. He talked as though Brad had been signaling them with a flashlight or reflector, but he had neither of these.

Brad pushed the control button at the side of his bed and the head slowly raised up. He felt the stiffness of his body as he came to a sitting position. A knock sounded at the door. "Come in," he called, surprised at the weakness of his own voice. He needed something to eat, something more than Jell-O and apple juice.

"Hey there," said London tentatively stepping into the room. In her hand she had a small bouquet of daisies. "These are to brighten things up around here," she said, holding them up. "And this," she said, holding up a pink bakery box, "is contraband, so you better eat quickly."

"I knew there was a reason I love you," Brad quipped, taking the box from her. Peeking into the container to find a giant cinnamon roll from his favorite bakery, Wheat Montana, he realized that, for the first time in months, it didn't feel awkward or painful to see London. And though he still loved her, it was different. Something had changed.

He had changed.

His once wounded heart had healed and in its place was a deeper love for a woman he knew he could never have.

"You look awful." Only the best of friends could joke with you at a time like this and it made his heart swell as he realized just how strong the bond of friendship between them remained.

"Gee, thanks. And here I was thinking how wonderful you look," he complimented her.

"Well, you know... a few more worry lines around the eyes is considered very attractive..." Her face grew more serious and she took his hand, holding it tight. "Don't you ever scare me like that again Bradley Stevenson!"

"Not if I can help it," he confirmed.

London pulled up a chair next to his bed. She tossed a copy of the *Missoulian*, the local newspaper, on his lap. "They're calling you a hero again. You've really got to stop all this rescuing business. I'm starting to think I should buy you your own superhero cape for Christmas."

Brad glanced at the headline and the cover photo below. It showed Emma and Amanda being helped out of a helicopter with Annie behind them waiting her turn. He recognized Laela in the foreground hugging a man and woman. The girls looked dazed but happy, dirty and definitely thin. He could imagine Laela complaining that the cameras hadn't snapped her from a_good angle and had shown her looking horrible—all the things a young girl would worry about when life had returned to normal. He had come to love these girls like they were all his kid sisters. Already he missed them and their constant stream of "girl talk." The headline read, "Out of the Ashes."

"It wasn't me that saved them," he said to London.

"Of course it was. They'd have been killed in the fire if not for you."

"Maybe," he reasoned. "But I didn't save them."

London waited patiently for him to read the article detailing the ordeal that he'd just lived through. There were quotes from the girls that made him chuckle. His own words from the night before were printed there as well.

"I didn't save them," he repeated, folding the paper back together. He looked at London, his brow puckered in confusion. "Do you believe in miracles?"

"Yes," she said without hesitation.

"Not just coincidences, or things you can't quite explain, but honest to goodness miracles?"

"What happened out there Brad?"

"That's just it, I don't know what happened." He proceeded to tell her about how he'd found the girls and they'd had to run from the fire. Much of what he shared was the same story that was printed in the paper, only with more detail. He told her about the bear attack, his complete and absolute fear that Sky would die. As he spoke of her, his face, his words, and his countenance revealed his feelings. "And then I left them there alone."

London tried to console him, "You had no choice."

"I know, but…"

"And the way you signaled the helicopter—"

"But that's just it, I didn't."

"What do you mean? Ammon said it was you flashing something at them that signaled them to land and find you."

"That's the miracle. Look in that bag," he said, pointing to a plastic bag that sported the hospital's logo on the outside. London picked up the bag and looked inside. It was all of his personal items, the things he'd had on him when he got to the hospital. There was a water bottle, the pocket knife....and the broken compass. He said, "That's everything I had with me. No flashlight. Nothing shiny. Nothing reflective. Just my broken compass and it was still in my pocket when I got here."

London looked at him, confused.

"I didn't signal them. I was under a tree, completely blocked from view. I was ready to die, London," he said gravely. "I didn't know what else to do so I said a prayer of sorts and then I got ready to let death take me and the next thing I know Ammon's there. I know he says I signaled him, that they saw a flashing light from right where I was sitting. But it wasn't me. The only thing it could be, is a miracle."

"And that's a problem...?"

"It's just hard for me to comprehend. I mean, why me? I'm nobody special. Why would God send a miracle to save Brad Stevenson from Kalispell Montana? Why not just send one to the girls? They're the ones that were praying, that believe He listens."

"Behold, I have graven thee upon the palms of my hands," London quoted. "You are no less special to Heavenly Father than any of His children. He's aware of each and every one of us. He knows who we are and has a plan for each of us. His plan for you isn't finished so he sent a miracle to make sure you get that chance."

"I think I may actually be starting to believe that."

"Well, it's about time! I've got a couple of friends that would love to tell you more about it once we spring you out of here."

He knew she was referring to the missionaries, and for once the idea appealed to him. Could they really explain what he'd felt out there, what had happened? He hoped so. He also knew he'd have to eat crow for a while though, see the gloating smile on London's face.

"Okay, okay. You win! I bet it's no coincidence I was lost in the wilderness for a week with a group of Mormon women. They've got to be the most persistent people on earth."

"You won't regret it!" She kissed him soundly on the forehead.

"Hey, can we come in?" Ammon called. He stood in the doorway, Marty and Corkie at his side. "Seems I can't leave you two alone."

"Come in." London smiled at him then turned back to Brad, a mischievous look in her eyes. "You're just in time. We were speaking of Mormon women…Brad was just about to tell me more about *Sister* Ryder."

Three days later Brad was cleared to be released from the hospital. The surgery on his leg had been successful. He now had four pins holding his tibia and fibula together. He would have to be off it completely for three weeks and then, if all was healing properly, he could move to a walking cast. He'd be going home with a rented wheelchair and a pair of crutches. He hated the idea of missing work for three weeks. On the other hand, after what he'd been through in the past week, the idea of sleeping, resting, and reading at home appealed to him.

He'd had frequent visitors during his hospital stay; his family, the Moffatts, even the young women he'd grown to love and respect. Their story continued to be written and talked about. It was a story that would forever bind them as friends.

The girls were happy to be home and seemed no worse for their experience. They were all on the thin side, but had regaled him with full details of all they'd eaten since their rescue. Since he'd been subsisting on hospital food, the descriptions of greasy hamburgers, French fries, pizza, and ice cream made his mouth water. They did manage to sneak a large Dairy Queen Blizzard past the nurse's station for him, which he fully enjoyed as they talked and laughed.

One friend he had yet to see. Though he'd received reports about Sky, he hadn't been able to visit her hospital room. She was slowly recovering from her wounds and the ensuing infection. She had required hundreds of stitches and would bear the scars of her bear encounter for life, but she would fully recover.

With his sore ribs and heavily cast leg, Brad maneuvered slowly to a sitting position on the bed. He managed to grab any personal items within easy reach and put them in the bag his mother had brought him that morning when she came to say goodbye. Because his parents lived in Polson, London had volunteered to drive him home. He looked around the sterile hospital room for anything he might have forgotten.

A knock sounded and soon London's cheerful smile was pushing past the door. "Hi there. You ready to go?" she asked, pulling a wheelchair in behind her.

"I think so. If you could double check the bathroom for me."

London opened the door to the small bathroom and peered around for any items that looked like they didn't belong. She found a disposable razor on the sink and grabbed it. "You want this?" she asked, holding it up for his inspection.

"Nah, you can toss it. I can hardly wait to get back to my own electric razor." He rubbed his face, now smooth. "Where's the rest of the crew?"

"Ammon took the kids back home last night. We thought it might be easier on you if you didn't have to listen to Corkie for the next two hours."

"You know I wouldn't have minded."

"Anyway," she continued as though he hadn't spoken, "it'll give us a chance to talk more."

"Well, okay then. I've got my discharge papers signed so we can get going. I just want to make one stop if you've got time...If you don't mind pushing me down there."

London pushed Brad's wheelchair to the elevator where they rode it down to the first floor. He had learned from the nurses that Sky had been released from ICU and moved to her own room. He was nervous. The thought of seeing her made butterflies float in his stomach, but he was also excited. He had missed her and their often-times impassioned conversations. He missed her smile and the way she laughed. He missed the intensity of her dark eyes when she was mad and the soulful reflection when she was thoughtful. He just plain missed her.

The door to Sky's room was slightly ajar. Brad lifted his hand to knock but paused when he heard voices inside. He recognized Sky's right away, talking with someone. Whoever it was had a deep voice and was relating a story.

"...so then, the guys and I start bookin' it out of there thinking a moose is chasing us. Scared us half to death."

Brad heard her laugh. "Stop, don't make me laugh. It still hurts."

"Sorry, Babe. You know I'm just glad they found you."

"Thanks. I missed you, Tom." Sky's voice was soft and endearing. Brad could picture her face as he heard her voice inside the room and it made him seethe with envy.

Tom.

Her fiancé.

"I missed you too, babe." There was the sound of a kiss. Brad didn't even want to imagine it. "I was going crazy without you. I can't wait 'til you're mine and then I'm not letting you out of my sight ever again."

It was the cheesiest line he'd ever heard—and Brad had heard more than enough. He turned away from the door and said to London, "Let's go."

"But Brad—"

"I said, let's go." His voice was cold, his words stern. How could he have been so stupid? He'd forgotten all about Tom, or at least hadn't thought about him. He'd been so caught up in his own feelings for Sky, he'd not stopped to consider hers.

Nothing had changed. She was still engaged to be married. She was in love with someone else. It didn't matter what she had shared with him. There were moments out there in the wilderness when he had gotten the distinct impression that there was something between them, something more than a shared need to survive. They had…connected. And he'd blown it all out of proportion in the excitement of being rescued and Sky nearly dying. But no. Nothing had changed. Not for her.

His heart was in danger of seizing if he heard another word from the happy couple.

"You can't just leave, you've got to say good bye." London urged. "I thought you really liked—"

"London, I don't want to talk about it. Now would you please wheel me out of here or I'll have to hop."

Sky waved goodbye to Tom once more and stared after him as he walked out the hospital room door. He had been so attentive to her since she'd been rescued, but she was grateful for the solitude now.

She kept her eye on the door, wondering—wishing—Brad would walk through it. Why didn't he visit?

When she first arrived at the hospital she had been hours, maybe only minutes away from death. She didn't remember any of it. She remembered Brad kissing her before walking away. Then she had slept and dreamed.

In her dreams she was safe and warm. Her stomach was full and there was no pain at all in her arm or belly. Her surroundings were beautiful and bright. She sat on a marble wall, dangling her toes in refreshing, blue water while looking up at majestic mountains. Birds sang and animals came, unafraid to drink from the water beside her. It was peaceful and refreshing. A man—a friend--sat beside her. She wanted to stay there forever. He told her she couldn't stay, that she needed to go back. "But it's cold there. It'll hurt if I go back," she told him. "I know, but you must go back," he insisted. "You aren't finished with your work. There is more to do. You are strong and there will be those who can help you. They love you, as do I. They need you."

When she woke three days later, she remembered the dream, but nothing else. At first, she wasn't even certain where she was. She recognized some of the nurses and doctors who hovered over her. She worked with some of them.

She felt pain in her arm, in her belly. She had an IV in her other arm. "Brad?" she asked still dazed before turning her head to see her parents smiling and crying. "Where am I?"

"You're in the hospital dear," her mother informed her. "We've been worried sick about you."

"I'll be fine, Mom," she whispered, thinking about the dream. She had to be fine, she had more work to do.

Mostly she slept after that. The days and nights ran together. Different faces appeared in her room from time to time. Eventually the room changed. Over time she was awake for longer and longer periods. She was so happy to finally eat real food, even if it was only Jell-O. And though she enjoyed seeing her friends and family that trickled in with balloons, flowers, and well wishes, there was one person she had yet to see.

How could he have kissed her like that and not come to see her? She wondered. She could still remember the feel of his lips against hers like a balm to her soul and body. People said he had been hurt. Was he okay? She wanted to see for herself, but she couldn't leave her room. Why didn't he come?

And so she waited.

And waited.

They drove in silence for over thirty minutes. London kept the car stereo on low but didn't sing along as she usually did. Brad kept his eyes glued to the passenger side window, watching as the world whizzed by outside.

They ascended the rise outside of Arlee and Jocko Canyon to the high plateau that looked out on the Mission Mountains. They looked tall and menacing, an impenetrable fortress. He'd always loved the mountains and their constantly changing façade. Today they just acted as a painful reminder of where he'd been and where he was now. The mountains hadn't conquered him. He'd survived. But a large part of him—his heart—would forever be lost in the wilderness.

London pulled the car to a stop on the side of the highway at the top of Polson Hill. Flathead Lake stretched out before them in one of the most breathtaking views along the shore. The sun was still high in the summer sky, reflecting off the aqua blue surface of the water. She killed the ignition and the radio went silent. Nothing but the sound of the occasional car or semi-truck passing them disturbed the silence. After several minutes she spoke, "I love this view."

Brad didn't say anything, just continued staring ahead.

"Perspective is a wonderful thing," she continued. "From up here you can see how big the lake really is. It seems to stretch forever. You can see the hills and mountains that surround it; things that aren't so easy to see when you stand at the edge."

"London, I appreciate—"

"I stood at the edge for most of my life and all I ever saw was what was directly in front of me. I didn't know how to get past it. I didn't know just how much more there was to see, how much more was available to me."

"I appreciate you trying to be philosophic," Brad said. His voice wasn't angry anymore, but he sounded defeated.

"My point is, things may look different than they do right now when you've had some time to get some perspective."

"I don't know what I was thinking. I guess that's just it, I *wasn't* thinking. All those days in the hospital, but I was still up there in those mountains where she needed me. I just forgot is all. She doesn't need me. She never really did." Brad smirked, shrugging his shoulders. His act wouldn't have fooled his enemies, let alone his best friend.

"Of course she needed you. I'm sure she still does, but you wouldn't let her tell you."

"I didn't need her to tell me, I could hear just fine." He ran his hand through his hair in frustration. "You know the really ironic part," he said, looking directly at London, "is that I left town thinking it would help me get over you."

London reached her hand out and finding his, held it tight. "Brad…" she began.

"No, let me finish. I'm okay," he told her. This was a conversation they needed to have. "It's not been easy for me to watch you and Ammon. As you probably guessed, I tried hard to avoid you whenever I could."

"I'm sorry. I didn't mean to pester you, I just couldn't let you go."

"I know. And I couldn't let you go. I don't *want* to let you go either—not as my friend. I hope we'll be friends for a long time, even though you're an old married woman now," he teased. "I don't know if I've told you this, but I'm happy for you. You two are good for each other. I see that. I think what was really bothering me was seeing what you have, what I want and not being able to have it, to find it."

"Thank you," she said, tears welling up in her eyes. "I've been so worried all along. I've found this great happiness and I want to shout it from the roof tops, but that's hard to do when your best friend is unhappy. It feels kind of in your face, you know?" He nodded and she continued, "But I know you'll find it too."

"You're not going to keep playing match-maker are you?" he asked dubiously.

"I'll try to restrain myself from now on." She smiled at him, and he leaned over and kissed her cheek. "I still think you should have said goodbye," she confessed.

"I said my goodbye on the mountain."

"It's not the sa—"

"Let her go, London. She's getting married." His mind knew it was true, but his heart didn't want to believe it. "If I'm going to survive, I have to let her go."

Chapter 27

Brad pulled the corners of his coat tighter around his neck, securing them against the stiff November wind as he exited the fire hall. Needle-like pellets of rain stung his face as brown, orange, yellow and red leaves danced around his feet, swirling in mini-tornadoes along the sidewalk.

The hot, dry summer had given way to a wet, cold fall. The Flathead Valley was gloriously arrayed in the colors of autumn. Dark gray skies were the norm now, but few complained. Everyone was grateful for the return of the rain. The Farmer's Almanac predicted a harsh winter with heavy snow both in the mountains and in the valley. Come spring, the rivers and lakes would be full again. The drought was over.

Brad had taken to walking around the neighborhood during breaks at work and after his shifts. His leg still had a tendency to become stiff, particularly when the barometer fell. After his cast was removed in August, he'd had to wear a walking boot for two months. He was glad to be rid of the clunky thing as it made work difficult and often awkward. He'd been forced to a desk job when the chief felt it was a hindrance to his performance. He no longer had to wear the boot, but his leg was still gaining strength. He saw a physical therapist twice a week and was religious about exercising it whenever he could.

The walks were not only helpful for his physical state, but had been healing to his mental state as well. He'd had time in the past months to think and reflect, and though in his heart he would always love Sky, he had come to terms with all that had happened.

It helped that he was finding a new direction for his life. He'd found new purpose as he learned more about the gospel of Jesus Christ. London and Ammon had been instrumental in teaching him, along with a set of Mormon missionaries—two young men—whom he'd come to respect. And he no longer scoffed at the message they had to share. Life was good and he was happy to be alive. There were times when he looked back on that pivotal moment against the tree when he'd finally given up his own will and put his life in the hands of God. It had changed everything, especially his perspective. His gaze was no longer on just the sand of the shore immediately before him. Now he could see a great distance beyond. And it really was a glorious view.

With his head bent in protection against the wind, Brad stepped off the curb towards the park where he liked best to walk. A set of small feet stepped in front of him. Startled, he looked up past long strands of silky black hair being blown by the wind into a set of chocolate brown eyes.

Thundering Sky.

"Hi," she said.

For what seemed like hours he stared at her, drinking her in like water in the desert. She looked amazing. He had never seen her with makeup on her face or her hair tied back so artfully. He'd never seen her in a skirt with her shapely legs outlined by silk stockings. It was as if he'd never seen the woman who stood before him at all, but his whole body felt the jolt of recognition.

"Thunder?" He stammered.

"In the flesh."

"What are you doing here?" He realized his words sounded accusatory which wasn't what he meant. He was just so stunned. "I mean, it's good to see you."

"It's good to see you too."

"How are you doing?" He felt like an idiot making small talk with her this way, but the question was genuine. He had thought about her so often in the past months, wondering how she was recovering from her injuries. He wondered how her life was now that she was married. Was she happy? Did she ever think about him?

"I'm good. I'm moving actually." He remembered the conversation they'd shared under a tree in a rain storm when she told him her fiancé was going to school still.

"Really? Where to?" A list of well-known universities and their locations ran through his brain like ticker tape.

"Kalispell," she answered. She reached up and brushed away a piece of hair from across her face that the wind had gotten hold of. Brad noted the absence of the shiny diamond she always wore on her left hand. It had been a constant reminder to him while they were in the mountains that she was off limits.

Dare he ask? What did he have to lose? He had to know. "Kalispell? Will your husband be able to finish school here?"

"I took a job at the hospital here. I needed a fresh start." Brad stared, a perplexed look on his face as though not quite understanding her. She continued, "There is no husband. I…I, uh…I called off the wedding in late August."

"I'm sorry to hear that," he lied. His heartbeat increased at the possibilities…

"There were some differences between us that would have made marriage difficult..."

That's too bad," he said, trying to sound sympathetic even though he wasn't really listening. He was still stuck on the good news that she wasn't married.

"…like my being in love with someone else."

That caught his attention. His eyes searched hers, but he didn't dare speak. Finally she looked away.

Sky took an envelope from her pocket. She lifted the flap and pulled out a cream colored linen card. Brad recognized it at once. It was an announcement card for his upcoming baptism that was to be held on Saturday, just two days away. It had been London's idea to have them printed and sent to friends and family. He hadn't wanted the fuss, but she insisted on doing it herself, saying she'd take care of everything…

"Where'd you get that?" he asked, surprised.

"In the mail." Her hand dropped to her side. The wind continued to blow, whipping up strands of her dark hair. She stood staring up at him, tears forming in her eyes. "You didn't even say goodbye. I lay in that hospital bed for days wondering when you were coming, but you never came. I missed you so much. There was nobody that could understand…nobody that knew what I was going through. I wanted you there, but you just disappeared."

Brad closed the distance between them. He framed her small face in his hands, smoothing away the few tears that had escaped. He had had dreams like this, where he'd held her in his arms again, but if he was dreaming now, he hoped to never wake up.

"I'm so sorry, Sky. I was a coward. I came to see you and I heard you laughing—I heard him kiss you—and I had to leave. I thought I'd just imagined things…feelings. It hurt too much to see you again, knowing that I was in love with you. Knowing you belonged to someone else." He lowered his head and kissed her gently.

Sky reached up, lacing her fingers around his neck and pulled him closer. Brad deepened the kiss and she responded, both of them pouring out their feelings without words. Colored leaves danced past them in the chilly wind, rain drops splattered against their cheeks, but they felt none of it. There was only warmth between them.

When at last he pulled away, letting her catch her breath, he touched his forehead to hers and breathed in the scent of her. It was as refreshing as a cold drink on a hot summer day. "I love you Thunder," he confessed. "I love you so much."

"Are you really getting baptized?" she asked, pulling back to look in his eyes. "I thought you didn't believe in all that stuff."

"Yeah, well…it took a miracle, but I changed my mind."

"I'm glad, not just for you, but it will make it so much easier when I explain to my parents that I'm getting married."

"Married, huh?" He smiled and kissed her again. He could hardly believe what was happening. For months he had felt like the best part of his life was gone forever, burned away. But now here she was, in his arms. She loved him. She wanted to marry him. Could happiness really come…out of the ashes? "That sounds like your best idea yet. I can't imagine a better way to spend eternity."

"I love you, Brad," she said.

"And I love you," he repeated. "What do you say for our honeymoon we go anywhere but…"

They smiled at each other and in unison exclaimed, "camping!"

About the Author

Nothing makes Stephanie happier than snuggling up on the couch in front of a fire on a dark gray, rainy day with a good book. Born and raised in Salt Lake City, Utah, she traded in the desert for the clouds of northwest Montana where she loves to hike, ski, swim, and of course, write! She spends her days managing students at an elementary school and her nights managing her busy family of three kids and one husband. Stephanie holds a degree in Biology from the University of Puget Sound but hasn't let that stop her from exploring all kinds of other subjects like sailing, speech and Japanese. If she could travel the world she'd start with the Scottish Highlands and work her way down, delighting in chocolate confections along the way. She dislikes politics and can't juggle, but loves history and can bake just about anything. Her son calls her "well-rounded" but she prefers "eclectic." Stephanie loves hearing from her readers. Connect with her at:

Stephaniewellsmason.com
Facebook.com/ stephaniewellsmason
Twitter.com@stephanieWMason

www.ingramcontent.com/pod-product-compliance
Lightning Source LLC
Chambersburg PA
CBHW061130200626
46817CB00016B/574
9780692389423